What the critics are saying...

"*Passionate Realities* by *Nicole Austin* is a powerhouse of emotion and beauty! *Ms. Austin* has created a plot that is just superb with nice little suspenseful twists. *Passionate Realities* has made my bedside to-be-read-again pile and it is currently on the top." ~ *Keely Skillman, EcataRomance Reviews*

"*Ms. Austin* does a skilful job in creating wonderful scenes to build up the sexual tension between her characters. The ménage a trois scenario is fresh and interesting, and will have you glued to your seat until you finish the entire story. I wouldn't hesitate to recommend *Passionate Realities* to readers." ~ *Aggie Tsirikas, Just Erotic Romance Reviews*

"If you have a soft heart as I do, you will probably need Kleenex while reading this book. This is definitely a must read." ~ *Oleta M Blaylock, Just Erotic Romance Reviews*

"Even if you took out all of the erotic scenes the story could stand on its own with a *rating of 5*. *Ms Austin* tweaks every emotion that the human psyche can encompass. This book has everything that you want in a good read. *Ms Nicole Austin* has done what every author in the romance industry strives to do...give us a story with simply everything." ~ *Raashema, Euro-Reviews*

"The sex scenes are so smoking hot that I was literally panting when I had finished reading them...my eyes were riveted to the pages the whole time I was reading the book." ~ *Susan White, Coffee Time Romance*

Nicole Austin

Passionate REALITIES

ELLORA'S CAVE
ROMANTICA PUBLISHING

An Ellora's Cave Romantica Publication

www.ellorascave.com

Passionate Realities

ISBN # 1419952919
ALL RIGHTS RESERVED.
Passionate Realities Copyright© 2005 Nicole Austin
Edited by: Pamela Campbell
Cover art by: Syneca

Electronic book Publication: May, 2005
Trade paperback Publication: November, 2005

Excerpt from *Triple Play* Copyright © Rhyannon Byrd, 2005

Passionate Realities

Dedication

This one's for you, Donna. Without your unconditional support this would never have been possible. No adequate words exist to express how much your friendship means to me.

And for my wonderful family. Your belief in me is what keeps me reaching for the stars.

Trademarks Acknowledgement

The author acknowledges the trademarked status and trademark owners of the following wordmarks mentioned in this work of fiction:

Chivas: Chivas Brothers (Americas) Limited Company
Cristal: Champagne Louis Roederer Corporation
Jacuzzi: Jacuzzi Inc. Corporation
Mercedes: DaimlerChrysler AG Corporation
Saleen: Saleen Performance, Inc. Corporation
Volvo: Volvo Personvagnar AB Corporation
Chevy: General Motors Corporation

Warning:

The following material contains graphic sexual content meant for mature readers. *Passionate Realities* has been rated *E-rotic* by a minimum of three independent reviewers.

Ellora's Cave Publishing offers three levels of Romantica™ reading entertainment: S (S-ensuous), E (E-rotic), and X (X-treme).

S-*ensuous* love scenes are explicit and leave nothing to the imagination.

E-*rotic* love scenes are explicit, leave nothing to the imagination, and are high in volume per the overall word count. In addition, some E-rated titles might contain fantasy material that some readers find objectionable, such as bondage, submission, same sex encounters, forced seductions, etc. E-rated titles are the most graphic titles we carry; it is common, for instance, for an author to use words such as "fucking", "cock", "pussy", etc., within their work of literature.

X-*treme* titles differ from E-rated titles only in plot premise and storyline execution. Unlike E-rated titles, stories designated with the letter X tend to contain controversial subject matter not for the faint of heart.

Chapter One

Gloriously light bubbles tingled over her tongue as Cassandra McCarthy's senses became immersed in the rich, crisp, Cristal champagne. Keeping her eyes closed she focused on the slow, sensual glide of cold sparkling liquid down her throat. Immediate fingers of pleasure coursed from her mouth outward through every cell in her body, bringing every nerve ending to life.

Before the fresh fruity taste could leave her senses she placed a thin curl of dark chocolate on her tongue. The morsel slowly melted, spreading sweetly through her mouth. Immediately she took a bite of lush red strawberry, allowing the flavors to combine over sensitized taste buds.

Umm, who needs sex? There was not a pleasure on earth she could imagine being better than a fine champagne coupled with rich dark chocolate, and ripe strawberry. It just didn't get any better.

"So, what now?" queried Darlene.

"Hmm…start another book, I guess," she stated blandly. Anything but take her focus away from the sublime, titillating sensations coursing through her warm mouth.

"Cass, could you pay attention to the conversation," demanded Darlene.

"Damn it, why bring me the three most extraordinarily sinful pleasures of this world, and not allow me to thoroughly immerse myself in the erotic sensual fulfillment."

Darlene could not hold back her riotous laughter. "You need to write that down for your next book," she teased. "That's an incredibly sexy description of a few simple treats."

Finally opening her eyes, Cassandra gave her friend an arrogant look. "That's why I make the big bucks."

It was really more a statement of fact than a boast. Her romance novels brought in a great deal of money. The one she'd just completed was recorded on a CD-ROM, which had been safely tucked away into Darlene's purse.

She enjoyed writing. It was the career Cassandra had longed for, but without a college degree her options had been limited. For several years now she'd been writing romantic suspense e-books, which Darlene published on her website.

Cassandra wanted more. She'd always wanted to write stories with more substance, more reality, but depended on the income provided by the romances. All that was required in writing them was a good imagination. She was well-paid for following a certain basic scenario, but was free to be creative in the telling. Her real difficulty came with writing the happily-ever-after, undying love, and devotion she felt did not exist in real life.

She wanted to write compelling novels that captured the reader from the first paragraph. She would master every sense and emotion, taking them on a roller coaster ride. She wanted them laughing out loud, crying, biting their nails, and hanging on her every word, anxiously anticipating what surprises would be encountered when they turned the next page.

She would take the reader on a wild, twisting, turning journey, revealing seemingly random pieces of an intricate puzzle to which only she held the ultimate solution. Then finally, she would meld all the pieces together seamlessly into an explosive, climactic conclusion no one could have predicted. Now that would be an accomplishment Cassandra could savor.

"Why not take some time off," Darlene suggested. "Take a trip somewhere."

"A vacation?" Yeah, that would be a grand idea. Pack up Samantha and Aiden, and then take off for some secluded island paradise. She could vividly picture Aiden lying naked next to a shimmering pool of water. Tanned, muscular male flesh gleaming in the sunlight. Yum.

Cassandra's eyes snapped open, allowing reality to slam down around her once again. It had become a ritual for the two women to share a bottle of champagne in her large, comfortable kitchen upon the completion of each novel. Over the years Darlene Conley had become much more to Cassandra than her publisher. She'd become her best friend.

"Yes, a vacation. It's not that foreign of a concept. Pack some clothes, go stay in an exotic location where other people are waiting to take care of your every need and desire." Darlene laughed lightheartedly. "Most people take a vacation at least once a year."

A very unladylike snort escaped Cassandra's lips. "Well, there's the problem right there, Darlene. I'm not most people." Hell, she was nothing like most people.

Not once in her twenty-four years had she ever gone on a vacation, much less traveled outside her home state of Florida. Her lifestyle was anything but typical.

She had been abandoned by her parents. Then her first love had left upon learning of her pregnancy, leaving her a single, teenage parent. This was followed by becoming the widow of a heartless man. Left shattered and alone, Cassandra had adopted the quiet life of a reclusive author. It was a role she cherished.

She'd always been a painfully shy child. Her tomboy ways had led to her vast automotive knowledge, and kept her away from learning how to relate to other girls. She'd spent more time under the hoods of cars than socializing.

She loved to watch people, and write about their natures. It was much easier to express ideas and emotions to a blank computer screen than to another person. Not much else had ever mattered to her.

Now all she had, all she needed, was her writing and the beach house shared with her daughter, Samantha. While

Darlene's friendship was supportive and undemanding, she always pushed for Cassandra to be more socially active.

Oh, it's not like she was a hermit or anything. She socialized often enough. There was the small, exclusive group of friends who went out dancing together weekly. And she had Aiden, her brother-in-law.

Well, if only she had Aiden. Over the past three years the incredibly handsome man had worked his way past many of the barriers surrounding her heart, which she'd thought were impenetrable. Um, but what woman could possibly ignore his magnetic, insatiable sexuality?

Cassandra had always felt tall, standing five foot ten. Aiden easily stood six inches taller, making her seem short by comparison. His body reminded her of the sculptures of Greek gods she'd seen at a local museum. Recently she'd become increasingly more aware of his magnificent masculine form. His slightly long jet black hair made her fingers itch to feel the satiny strands flow between them.

Aiden's incredibly dark chocolate brown eyes held a boyish twinkle. When he smiled, deep dimples were revealed in his cheeks. His hair would hang down into his eyes, a devilish grin lighting up his face, giving him a rakish bad boy look. Entirely yummy.

The most enticing draw was that he had the whole package going on. The man was incredibly fun, engaging, energetic, sexy, successful, charismatic, and smart as shit. Okay, some people thought he was arrogant, but she knew that it was just his extreme confidence putting out that vibe. He knew what he wanted and staked his claim with no doubt as to his right of possession.

Then he would mysteriously surprise everyone with a burst of charming little boy shyness or deep emotion, keeping you slightly off balance. Aiden exuded charm, and people just loved to be near him. A real man's man. Guys wanted to be him, and women just plain wanted him. His seemingly casual disinterest in their obvious desires just made them want him all the more.

"Earth to Cass," Darlene snapped, pulling Cassandra's thoughts back to her friend.

"Hmm?" she mumbled.

"I said if you don't want to go alone, talk Aiden into going with you. I'm sure he could use a break from work." Darlene sat looking at her expectantly, one artfully arched eyebrow raised.

She fought to suppress her laughter, but ended up wearing a huge grin. "Darlene, if Aiden went on a trip he'd want to take some available hot young woman along, not me." With his cocky confidence the man always had the most gorgeous woman in the room draped over his arm, hanging on every small bit of attention he threw her way.

Despite her best efforts to push away the thoughts, Cassandra pictured Aiden lying wrapped in her arms in a hammock on a deserted stretch of beach. Heat spread through her abdomen, causing the muscles to tighten. Now that would be something to write about. Oh, or maybe sandwiched between Aiden and his equally sexy friend, Travis.

It suddenly hit home. She needed to get laid. How long had it been? The calculations performed quickly in her head left Cassandra shocked. That's what was wrong with her lately. She was having a seven-year-itch. Hell, the phenomenon was common knowledge.

Darlene's laughter once again brought her out of her thoughts. "What's so funny?"

"You dork. You just described yourself, Cass. You are 'an available, hot young woman'. I'm sure Aiden would be more than happy to take you on vacation, or into his bed."

"Darlene," she gasped. "I get enough insane ideas on my own. I don't need any help from you." It took several moments to get her soaring heart rate under control, and her brain functioning again. "Aiden is my brother-in-law," she stated in an exasperated tone.

Darlene just tsked. "So what. His brother's been dead for a long time. There's nothing wrong with starting something up with Aiden. In fact, I think it's a great idea!"

Scraping her chair back across the tile floor, Cassandra rose. She carried the flutes to the sink and washed them, giving her trembling hands something to do. She did not want Darlene to see how greatly the idea affected her.

Could she really "start something up" with Aiden? Sure, she was attracted to him. What woman wouldn't be? Aiden McCarthy was a living, breathing wet dream. He was also an incredibly giving, caring, honorable man. But could she take him into her bed?

Over the years she'd heard many rumors about Aiden. People were bound to talk about such an interesting, enigmatic man. It was said he did not like what many people referred to as "vanilla sex". The kind of sex Cassandra wrote about in her romance novels. Word was that Aiden had dark tastes which ran toward bondage and group sex. For some reason the thought excited her wildly.

Cassandra's limited experience involved only sex in the missionary position. Hell, she had never understood what the big deal about sex was anyway. She'd never experienced the earth-shattering release many women talked about. To her, sex was a sharing of closeness and warmth. She'd never even had an orgasm until she'd bought a vibrator last year.

Um, just thinking about that purple wonder got her hot. She had bought a spare, just in case. After all, a girl can never be too prepared.

Maybe she needed to try something other than "vanilla sex"? If anyone would be able to teach her to let go, it'd be Aiden. But could she actually take him into her bed? Such an intense experience just might kill her.

The more she considered the idea, the more confused Cassandra became. She loved Aiden as a friend, a brother-in-law. Could she love him as a man? And what if it didn't work out? Would she wind up all alone once again?

Coming up behind her, Darlene turned her around with a firm pressure on her shoulders. "Look, Cass. I know you are afraid. I can see it written clearly in your eyes. But if you don't take a chance, you'll lose him. He won't wait around forever just being your friend, but he won't push you either. You have to make the first move."

Darlene's voice shook with frustration. "How much longer can you go on just existing? Damn it, you're the most beautiful, intelligent woman I know, but you're dumb when it comes to life. You need to live again, Cass. You need to love again. You and Aiden belong together."

Unshed tears shimmered in her eyes, dulling the sparkling emerald color to an olive green. "Don't you see, Darlene? I can't risk losing him. I need his friendship too much. I can't risk complicating things by taking him to bed. And if he'd wanted me, he would have made his move by now."

Darlene shook her head. "Hell, look at Jared and me. I fought him tooth and nail. I just knew that if I let myself love him, I'd lose him. He had to bulldoze me into trusting him with my heart. I almost missed out on the most incredible love because of my pigheadedness."

She shook Cassandra fiercely. "Cass, don't miss out on Aiden because you're too stubborn and hurt. You'll regret it the rest of your life. Let the past go. Live. Go after what you want."

Chapter Two

"Cindy, where the hell are my notes," bellowed Aiden. "I can't find a damn thing."

Well, he was only getting what he deserved. It had been a stupid move hiring a friend to work as his administrative assistant. In frustration he raked a hand through his rumpled hair.

He had worked so hard to build his career, fighting against the doubts his father had instilled in him. His diligent studying had paid off with a full scholarship to MIT. With persistence he had ended up with a promising career as a computer programmer working for a prestigious organization.

Now, at the age of thirty, he was comfortable with his career. Working out his relationship with Cass would make almost everything perfect. The one thorn in his side was finding himself reduced to putting up with Travis' lover making his work life hell. The bawdy woman knew exactly how to push his buttons. How Travis put up with the woman was beyond Aiden.

Cindy waited a full minute before entering his office, fighting to hide her smile. She knew it drove him crazy when she made him wait. And heck if she wasn't enjoying messing with Aiden. Tricking him into going to Travis' house would be easy. All it would require was forgetting to give him a phone message.

Um, if only she could be there to see the sparks fly. It would be so wickedly delicious. She knew how he would react to what he found. The dominant alpha caveman he tried to keep hidden would rear his head, and maybe he'd finally grab what he really wanted.

Maybe Travis would also be pushed into taking some action. He needed more than the casual no-strings relationship he'd established with her. And wasn't it just ironic that both of the sexy men wanted the same thing. Yup, this little encounter just may become explosive.

She sauntered into the office, coming around the desk to stand next to Aiden. Her face held a practiced look of long suffering. "I swear, Aiden. No one would ever mistake you for a computer geek. Er...um, I mean programmer. All I did was organize your desktop." She pointed a long, fuchsia-glazed fingernail at the icon of a file cabinet on the softly glowing screen.

She always felt somewhat disconcerted looking at Aiden. It was amazing how he and Travis looked so much alike. Sometimes it was difficult to remember which man she was dealing with. It must be true what they say about everyone having a double out there somewhere.

Aiden was certainly Travis' double. They had such similar personalities, yet there was an innate difference between them. It wasn't anything you could put your finger on, just something you felt.

Cindy spoke in the tone of a frustrated teacher trying to explain a simple concept to a particularly dense child. "All your notes and documents are in here. I gave them very simple names. You should be able to figure this out." Cindy smiled at him indulgently. "Would you like me to walk you through it step by step?"

Aiden let out a deep growl of frustration. His teeth were tightly clenched. He tried to hold back his temper. Any patience he had once possessed was rapidly wearing thin. "No, Cin. Just show me where my frickin' notes for the new security program are hidden."

Cindy silently stared at him with one eyebrow arched, waiting until he added, "Please." Her bright, triumphant smile lit up the room.

"Sure, Aiden. No problem." After several mouse clicks the file opened up. "Is there anything else you need?" she sweetly asked.

He mumbled a negative response as she walked to the door, already deeply lost in thought.

Cindy stopped at the open doorway. "Oh, by the way…"

She stood patiently waiting for Aiden to spare her a small amount of his attention. After a long moment of silence he finally looked up.

"What?" he snapped.

The tall, luscious blonde stared back defiantly. Again he received her patented, you're-lucky-I-put-up-with-you look. She was so infuriating. He didn't understand how Travis handled the little witch.

"If you don't leave right now, you'll be late for poker night…again." She dragged out the words sarcastically.

With a bright smile, she closed the door. It took incredible control for her to keep from busting out hysterically. Her muffled, mischievous laughter vibrated through the office.

Aiden stared at the door in disbelief. How did she always manage to do that? He shouldn't have to feel bad about the one night a week the guys all got together to just be guys. It was the one time he truly relaxed.

Glancing down at his watch, Aiden decided she was right. If he didn't get going he wouldn't have time to shower before heading out. With a deep sigh he closed the file. Tomorrow he'd have to convince Cindy to show him where it was again.

He left the building quickly, driving a little faster than normal. If he timed things right there'd be just enough time for him to make it to his friend's house. The rule was the last man to sit down for the poker game paid for the pizza and beer. Aiden had paid the last two weeks, he wasn't about to continue the trend.

He'd chosen his condo for its desirable address, and the boat slip it came with. After all, boys had to have some big, impressive toys. His sleek, powerful cigarette boat had certainly made an impression with its clean lines and bold flashes of color. But the best thing about the boat was that Cass loved to get her hands into its engine.

Just the thought had sexual energy humming through his veins. There was nothing sexier than watching a beautiful woman get dirty tinkering with something mechanical.

Making it home in record time he anticipated the relaxing night ahead. Once showered and changed he drove the familiar route to the beach, wrapped up in thoughts about the new program he was designing.

Parking his Mercedes in front of Travis' house, Aiden couldn't believe his eyes. None of the other guys were there yet. How had he managed to be the first? Checking his watch again showed that he was indeed five minutes late.

He saw two pairs of legs were sticking out from under Travis' old truck as he walked up the driveway. "Where the heck is everyone, Travis?" he asked. When he got no response, Aiden lightly kicked one booted foot.

Travis slid out from under the truck on a mechanic's dolly. Although grease smeared both arms and his face there was no mistaking how strongly they resembled each other. Sometimes it even freaked him out a little bit. It was kind of like looking in the mirror and seeing a slightly different version of yourself.

"Hey, Aiden! What're you doing here?" Travis looked up at him expectantly. "Oh, man. Wait a minute. Didn't Cindy tell you?"

His laughter sent a cold tendril of unease along Aiden's spine. "What didn't Cindy tell me?"

Before Travis could answer a muffled, feminine voice drifted out from under the truck.

"Hang on, sugar. I'll be right there," Travis replied, before turning his attention back to Aiden. "I cancelled poker night due to problems with the Beast."

Aiden couldn't believe Travis still drove the same old dilapidated truck. He knew that Travis made at least as much money as he did at Danbury Industries. They both held executive positions within the organization. "When are you going to get a real car that works, and get rid of the Beast?"

Travis just shook his head. "And drive some flashy little German tin can like you? No thanks. Besides, the Beast has its fringe benefits," he joked, stroking his hand over one slender ankle sticking out next to him.

Aiden couldn't hide his broad, amused grin. "Who've you got under the truck with you, Travis?" he asked with a wink. "Damn, Cindy's gonna kick your ass if she finds out."

Travis' boisterous laugh ripped through the quiet neighborhood. A devilish look spread over his ruggedly handsome face. Keeping his eyes on Aiden's reaction, he reached an arm under the truck, pulling on a slender ankle. Long, shapely legs were slowly displayed, topped by a soft pair of grey jogging shorts. They were slender legs, with sleek muscles. The kind of legs a guy dreams of feeling wrapped around his hips while fucking.

Aiden found himself anticipating seeing the rest of the beautiful body being tantalizingly revealed. Her fabulous legs seemed to go on for miles. Her skin was nicely tanned, glowing with health, and appeared soft as spun silk. Gracefully curved hips were followed by a slender waist.

Something about the woman being slowly revealed struck a chord in his memory, and an insatiable longing in the pit of his stomach. Did he know who belonged to the incredibly fuckable body? She called to him in an elemental way, causing his cock to strain painfully against his zipper. Feeling his cock jerk, Aiden tried to tamp down his reaction. *Down boy*, he told his unruly dick. Damn, he didn't normally react like this. He just didn't drool over women.

"Come on out here, sugar. I want you to see who came to visit," Travis drawled, and continued to draw the woman out, inch by glorious inch.

Her bare navel drew Aiden's eye. He vividly pictured flicking his tongue into the shadowed little hole. Running his hands over the glorious expanse of flat, bare abdomen which led to a little scrap of T-shirt just covering a narrow rib cage. Firm, full breasts brought about another reflexive jerk from his suddenly unruly cock.

That was one hot woman Travis had under there. Her slender arms and hands were smeared with dark motor grease. A long caramel brown ponytail lay coiled over one narrow shoulder, then disappeared behind her back. Shock took hold of Aiden as her face slowly appeared.

"Hi, Aiden. What's happening?" Cassandra said in a sultry, husky tone.

He had to blink several times before his mind could accept that it was Cass who'd spoken. It was Cass' luscious body that had quickly brought his cock to full mast. Damn, he couldn't be lusting after her. A blinding, possessive rage had every muscle tensing. In two quick strides he stood over her.

"What the hell are you doing under the truck with Travis?" he snarled, leaning closer. His fingers sunk deep into her muscular deltoids as he held her arms in a viciously tight grip. He didn't know how to respond to the unfamiliar situation and feelings.

Before Cassandra knew what was happening, Aiden had grabbed her, pulling her roughly to her feet. What was wrong with him? She looked over at Travis, but he just sat there wearing a shit-eating grin, enjoying the show. What appeared to be a spark of jealousy flashed across his dark brown eyes, disappearing before she could be certain.

Anger, and what looked like jealousy, gleamed in Aiden's eyes. Surely that wasn't desire she saw reflected there too? What was going on with the two of them? And just what did Aiden have to be either angry or jealous about? She didn't understand what was happening.

"Aiden, you're hurting my arms. What the hell's wrong with you?" she questioned. He just stood there, staring. Without really thinking about it she reared back, and sucker-punched his rock-hard abs. All she wanted was to be free of that painful, iron-tight grasp. Now she had a tingling pain shooting up the length of her arm.

All the air rushed out of his lungs. Aiden doubled over, letting go of Cass. He saw Travis quickly jumping to his feet to intervene. After all, the situation was his fault.

"Whoa. Everybody chill out," Travis said with a chuckle. "Damn, Aiden. Cass is just helping me fix the Beast. You need to relax, buddy."

Turning toward Cassandra with a wide grin he said, "You pack quite a punch, sugar."

When Aiden was finally able to straighten up, he saw Cass rubbing her arms where angry red marks had been left by his fingers. What had gotten into him? He'd just hurt the woman that he'd spent the past three years trying to protect.

"Oh, Cass. I'm sorry." Slowly he approached her, and tenderly ran his fingers over the marks. He marveled at the shiver that went through her in response to the gentle stroke.

"Cindy's making me nuts at work. She's hidden all the files on my computer, and isn't giving me my messages." Yeah, and like that gave him a right to be short-tempered, and hurt Cass. It was a lame excuse, and he knew it. "Damn it, I'm sorry."

She just stared. The two large, muscular men standing side by side shared boyishly repentant looks. They were so handsome alone, but together the effect was magnified. Umm, she could just eat them both up, then come back for seconds.

They were so damn adorable, sexy, delicious, and incredibly hot. It was like standing in front of a gourmet smorgasbord and having to decide where to start. Umm, she suddenly had a ravenous appetite. A desperate ache began somewhere in her abdomen and spread as quickly as a forest fire through her entire body. She nearly trembled with need.

They were sin personified. Black wavy hair, smoldering chocolate eyes, and sexy full lips just waiting to be kissed. Their chiseled, masculine features with boyish dimples were just too hot for words. Both were slightly rumpled, looking like they'd just rolled out of bed after a good fuck. Their innate sexuality heightened all her senses. The magnetic pull she felt toward both men had always been incredibly strong.

Her eyes feasted on two sets of incredibly muscled shoulders, down wide chests narrowing to flat, muscular abs. Four long, powerful legs encased in faded denim, and temptingly large bulges that made her mouth water. Too bad she couldn't circle around to appreciate their tight buns without being obvious.

Travis looked cute with grease smeared across one cheek. Aiden raked a hand through his rumpled hair, the motion mimicking what she would like to do. *Get a grip on your raging hormones, girl. Damn, these are your friends.*

Aiden couldn't believe the look of smoldering passion he saw in Cass' eyes. She was looking at the two of them like she wanted nothing more than to take them both into the house and devour them. Was he reading her eyes right?

"Cass?" he questioned.

"Hmm." She visibly shook herself, an embarrassed flush heating her cheeks. She'd just been caught staring at their crotches. "Oh…um, Travis asked me to help him out with the Beast." She shrugged her shoulders dismissively. "You know I can't pass up a chance to mess with a greasy motor."

More than anything, she loved to work on Aiden's boat. Now there was a fun toy to play with. Forty-two feet of sleek fiberglass equipped with some major muscle in the engine compartment. The huge pair of supercharged nine hundred-horsepower V8s both looked and sounded intimidating. She loved to get out on the water, set free all those horses and bask in the throaty rumble. Now that was fun.

God, her distraction must be apparent. Aiden stepped closer, trailing his fingers over her jawline. The intense desire in his dark eyes sent a shiver of anticipation crackling through her abdomen, straight down to her pussy. She felt hot, wet cream spread over her swelling nether lips.

She gasped in horror as Aiden's nostrils flared. The sweet, intoxicating smell of her arousal filled the air, tempting him. Panic shot across her delicate face. A second wave of heated embarrassment stained her cheeks.

His fingers brushed delicately along her jaw. "You've got some dirt on your face," he said in a velvety tone. Slowly he lowered his head, intending to kiss her pouty lips. His lips hovered so close he could feel her warm breath. The sound of Travis clearing his throat had Aiden quickly jerking back. Christ, what the hell was he doing?

Without looking away from her eyes, Aiden asked, "Travis, you don't need her help anymore tonight, do you?" His tone made it clear that three was becoming a crowd.

"Uh, no. I think I've got it under control now." After picking up some stray tools he said, "I'll see you guys later. I'm just gonna go wash up." He paused for a moment in his retreat. "Thanks for the help, Cass."

Knowing she would be unable to form a coherent sentence, Cassandra just shook her head in acknowledgement. She couldn't take her eyes away from Aiden's intense stare. Heat pooled between her legs, and she could feel the slick juices saturating her panties.

She imagined trailing her hands down his abdomen and jeans to feel his hard cock. She was certain that his erection would be wonderfully long and thick. She wanted to feel all that hard masculine power inside her so badly it hurt.

"Where's your car?" Aiden asked.

She could not hide the huskiness in her voice. "I walked over."

He nodded slightly. "Come on, I'll drive you home."

* * * * *

The two-block drive rolled by in silence. They both remained focused on their own thoughts. Cassandra could not comprehend what had just happened. She loved Aiden as a brother. How the hell could she be getting hot for him sexually? And how could she lust after Travis? Frigid women didn't get hot and bothered like this.

That's what her husband, Mike McCarthy, always told her anyway. He'd been attracted to her, regardless of her rapidly expanding abdomen, but found her sexual prowess lacking.

They had gotten married two weeks before Sam was born. Mike had promised to take care of her and the baby. The marriage had seemed the perfect solution to her problems. She'd been so wrong.

Mike was a big man, like his brother. His muscular strength had made her feel safe, protected. As soon as Sam had been born though, Mike stopped touching her, and began with the verbal abuse. His painful words still echoed in her ears.

"You're a frigid bitch who can't even get wet," Mike had told her on more than one occasion.

Oh, she could get wet all right, just not for Mike. He had proceeded to break her spirit in the worst way possible. She could have dealt with physical abuse by simply walking away. But not the systematic psychological abuse meant to strip away her confidence, pride, and lust for life. He'd kept her isolated from friends, codependent on his mistreatment.

She remembered the day police had informed her that Mike had been killed in an accident while driving drunk. She'd felt nothing but relief. Finally she had been freed from his constant badgering.

Then Aiden had walked into her life. Thankfully, the brother's striking good looks were where the similarities ended. Aiden's sparkling personality was the opposite of Mike's dark, brooding persona. And Aiden was different with her than he was with anyone else. Around her he became protective, sheltering, caring. Most of all he had become an important part of Sam's life, a father figure.

Cassandra wished she did not have to depend so much on Aiden, or take so much of the support he so unselfishly gave. She wished he'd fall in love with a good woman, settle down, maybe have some kids. Without a doubt he would make a wonderful father. He had so much love to share, and gave of himself so freely.

A sharp little pang of regret pierced her heart at the thought of Aiden in love, married. Old impossible dreams returned with a vengeance. Could Aiden possibly be the one that could make her dreams come true? Could she even still believe in such a perfect life, cynical as she'd become?

What about Travis? The two men were reviving feelings that she had buried long ago. She was incredibly attracted to both of them. A sexual triangle? Yeah, right. Maybe for one of her stories, but not in real life. She forcefully pushed the strange thoughts from her mind.

Her feelings for both men were so strong. They had both come to be such a big part of her life. She loved them both. Was it possible she was in love with them?

Giving herself a mental shake, Cassandra dismissed that thought. She couldn't possibly be in love with two men. If she was in love with either, then it was Aiden, right?

Her feelings were turning into such a jumbled, convoluted mess—running in wild circles. Eventually she'd have to sort everything out.

Chapter Three

Arriving home, she overpaid her teenage neighbor who often babysat Samantha. Aiden saw the girl home safely, while Cassandra checked on her sleeping daughter.

She would not trade a moment of the past for the precious girl lying beneath the covers. Every hardship was worth one sweet smile from her beautiful little princess. She tucked the covers in tightly, and feathered a kiss across Sam's forehead. Just as she was getting up, Sam stirred.

"Mom, why can't Uncle Aiden be my Dad?" she sleepily asked.

The innocent question nearly stopped her heart, wedging it painfully up into her throat. Gently she smoothed the soft hair back from her daughter's face. "Oh, pumpkin. You can't change who's your father, but Uncle Aiden will always be here for you. And he loves you just as much as if he were your father."

Staring down, it was Bryce's piercing blue eyes she saw looking back. Fierce waves of pain threatened to engulf Cassandra. She knew the day would come when her daughter began to ask questions about her father. She had yet to figure out how much she wanted to tell Sam about her first love and their summer romance.

"It's sad that you don't know your father, but you know what? You have his beautiful blue eyes. And you'll always carry him with you in your heart." She feathered a kiss across Sam's cheek.

"Go to sleep now, pumpkin. Sweet dreams," she whispered.

"But Mom, if Aiden were the daddy I could have a brother or sister. I really want a sister."

Feeling tears welling in her eyes, Cassandra fought to push her yearning for another child away. "Pumpkin, little sisters are a pain. They take all the attention, and all your stuff." Her fingers trembled as she rose from the bed. "Trust me, sweetie. They are more trouble than they're worth."

From the doorway she blew a kiss to her daughter. "Good night, Sam. Sleep tight."

Samantha immediately picked up the nighttime ritual. "Don't let the bedbugs bite."

"Bite 'em back," Cassandra whispered.

Caught up in her thoughts, she walked right into Aiden after softly closing the bedroom door. Looking into his turbulent brown eyes, she knew he'd heard everything.

Strong arms wrapped her in a warm embrace. His big hands smoothed down over her long hair and back soothingly. She let her forehead rest against his warm chest.

"Aiden?" Her voice was filled with longing.

Gentle fingers lifted her chin, forcing her to look up into his eyes. Her slightly parted lips called out to be kissed. Aiden could not resist the fierce need to taste her, just once. Lowering his head, he brushed his lips over Cass'. Her soft moan vibrated against his mouth, tearing at his restraint. His tongue slid over her soft lips slowly before delving deeper.

The second their tongues touched, Aiden knew he was a goner. She tasted so sweet, and felt so good in his arms. Kissing Cass ignited the passion he'd fought so valiantly to suppress. He knew in that instant that one taste would never be enough. It would take centuries to slake his thirst for this woman.

Her response was instinctive. All thought left her mind as his tongue slid over her own. He boldly explored her mouth, and she sucked his tongue in deeper. Her entire existence narrowed down to the intimate mating of their mouths.

Long denied desires flooded her senses, making her hunger deep within her belly. Aiden's kiss was far better than she'd ever imagined, and she had a good imagination. He tasted slightly of peppermint, warm and masculine. In his kiss she felt his desire and need, as well as his caring and love. Why had she never kissed him before?

Her nipples puckered, straining against the material of her shirt. Moving slightly had the taut peaks brushing over his chest, sending electric currents straight to her clitoris. Feeling the hard bulge of his erection pressed against her soft belly nearly drove her insane with need. He felt so good. She wanted to feel that rock-hard shaft pounding inside her body. But thoughts about Mike invaded her bliss, and a shiver of fear racked her body.

Aiden pulled back first, the dark look in his eyes sending her frantic pulse beating triple time. That look left no doubt as to what he wanted. It was what she wanted too. She could clearly see his struggle to hold back.

She met his gaze, facing the raw, burning hunger reflected in those dark eyes. The drugged, heavy-lidded look only increased the hot, burning hunger raging through her tightly clenched abdomen.

"Three years I've waited. I can't hold out much longer, Cass. I've tried to be just a friend, do the honorable thing, and take care of you. I don't want to be just your friend anymore. I want you." They stared into each other's eyes until he turned and walked away.

Cassandra walked in a daze to her bedroom. She needed to gather her self-control. And her rapidly pounding heart was threatening to leap from her chest. The sexual fog created by the best kiss she'd ever had was making her mind feel fuzzy. The warm, sweet taste of his mouth still lingered on her tingling lips.

The hard contours of his body would forever be branded on her memory.

Tingling sensations raced through her breasts as her soft T-shirt rasped over sensitive, needy nipples. Silently cursing her newfound hormones, she quickly stripped off her clothes. Her panties were soaked, and she needed to cool off.

Biting her lip, she stepped into the cold cascade of water in the shower. Images of Aiden in her bed continued to warm her body despite the cold water sluicing over her heated flesh. She could vividly picture his large body covering her own as he thrust deeply into her core. And now she knew without a doubt, his cock was both long and thick.

Shutting off the water, she wrapped herself in a large, fluffy towel. After drying off, she dressed in silk pajamas, and then towel-dried her wavy hair. Her mouth felt dry. Licking her lips she could still taste his kiss lingering there. *Holy cow!*

She headed into the kitchen for a glass of water, shocked to find Aiden waiting in the living room. He'd opened a bottle of wine, and already poured two glasses. She quietly joined him on the couch, tucking her legs under her bottom. Confused by the evening's events she sipped the offered wine, waiting for him to say something.

While Aiden was accustomed to seeing Cass in her pajamas, his gaze slid longingly over the silky cropped shirt that left her navel bare, down the baggy drawstring pants that did nothing to hide her long, curvy legs. Heat arced between their bodies.

She was most likely unaware that her long, wet strands of caramel hair had dampened the front of her top. He could just make out the dark, puckered circles of her areolas. The sight just might make him lose his legendary control. But Aiden's mind was troubled, drifting in a different direction.

He needed to know more about what drove Cass, her fears, her past. Then maybe he would know how to proceed, and how to win her heart. "I know you don't like talking about Mike, but I need to know, Cass. What did he do to cause you so much pain, and put such fear into you?"

Her hands began trembling so hard that she almost splashed wine all over herself. She'd never talked to anyone about Mike. How could Aiden ask her to do so now?

He slid closer. Taking the glass from her hands, he set it down on the table. Then Aiden began rubbing warmth into her shaking arms. "It's okay, Cass. He can't hurt you anymore. I really need to know, and I think you need to get it out. Until you do, we won't be able to move forward."

He continued sliding his hand up and down her arms, providing warmth to replace the cold that was always there. "I never understood how you could've ended up married to the sadistic bastard."

Oddly, Cassandra found that she did want to share her pain with Aiden. If anyone was strong enough, loving enough to accept the burden of her past it was him. He would not think less of her for her weakness.

Where should she begin? How could she explain the fear, and solitude of her life? It started all the way back with her parents.

"It's okay, baby. Start as far back as you need to," he said as if reading her mind. "I've got all the time in the world."

Steeling herself for the painful journey ahead, Cassandra reached for the glass of wine. She drained its entire contents before she was ready to start. Her voice came out as a soft whisper at first, but gained confidence the more she spoke. Soon the words and pain flowed forward steadily. She could not stop now even if she tried.

Her parents had been Cassandra's first example of relationships gone wrong. They had fought constantly about everything, but most especially about her. Neither had wanted a child, but had married upon learning of the pregnancy.

Everything finally blew up in their faces on the day of her seventh birthday. Her grandmother had worked hard to give her a beautiful party befitting a princess. The big fight had occurred in the middle of the party, amidst a dozen shrieking children running around in wild abandon. Angry shouts and words had cut through the festive atmosphere as effectively as a scalpel through soft flesh. Even putting her fingers in her ears had not kept out the hateful declarations.

The party had ended abruptly with her parents each packing separate suitcases, and walking away from the life they had built. With tears streaming down her beautiful face, her mother had told Grandma Hazel that she could not start over with a child in tow. She had never seen either parent again, never looked for them. They had made it clear she wasn't wanted.

Aiden pulled her into his warm embrace. She vaguely felt his fingers wiping the tears from her face, his feather-soft kisses easing the pain fractionally. She was trapped in memories now, barely noticing his attention.

Over the years of growing up with her grandmother, Cassandra had thought one day she would find her prince charming, have a family, and hold them all together through the sheer force of her love. Of course, that had been just a childhood delusion. She'd had no better chance than her parents to get it right.

She had inherited her love of reading from her grandmother. Cassandra had been a good student in school with perfect grades. She had won several writing competitions, and even had one of her stories published in a magazine. During her junior year of high school she'd been awarded a full scholarship to the University of Florida, College of Liberal Arts and Sciences.

Dreams had not been enough though, and college just wasn't in the cards. All her bright plans for the future drastically changed the summer she was seventeen and Bryce Martin walked into her life.

Cassandra had felt her heart stop beating. Walking toward her was the most striking boy she had ever seen. His dark blond hair had been neatly cut, and feathered back along the sides of his head. His beautiful face like a picture cut from a teen magazine. Dark brows rose over sultry blue eyes, which stared down at her as if seeing inside her soul.

His nose was a straight slash between wide-set eyes. A square, masculine jaw and the most sensuous lips Cassandra had ever seen. His intense, crystalline blue eyes seemed to gaze right into her soul. She had fallen in love instantly.

The summer had been pure bliss—hanging out at the arcade, lying on the beach. She never got tired of watching Bryce surf the waves. Joy filled her at his every touch, and every kiss seared her soul. They spent every free moment together. He filled her heart, and taught her body to please him. They made love everywhere and anywhere with a desperate, never-ending need.

Aiden did not speak, but sat silently absorbing her pain. He continued to rub warmth into her trembling arms. His soothing touch allowed her to get the rest of her story out. Leaning into his chest she continued.

With only two weeks left of the summer, a home pregnancy test had confirmed her suspicions. Cassandra had been terrified, but also thrilled. *A baby.* She would have Bryce's baby. They would be forever joined together in the child that was the result of their all-consuming love. Of course, she thought they would get married and be together forever.

Bryce had convinced her to wait a few weeks before telling anyone so they could make some plans. She had not been aware that Bryce's father was being transferred across the country by work. Her blissful ignorance had lasted for little over a week.

She first knew something was wrong as she tried to call Bryce. At first she thought she'd dialed the wrong number. Starting over she again heard the horrible recorded voice state, "The number you have reached has been disconnected. If you feel this recording to be an error, please hang up and try your call again."

Grandma Hazel had passed away during her pregnancy, and she'd had to give up their little house. She had gotten her diploma three months after the rest of her class by taking the high school General Equivalency Diploma test. By that point she had been working two jobs to bring in enough money to help support a baby, a husband, and herself. The three of them had lived in a small apartment above the garage of a couple who were always fighting.

"I was so afraid and alone when I met Mike. He promised to take care of us. God, he was so strong, so sure of himself. I knew I needed help, so I took what he offered."

Cassandra looked up into Aiden's eyes hoping to find understanding. What she saw shocked her. Fierce anger gave his eyes a stormy appearance. After a brief pause she continued.

"As soon as Sam was born, I knew that I'd made a big mistake. Mike was so cruel. He humiliated me at every opportunity. Nothing was sacred. He would follow me, and make me account for every mile I put on my car's odometer. I thought about taking Sam and running, but where would I go. I had no money, no family, nothing."

Finally, having told him her painful secrets, Cassandra felt weak with exhaustion. Conflicting emotions twisted within her gut. Unable to bear waiting she looked up into Aiden's eyes. A myriad of emotions swirled across his strong features. *Oh God, please let him understand.*

Aiden fought past the anger to find his voice. "Oh, Cass. I'm so sorry, baby. I should have been around, should have been there to protect you and Sam."

Tears of relief flowed from her puffy eyes. He didn't think less of her for what had happened. He held her sheltered against his warm body, and tried to provide comfort. How could one brother be so maliciously hateful, and the other so wonderful? If only it had been Aiden she'd met first, things would have been so different.

"I'm so tired," she huskily whispered.

Aiden rose from the couch with her held in his arms like a child. He carried her to her room, gently tucking her into bed. He gently stroked her hair away from her face, and then planted a tender kiss on her forehead. More than anything he wished he could heal her.

"Thank you for having enough trust to tell me, Cass. It means more to me than you could know." He rose and stared down at her for several moments. "Rest now, baby. You need sleep."

She held out one trembling hand toward him. "Aiden, please don't go. I've been alone so long. Please, stay and hold me. Just for tonight. I need you."

Her request stopped him cold. Emotions crossed his face so quickly that she was unable to tell what he was feeling. Silently he climbed into the bed, fully clothed, and pulled her into the shelter of his body. She snuggled into his side, quickly falling asleep. With her head on his shoulder, his heart beat steadily beneath her ear. She drew strength and warmth from the man who gave so freely when she needed him the most.

* * * * *

Aiden lay awake through the night, holding Cass close to his side. He wished Mike were still alive to provide an outlet for the rage boiling through his veins.

As much as he could, Aiden had taken her pain into himself. He could feel the shame, humiliation, and helpless fear. How she had ever come out the other side such a caring, loving woman amazed him. She was so much stronger than she gave herself credit.

Thinking back over his own life, Aiden was amazed how differently he'd turned out from his brother. Mike had taken the brunt of their father's cruelty. He'd never been more thankful than the day the bastard had finally packed up and taken off.

One of the things that had saved Aiden was his friendship with Travis. When he'd started high school people he didn't know would walk up and start talking to him. Finally one day he'd met Travis. It had been so surreal coming face-to-face with someone who looked like his double.

The bond between them was immediate. There was so much about them that was similar, yet a great deal that was different also. Playing on the high-school football team together had been some of the best times of Aiden's life. They were able to connect on a level that required no verbalization, making them a tough team to beat.

It was crazy the way so much changed over the years, yet so much stayed the same. His enduring friendship with Travis and a small group of friends from high school were the constants he could count on. These things endured even when he hadn't been able to count on his own brother. But Mike was dead now, and Aiden lay holding his widow.

He felt a blistering need to have Cass as his own, to possess her. Picturing turning her over and thrusting his cock deep into her brought the ever-ready organ to attention. It had been a long time for Cass. Her tight pussy would grip him like a fist. He groaned inwardly at the vivid images that flashed through his mind. He wanted to be inside her pussy with a nearly violent desperation. Not yet, but soon.

Things would be different now. He could no longer hold back his feelings. They belonged together. It didn't matter to him who Sam's father was. He would always treat her as his own daughter, and love her as much as any other child they had together.

Imagining Cass pregnant with his child sent shivers through his body. Her lush body swollen, ripe with new life. She would be so beautiful. She would finally be his.

Rising early, Aiden wandered into the kitchen to make breakfast for his girls. Before everything was ready Sam padded quietly into the large kitchen. She looked so sweet rubbing her sleepy eyes with a small fist. He'd make sure she never experienced pain like her mother had.

"Uncle Aiden?" Samantha questioned with a yawn. "Where's Mom? Did you spend the night?"

"Mornin', sunshine. Mom's still asleep. Are you hungry?" Love surged through Aiden. He'd always felt more like Sam's father than an uncle. He knew from her conversation with Cass that she'd quickly accept him as her father. Would she call him Daddy? His heart swelled at the thought.

"Is she sick? Mommy never sleeps this late." Concern etched her delicate features.

"She's fine, sweetheart, just tired. So, how about some breakfast?" he asked, ruffling her sleep-tousled hair.

"Mmm. Smells good, Uncle Aiden."

Kneeling down to her eye level, Aiden pulled Sam's tiny body into his arms. She was so small and frail. He would protect her, keep her safe, and shower her with love.

"Uncle Aiden?"

To hide his emotions, Aiden swept her up into the air. He tickled her without mercy before depositing her in a chair at the table. "So, what'll it be, sunshine. Eggs and bacon, pancakes, or a little bit of everything?"

"Everything," she squealed with delight. "Wow, did you cook all that?" she asked with admiration clear in her eyes.

"Sure did, sunshine. Just for you and your mom."

After she ate her fill, Aiden sent Sam off to get dressed, and then headed her outside to play on the beach. As difficult as the night had been for Cass, he had figured she deserved a break. He'd turned off the alarm clock before finally falling asleep. Sure, Sam would be missing a day of school, but that would be okay. She was an incredibly smart little girl, and way ahead of her class. It was more important that she be close to her mom today.

He made up a tray of food for Cass. Even took the time to gather some pink hibiscus flowers from the front yard, and arrange them in a small vase on the tray. He wanted to spoil her. Humming happily to himself he headed toward her room.

After spending the night in his arms she'd finally have to admit her feelings for him. Then they could begin to develop a real relationship. He wouldn't wait long before springing the idea of marriage. That thought sent his emotions soaring.

Chapter Four

Stretching out, Cassandra kicked off the covers. She had slept better last night than she could ever remember. Umm, and she must have had one hot, sexual dream too. She felt sexually frustrated, her pussy aching.

Taking a deep breath she smelled Aiden's distinctive scent. Sexy, clean, masculine heat caused her nostrils to flair. She could smell his scent and cologne clinging to the sheets, pillows, even her pajamas. That's why she'd slept so well, because Aiden had held her all night.

Fleetingly she wondered when he had left. The cold sheets let her know it had been a while since he had lain there. Pulling the sheets up to her face she breathed deeply, which only redoubled the ache between her legs.

Damn, she needed to be fucked. She didn't want a slow bout of making love. No, she wanted hot, sweaty, wild monkey sex. Hmm, this seven-year-itch thing was only getting worse.

Stretching her arms up over her head, Cassandra arched her back to loosen the muscles. The motion brushed her silky pajama top over already taut nipples. With a deep moan she stroked the sensitive peaks. Nerve endings sent the sensations straight to her clit.

A little early morning delight was in order. She listened carefully for several minutes for any indication that Samantha was awake. Hearing nothing, she reached into her bedside table for her trusty vibrator. It had been getting a lot of use over the past few months.

Turning it to the lowest speed she stroked the vibrator slowly over her nipples. Oh God, that felt so good. But what she really wanted was Aiden's mouth sucking the distended peaks.

She stripped out of her pajamas and trailed the vibrator slowly over her abdomen. Umm, this was going to be good. She hadn't been this worked up since before Sam was born. Her hot juices coated her slit, and dripped down over her anus.

Stroking her drenched folds with a finger she marveled over how wet she'd become. For several moments she slid the vibrator along her slit, coating it in her hot juices. Deep moans of anticipation slid from her throat.

The first stroke of the humming device over her swollen clit caused her to cry out. She was so close already. It would not take much to reach satisfaction.

She cranked up the speed. In one swift motion she buried it to the hilt within her sopping pussy. Normally she would slowly build her orgasm. This morning she was already soaring. She imagined it was Aiden thrusting into her wet pussy, driving her higher.

"Oh, yes!"

Taking on a fast, hard rhythm, Cassandra fucked herself with the purple device. Her hips rose up off the bed to meet each thrust as she rolled a taut nipple between her thumb and finger with the other hand. Her orgasm steadily built within her fevered body as she rode the vibrator for all it was worth.

* * * * *

Aiden continued to hum contentedly as he set the breakfast tray on the hall table. He would have to leave soon for work, but could spend a few minutes watching Cass enjoy breakfast in bed.

He first noticed the low humming sound as he reached for the doorknob. Confusion was his first reaction. He could not imagine what would be humming in her bedroom. A low, throaty moan penetrated his fogged brain. *What the hell?*

Slowly pushing open the door, Aiden stood in shock. He would have never imagined Cass pleasuring herself. Hell, he would never have pictured her owning a vibrator. The scene before him was the most erotic thing he'd ever seen. His cock was instantly hard.

Her hips bucked violently off the bed with each deep thrust of the device. The other hand fondled an engorged nipple, before reaching lower to rub her clit. Sensual moans of pleasure rose from the back of her throat as she brought herself closer to orgasm. A light sheen of sweat coated her luscious body. Her sleep-tousled hair framed her face in wild disarray.

"Fuck."

The bed faced the doorway, giving him a clear view of her luscious, swollen pink pussy lips. Neatly trimmed dark curls covered her mound. The heavy scent of her sweet cream filled his nose. He longed to slide his tongue over her silky folds, lap up all the delicious juices pouring from her pussy.

Her breasts were fuller than he had imagined, the pink areolas puckered, nipples hardened. His hands itched to feel the weight of those swollen globes, to tease her ripe nipples between his fingers.

His cock pressed painfully against his zipper while Aiden watched a violent orgasm overtake Cass. Her body shuddered, muscles rippling as waves of pleasure washed over her. Her back arched like a bow, and her head was thrown back. He almost came in his pants, which hadn't been a threat since puberty. Images of her sexual abandon would forever be seared into his mind. Damn, she looked so beautiful.

As she slowly stroked herself back down to earth his desire was replaced with rage. Aiden stood unconsciously stroking his erection through his soft denim jeans. Once she had her breathing under control he found his voice. He issued a low, intense growl from the darkened doorway, startling Cassandra.

"Damn it, the next time you come it will be for me," he said in a dangerous tone.

Cassandra screamed. Embarrassment flooded her body, turning her cheeks bright red. Frantically she grabbed for the sheets, trying to shield herself from his piercing gaze. Her mouth gaped open watching him stand rigidly across the room, calmly stroking his cock. She verbally tore a strip out of his hide.

"Aiden, what the hell are you doing. Don't you know how to knock? Oh my God, get out," she screeched. She blindly searched the nightstand for a projectile. Her hand settled on a thick crystal vase, which she flung at his head.

The vase smashed into the wall mere inches from his face. Shards of glass tinkled down the wall, and fanned out over the floor. Still Aiden just stood there staring. He never even flinched.

Calmly he walked into the hallway, and retrieved the tray. He casually walked over, setting it down on the nightstand. Looking down at her fiercely, his tone was matter-of-fact. "I made you some breakfast. I have to go to work now, but we will talk about this later."

He walked to the door, and then turned to face her once again. "Sam's playing on the beach with your neighbor and her daughter." Turning he slammed the door shut, and strode out of the house.

Cassandra collapsed back against the mattress. Rage surged through her. She would not be embarrassed about masturbating. He'd just have to deal with it. Throwing off the covers she prepared to face the day, unashamed.

* * * * *

Anger and need warred for control of Aiden. Why the hell didn't she come to him if she needed release? He would have gladly helped her. Visions of her wild, sexual abandon taunted his painful erection.

His need won out. Taking his hard cock into his hands, Aiden stroked himself in the parking garage at his condo. He replayed the images in his mind of Cass writhing on the bed. Her hips had bucked forward to meet each forceful thrust of the vibrator. He'd timed his strokes to the pace she had used, sliding his thumb over the sensitive crown on each upward movement.

He imagined how it would feel to make love with her. Aiden would pound inside her gripping pussy like a jackhammer. He would thrust powerfully over and over, again and again, giving her what she needed, never stopping until she screamed his name. He wouldn't stop until they both collapsed into a sated heap.

His strokes became firmer, faster. His fingers exerted more pressure. Soon his balls drew up tightly against his pelvis, signaling eminent release. Aiden continued to picture the way Cass had looked as her orgasm had rolled through her luscious body.

Hot streams of cum splashed against the quivering muscles of his abdomen. Pulling a towel from his gym bag, Aiden cleaned himself. The brief relief did nothing to still the raging desire that now plagued his body. He needed Cass.

* * * * *

Rushing through his morning routine, he was showered, dressed, and on the way to work in record time. Still, he would arrive later than normal. One of the perks of being an executive meant that no one would question his tardiness.

By the time he stepped into his office, rage had taken over. He stormed past Cindy, slamming the door shut behind him. A day spent dealing with her would only serve to increase his foul mood. Why the hell had he ever offered her a job? What a dumbass he'd become.

He paced the plush office like a caged animal. Why had he even bothered to come to work? It was not like he'd be able to accomplish anything in his current state. He should have called in sick, and gone to the gym. That's what he needed, an intense physical outlet for the endorphins surging through his veins.

When the door slowly opened, Aiden turned and poured out his rage and frustration on his assistant. Cindy didn't deserve to face his wrath, but she got it anyway.

With his jaw clenched, his entire body rigid, Aiden attacked. "Don't you know how to knock, Cin?" He heard the echo of Cass' earlier words in his own. "I swear. A two year old would make a smarter assistant than you." His hands fisted at his sides. "What do you want?" he spit out venomously.

Shutting the door behind her, Cindy stood up to Aiden. "Who the fuck pissed in your cornflakes this morning?" she boldly questioned.

"Cindy, I'm warning you. I'm in no mood for this shit." Heat poured off his body in waves.

Fisting her hands on her hips she faced him defiantly. "Look, whatever has made you so foul, it's not my fault." She stared at him intently for a moment before continuing. "I just got word from the higher-ups. You're scheduled to fly to the Knoxville office Monday morning for meetings. I thought you'd like to know."

Without another word she turned and left the office, quietly closing the door. She smiled to herself, knowing instinctively it was Cass who had him so tied up in knots. "You go girl," she whispered softly.

* * * * *

Not wanting to spend the evening in his empty condo, Aiden went to a local swing club. Normally he only went there on Friday nights when Cass went also. They would spend the night laughing with their little group of friends, and dancing.

Tonight he needed the companionship of his friends, and to work off the tension. He found almost everyone at their regular table. Markus, Eric and Trina, Devin and Katie, Nick and Sandy, Travis and Cindy were all there. Shouts of welcome went out as they saw him approach.

Travis jumped up and gave him a one-armed hug. Aiden was closer to him than anyone. The two men shared almost everything. Travis clearly read his mood, and signaled the waitress for another beer mug.

Over the years they'd had some wild times together. They'd even switched identities once. Several times they had even shared in pleasuring the same woman. He couldn't imagine two people being closer than their bond kept them.

"Hey, Aiden. What's going on?" Travis asked with concern.

Taking a mug from the waitress, Aiden poured from the pitcher, and drank deeply before answering. "Nothing new. Just the same old crap piling up." He looked around the table, and spoke briefly with the others gathered together.

The small group was very close-knit. Growing up, the men had formed indelible bonds. All of them had played football together in school. Their friendship had just naturally progressed from there.

They had occasionally participated in a ménage à trois with each other. Although no man really wanted to share his woman with another man, they wanted them to experience the ultimate pleasure and closeness the experience could bring. It was unconventional, maybe even socially unacceptable, but an act of deep love and emotion nonetheless. One that cemented their steadfast brotherhood, and brought great pleasure to all the participants.

Aiden had been involved in pleasuring most of the women in the group. The experience was what kept them all so tight. The men all enjoyed the knowledge that if anything was to happen to them, the others would all be there for his lady.

The one person Aiden had hoped to see tonight was not seated at the table. He needed some sexual relief. Looking around the room he finally spotted Tammy on the dance floor. Relief washed over him.

Tammy was the only woman in the group who was not part of a couple. Over the years he had formed a casual relationship with her built on taking care of each other's needs. It wasn't that different from Travis' relationship with Cindy. Aiden loved Tammy as a friend, but not the way he felt for Cass. Tammy understood and accepted this completely.

Watching her swing dance always brought a smile to his lips. Shiny, blonde shoulder-length hair swirled around her slender shoulders. Tammy's petite form twirled around, over, and under her partner. While not as graceful as Cass, she still drew the eye as she moved with skill and exuberance. Aiden admired her unadulterated love of life.

Noting where his attention was drawn, Travis smiled. "Tammy will be glad to see you here tonight." He chuckled softly. "Hell, we all know what it means when you show up here on a weeknight." He clapped Aiden on the back. "Why don't you go cut in?"

Secretly, Travis was thrilled to see Aiden turning to Tammy. That meant things with Cass were not going well. It would kill him to see them get closer, but he would not make a move on Aiden's territory. Nothing would be worth sacrificing their friendship. Not even his fierce feelings for the gorgeous writer.

After finishing his beer, Aiden moved to the edge of the floor and caught her eye. He watched the knowing anticipation cross her delicate features. Tammy immediately excused herself from her dance partner, coming to Aiden.

Without a word they began to dance. The strenuous moves, combined with the easy feeling of her body moving over his allowed him to relax. Tension rolled off his shoulders with the knowledge that Tammy would take him into her body and relieve his aching need. She would generously open herself, slender thighs would wrap around his waist as he thrust into her cunt. He would be imagining it was Cass he was fucking. He would picture her writhing beneath him, calling out in passion.

Wild thoughts of Cass brought an engorged need to his throbbing cock. Tammy immediately sensed the changes in his body. After several minutes she took his arm and led Aiden off the floor. They said their goodbyes, then left the club.

Tammy was a skilled, talented lover. She pulled out all the stops as he fucked her long and hard, hour after hour. Yet the blinding need riding Aiden refused to be tamed. No matter how hard he pounded his cock into her hungry flesh or how many times she cried out as her body spasmed in release, he could find no relief.

Eventually he climaxed, quenching his immediate ache, but never touching his consuming need for Cass. When he left, Tammy had fallen into an exhausted sleep still covered in their combined sweat.

Aiden silently cursed himself for being such a prick. He'd just treated Tammy badly. The truth slapped him in the face with a one-two punch. There would be no satisfaction for him with anyone but Cass—his wandering bachelor days had just come to an abrupt end.

Cass was the one. The only one.

Lying alone in his own bed, Aiden thought about when he'd first met Cass. She had tracked him down when Mike died. The breathless, nervous sound of her voice on the phone had touched something deep inside him. He'd rushed over to her apartment immediately. Nothing could have prepared him for what he found waiting there.

Cass was everything he had searched for in a woman. Long caramel brown hair fell in warm waves over her shoulders, down to her slim waist. Big emerald eyes reflected reluctant passion and pain. They also revealed her strength and deep intelligence.

Her nose was slender, and slightly turned up at the end. Rosy, pouty lips had trembled in a valiant attempt to form a smile. A worn T-shirt revealed full, firm breasts. Soft, faded blue jeans conformed to long, shapely legs.

Aiden had wanted to take her right then and there, feeling no remorse over his attraction to his brother's wife. The small, fragile arm snaked around one of her slender thighs was all that stopped him. After talking for a few minutes he finally caught a glimpse of the shy girl hiding behind her young mother. Clear, crystalline blue eyes stared out at him in wide-eyed fascination.

Both of them seemed so wary and innocent. He'd wondered what could have ever drawn Cass to his dark, brooding brother. It had taken a great deal of time and patience to get her to reveal even a small amount of Mike's abusive ways.

It had also taken a long time for her to learn to trust him. Day by day she revealed more strength and determination than he could have ever imagined. At times, he was still surprised by her strength of will and spirit.

He despaired that she would never accept the instant attraction that had sparked between them, and only grew stronger with time. Aiden knew that she was physically very aware of him. Desire was clear in her eyes, as was her fear of intimate relationships. As much as possible he'd tried to counteract the damage of Mike's abuse. No matter how sincere Aiden was, she still did not trust his words.

He decided that soon he would have to confront Cass. While he hated the thought of losing even the small part he played in their lives, Aiden knew he could not continue on this way much longer. He would force her to face the reality of their feelings. She could not hide from him indefinitely.

Chapter Five

Friday nights at the club were a staple of their weekly routine. Sam would go home from school with Darlene's daughter, Jessica, for a sleepover. Aiden always picked Cassandra up at eight o'clock. She'd wondered if he would show up this week, and if he was still angry.

It was only natural to take care of a physical need. She would not allow herself to be embarrassed that he'd seen her masturbating. When he picked her up she would behave like nothing had happened.

While Cassandra was an unofficial member of the small group of friends, she was unaware of many of their activities. Sure, she'd heard talk over the years, but chalked it up to crude gossip. The handsome men in the group were very devoted, and protective of their girlfriends. She could not imagine them inviting other men to participate in their sexual encounters.

She had danced with all of the men at one time or another, but most enjoyed taking the floor with Aiden. The fast-paced moves required that partners be closely in tune with each other, and dancing with Aiden was like a dream. They moved together with complete confidence, easily anticipating the other. They had even won several competitions together.

Cassandra was anxious to take the floor with Aiden tonight. They excelled at many forms of swing dancing, from the East Coast to Country-Western and Cajun Swing. The fast, high-energy music always lightened her spirits, and dancing with Aiden always made her feel closer to him.

Dressed in a silky leotard, twirly skirt, and strappy leather rug-cutter shoes, Cassandra was ready for some fun. She'd spent time in front of her mirrored closet doors observing the way the mid-thigh-length skirt accentuated her long legs. She loved the way the fluid material danced playfully over her tanned skin. The formfitting leotard revealed a daring amount of cleavage.

Regardless of her efforts, Cassandra knew that her nervousness showed through the mask of calm she tried to maintain. She was thankful when Aiden arrived right on time as always. His demeanor was relaxed, confident, and in command.

"You look great, baby. How was your day?" he asked, casually sweeping her into a friendly embrace.

Relief washed over Cassandra, but she did not fully relax yet. He could be just putting on an easygoing front, similar to hers. She knew that her overly cheery laughter over his quirky attempt at a joke did not go unnoticed. She fiercely battled her nerves while waiting to be sure that she could once again breathe easily.

On the drive to the club, the built-up anxiety slowly dissipated as they made normal small talk about work. They both chose to ignore the events of the other morning. Cassandra breathed a sigh of relief that she would not have to defend her actions to him. She was just not ready to discuss something so intimate.

They were on the large dance floor within moments of arriving. Cassandra could tell that Aiden shared her anxious need to move together. Like one body, they moved in perfect synchronicity. The intimacy of her body flowing over his often made her feel restless, but the energetic dance allowed a physical outlet for the adrenaline surges.

Many times when they danced Travis would join the couple. The two men would send her to new heights of euphoria as they expertly swung her between their big bodies. She felt the most alive when the three of them danced together.

Over time she had become as comfortable with Travis as she was with Aiden. She trusted both men implicitly on the dance floor. They would never allow her to be hurt. If only all things could be so simple and straightforward in life.

Aiden's hands flew over her body, cradling, pulling, pushing, and sliding her in new directions. Travis was quick to join them, and Cassandra literally sailed through the air under Aiden's legs, over Travis' shoulder.

The three of them read each other's eyes and body movements in silent communication. It still amazed Cassandra how attuned the two men were. She felt so relaxed, open to the intimate touch of their hands. It was truly extraordinary how the three of them moved together so fluidly. A perfect mating. She was beginning to realize an absolute rightness in how flawlessly the three of them joined together.

The DJ played the Brian Setzer Orchestra's "Jump, Jive and Wail", and the trio burst into motion. The other couples on the floor moved away to watch. Before long everyone in the club was on their feet, cheering the trio on as they danced with wild abandon.

The ending of the song brought on a riotous round of applause. The two men sat down to take a break, and Cassandra took the floor with Eric. There was too much adrenaline pumping through her system to sit down now. She always found it challenging to dance with the thin, wiry man. It required more strength and effort on her part, reinforcing how perfect her union with Aiden and Travis felt.

Aiden observed her movements from the table. He trusted his friends to treat Cass with respect. They all knew she belonged to him, and would not step out of line. Seeing his friends touch her intimately sent a delicious thrill through his body, but also a slight pinch of jealousy.

A friend of Eric's interrupted their dance and he went off with the woman, leaving Cass on the edge of the floor. Before he knew what had happened she'd been swept away by a stranger. Jealousy burned in his dark eyes as he watched the other man's hands move intimately over her.

He was on his feet and moving instantly. He noted Cass' distress in her every movement, which had turned jerky instead of her normal smoothly flowing motions. Within a few quick strides he was at her side, separating the other man's hands from her body.

Holding her sheltered protectively in his arms, Aiden headed away from the dance floor until stopped by the stranger. The idiot had decided he'd object to Aiden's interference.

No sooner had he turned around to knock the stranger down a peg than Tammy appeared, sweeping the man away. She had quickly assessed the situation, and taken action to prevent the inevitable fight.

Silently, Aiden thanked Tammy for her quick, unselfish actions. Once he had Cass off the floor and safely seated at their table, he saw Travis go to Tammy's rescue, quickly sweeping her away from the obviously inebriated man.

"Damn it, Tammy," Travis hissed. "You care about him too much, and it's only going to get you hurt." Looking into her eyes he saw the truth clearly written in their expressive hazel depths. He growled in frustration. "You know his heart belongs to Cass."

Looking down at their feet, Tammy said, "I know, but I worry about him."

Travis gave her a stern look. "Don't. Aiden's a big boy. He'll work this out between them, then where will you be? Don't let him break your heart."

She shook her head slightly. "Don't worry about me, Travis. I'll be fine. I know there is no future for me with Aiden. That doesn't stop me from caring about him though."

The group's men closed in on the stranger who had dared to dance with Cass. They pulled him to the side, and in explicit terms explained that it would not be wise to touch any of their women. Before long he had been convinced that it would be a good idea to leave the club.

The fun had abruptly ended for everyone in their little group when the club's bouncers became involved in the situation, ushering everyone out the door once their tab was settled. It was a relief not to find the drunk in the parking lot, but the men did not so easily let go of their anger. Aiden was especially riled, needing to blow off some steam.

Turning on their feminine charm, the six women were finally able to convince the reluctant men to call it a night. Cassandra was too shaken up to realize what had happened, or to pick up Aiden's dark mood. The stranger had put his hands on her body in ways that made her skin crawl. She felt dirty, and in need of a long shower.

* * * * *

They both remained absorbed in their own thoughts during the silent ride home. This was becoming an awkward habit. Cassandra missed how they normally talked easily about everything. She had been scared by the cold, possessive gleam in Aiden's normally warm eyes at the club. And the tension surrounding him now was palpable. What was up with that?

In the quiet of the car she was able to reflect back on the actions of their friends. Tammy had put herself between the two men to prevent bloodshed. The other woman's eyes had been filled with both care and concern for Aiden.

Angry energy surged through Cassandra from just thinking about Tammy. She knew the rumors about Aiden and Tammy. She saw the way they looked at each other, and acted around each other. She wasn't stupid. She could easily put together two plus two. The more she thought of him sharing himself with Tammy, the angrier she got. But what right did she have to be mad? Aiden could sleep with whomever he wanted. Yet just the thought of him and the petite blonde woman made her want to strike out.

The group had rallied, clearly determined to protect one of its own. She had never experienced anything quite like the way they quickly jumped to each other's aid. She was not sure how she felt about their actions. It felt good to know she had the protection of the group, but it also felt somehow restrictive.

She turned on lights as they moved through the house. In the living room, she stood with her hand hovering over the light switch. Cloaked in the darkness, she posed the questions that haunted her. "Do they always close ranks so quickly for each other? And why would they do that for me?"

Aiden could just make out the angry and confused look in her eyes in the dim light from the hallway that penetrated the darkness. He tried to relax for her benefit, and let his simmering anger go. "Oh, baby. They will always protect you and care for you, because you belong to me. You never have to worry about anything. Even if I were unable to take care of you, the group would." The intensity in his eyes let his words sink past her frazzled nerves. "You belong to me."

Had she heard him right? "But why?" she asked innocently, choosing to ignore the possessive comment. That was something she was just not ready to address.

"It's just the way we feel about each other, Cass. We love each other, and take care of anyone important to us. They all love you and care about you for the person you are, but all the more so because I love and care about you."

Emotions threatened to overwhelm Cassandra. Had he just said he loved her? The words were made all the more powerful by his honest tone, and the warmth reflected in his dark eyes. Dare she hope he was referring to something more than friendship?

Until his fingers wiped away her tears she wasn't even aware she was crying. The entangled emotions assailing her brought no answers, only more questions. She felt fear, uncertainty, and pain, as well as warmth, caring, and deep abiding love.

Pulling her into his sheltering embrace, Aiden gently rocked her. "It's all right, Cass. I know you feel disconcerted and scared right now, but you know the truth in your heart." His hands soothed over her hair and back, calming her abraded nerves.

The internal war being waged between heart and mind was clear. She wanted to trust in his words and feelings, but was terrified to take such a risk again. She wanted to take him deep into her body, but felt she should pull away.

Aiden could see that she still needed time. He had pushed her enough for one night. Pulling her against his chest he tucked her head under his chin. "It's all right, Cass. I'm not going anywhere. I'll always be here for you. Get some rest and we'll talk more later."

Shit. What was she supposed to do now? She had kept him at a distance for so long, but not lately. She'd needed the feelings of warmth, safety, and protection she got from being held by Aiden. It felt so right to be sheltered against his strong body. She'd lain with her head cushioned on his shoulder. Her greedy body had absorbed his warmth. She felt cold and alone without his touch.

If she hurt him now, drove him away, it would be kinder than the greater hurt that would surely come later. She had to push away the warmth he offered, allow the cold to seep into her soul once again. Summon all her strength to push him away before it was too late. It was the cowardly thing to do, but it would also be the kindest.

He deserved more than she could offer. Yes, hurting him now would be better for Aiden. She would be strong, stand up and protect the man she loved. It was the only gift she had to give.

She gathered her courage and strength for the inevitable look of pain in his eyes that would brand her heart with misery. Icy fingers of regret were forcefully shoved behind her carefully built walls. Mentally she heard the slamming of the door, the metallic click of the lock sliding home.

For a moment she almost turned and fled. With a mental slap, Cassandra forced herself to do what needed to be done. Every muscle in her body tensed, preparing for what lay ahead.

Sensing the change in her, Aiden froze in her arms. It was clear that she'd closed herself off to him again. The small chink he had managed to make in her defenses the other night had been built back up, stronger than ever.

He wouldn't stand there and let her close him out. He'd be just as stubborn and pigheaded. "Ah…I have to get going. I have to leave for the Knoxville office early Monday for a few days." Brushing a kiss over her cheek before she could protest he said, "I'll talk to you later, baby. I've got a lot of work to do before I go."

Turning, he left before she had a chance to say something he did not want to hear. He'd give her some space and time to think. But as soon as he got back from this trip they were going to have a serious conversation. He wouldn't let her escape again.

Chapter Six

Early Saturday morning Darlene arrived at the house with Sam and Jess. Once the girls headed into Sam's room to play, the two women sat down at the kitchen table to talk.

"Have you thought any more about taking a vacation?" Darlene questioned.

Cassandra just shook her head. "I can't take a vacation right now."

"I think you're going to need some time off before you start your next book, Cass. I need something different from you. The romances are very popular, but my readers want more erotic, explicit fantasy novels. I have plenty of short stories, but need full-length books."

Seeing no protest forming yet, Darlene continued. "I specifically want you to work on something with overwhelming lust, hunk with dark tastes sexually falls for timid woman, introduces her to toys, some light bondage, maybe a ménage à trois. The housewives can't get enough of the ménages."

Darlene laughed inwardly. She'd just described Aiden and Cass, and what she hoped would happen between them. Hell, she was well aware of the rumors of Aiden's sexual tastes and practices. She knew what would happen when the two finally came together.

A startled, wide-eyed look crossed Cassandra's features. "I can't write like that, Darlene," she anxiously gasped. "I have no experience with those kinds of relationships."

Darlene ignored the objection. *Not yet you don't, but Aiden will teach you.* "I know this is hard-core for you, but I'm sure you can come up with stories my readers will die for. The best part is these stories will pay twice the fee of a romance, and the residuals are much greater. I've already put some examples of other works similar to what I'm looking for on your electronic bookshelf. Maybe they'll bring some inspiration."

Darlene inwardly chuckled again. *Yeah, and maybe Aiden can bring some inspiration.* She'd brought everything needed to tease and play with him. Now she just had to get Cass to play along.

She patted the box sitting on the table. "I brought some research material. Explore, have some fun, and then write some mind-blowing sex." Darlene smiled suggestively. "Maybe Aiden can help out with the research."

Cassandra groaned in frustration. "Great. Thanks, Darlene. Turn me into a major porn writer." A deep red flush colored her cheeks as her friend's words penetrated her embarrassment. "And I can't research sex with Aiden. Our relationship is not like that."

Images of Aiden naked flooded her body with heat. She had no doubt that he would be an incredible lover. His gorgeous body poised over her, ready to fuck her senseless. She knew his cock was long and thick. She also knew from rumors that he was an insatiable lover who could last for hours.

She pictured him thrusting between her legs. He would fill her completely, each powerful thrust sending her closer and closer to climax. It would be so incredible to abandon her body to Aiden. He would be so careful of her. Hell, maybe she would experience an elusive orgasm without use of her vibrator. They would make love like she wrote about in her romances, cherishing each other's bodies, then they'd fuck like wild animals.

"I can't play sex games with Aiden," she gasped.

Her friend sat shaking her head in disappointment. "Damn it, Cass. Why not? He is hot, available, and most definitely willing. Shit, if I was ten years younger, I'd go after him myself."

It was impossible. What Darlene was suggesting would ruin her friendship with Aiden. He would discover her severely lacking skills in the bedroom, and run for the hills.

When Darlene and Jess finally left, Sam walked them out, and Cassandra began sorting through the contents of the box in her office. Her jaw hung open in shock. She had never seen anything so exotic.

Inside were packages containing all manner of sex toys. Some of the packaging was incredibly shocking, containing pornographic pictures of women using the toys. She discovered devices such as butt plugs, vibrators, cock rings, bullets, eggs, nipple clamps, and pocket rockets. Darlene had even included a large supply of batteries in various sizes, padded leather restraints, lubricants, and a bungee cord swing.

One package in particular was mind-boggling. The Golden Bumble provided clitoral suction and vibration. A jelly suction cup was fitted over the clitoris and inside the vaginal lips. The squeeze pump created suction, which held the device in place. Then a vibrating egg delivered stimulation to the clit.

OHMIGODOHMIGODOHMIGOD!

Just looking at the items in the box caused Cassandra to blush hotly. She could not imagine actually using any of the implements, much less writing about their use. Yeah, like she would hang a pleasure swing in her home. She was a member of the PTA for crying out loud.

Darlene must have lost her mind. How was she supposed to write about things she had never experienced? A ménage à trois of all things. She couldn't imagine many women having participated in a threesome, though it did sound blissfully decadent.

Darlene's words hung in the air. "Maybe Aiden can help you out with the research." *Yeah, thanks for putting that image in my head. As if I need any help fantasizing about Aiden.* Cassandra had caught herself many times recently in just that activity. Seeing him without a shirt on would be forever burned in her memory.

After a late evening, Aiden often spent the night in the guest bedroom. One such night, Cassandra woke from a bad dream to find him sitting on the edge of her bed, gently stroking her shoulder. "Shh. It's okay, baby. Just a dream," he'd whispered in a husky voice.

She'd reached out and turned on the bedside lamp. Soft light glowed over his golden skin. The primal urge to run her hands over his broad chest almost had her reaching out. Dark hairs dusted his well muscled chest, and tapered down his stomach. A thin line of hair descended from his navel, down into the waistband of his boxers.

Pulling her eyes back up quickly she'd allowed them to roam over his chest again. While not a weightlifter, he had the well-muscled body of a healthy, active man. Broad shoulders led to sensually curved, muscled arms. His pectorals were nicely shaped with a shallow cleft running down his breastbone. His flat abdomen displayed a washboard pattern of lean muscle.

She had wanted nothing more than to spread her fingers over his abdomen, and feel every swell and curve so wonderfully displayed. She'd longed to flick her tongue over the intriguingly small male nipples. It had been so long since she'd touched a man sexually. Touching Aiden held such a strong appeal.

After assuring Aiden that she was fine she'd watched his back as he retreated from the room. It was certainly not the first time Cassandra had noticed the way his body moved with powerful, masculine grace. His upper body formed a v-shape, down to a slim waist where boxers rode low on trim hips. The thin material slid enticingly over tight, perfect male buttocks. She could see herself holding tightly onto his ass while he thrust into her. The images made her groan.

Giving herself a mental shake, Cassandra forced her mind back away from Aiden. She should not be thinking of him in a sexual way. He was her best friend. She had to get a grip on her raging hormones.

She would have to call Darlene and straighten out this mess. There was no way she could write the type of book the publisher wanted. Hell, she hadn't even had sex in years.

It wasn't that she was a prude. In the locked drawer of her nightstand were lubricating gel and her vibrator. It was a nice, plain, normal vibrator. Nothing fancy, but it did the job, slaking her needs.

Could she actually launch Lacy Harte, her pseudonym, into a world of dark fantasy sexual exploits? And how was she supposed to research such activities? Experimenting with the provocative toys Darlene had sent would be a start, but participating in a ménage was out of the question.

The visual images pouring through her mind sent heated sensations coursing through her body. Her nipples pebbled in anticipation, and hot juices coated her sex. God, she was getting hot just thinking about the possibilities. Heck, she could admit the truth. It would be utterly delicious to be sandwiched between Aiden and Travis.

She had strong feelings for both men, which in itself was scary. God, she was so messed up. How the heck could she love two men at the same time? Feelings like that could only lead to misery for all of them. Hell, they were best friends. Loving either one would make their current friendship uncomfortable. She did not want to see anything ruin the incredible closeness the two men shared.

At the sound of the front door opening, Cassandra quickly closed the box, shoving it under her desk. She stood up just as Samantha blasted into the room. Catching her daughter in a tight embrace, she fought to return her breathing and pulse to normal.

"Hey, pumpkin. Did you have fun with Jess last night?"

"I always have fun with Jessie, but I missed you and Uncle Aiden," Sam said.

Hugging her daughter close, Cassandra fought to bring herself under control. She decided to spend the rest of the weekend doting on her beautiful little girl. "How about we have a makeover day?" she asked.

Sam's squeal of delight cut through the quiet house. "We haven't done that in a long time, Mommy."

"Well, this weekend is all about us. Let's have some fun."

They spent the rest of the day putting makeup on each other, twisting their hair into outrageous styles, and dressing up in Cassandra's clothes. Later they went out to dinner at Sam's favorite restaurant for pizza and video games.

* * * * *

Sam and Jess cavorted gleefully on the playground as their mothers watched from a nearby bench. The park was nearly empty, most people choosing to stay inside where air conditioners kept the scorching Florida summer heat and humidity at bay.

Sweat trickled down between Cassandra's breasts as she fought to explain what she did not fully understand herself. There was just no way she could write what Darlene wanted.

"Damn it, Cass. It's much simpler than you'll let it be. Aiden loves you, and you love him. He's the one man strong enough to love you. You just have to drop your defenses long enough to let him inside."

Darlene's fists clenched, revealing her frustration. "I know you better than you think, maybe better than you know yourself. You're acting like a big chicken, but you're strong. Let go of your fears, his love could save you, Cass."

Dropping her face into her hands, Cassandra fought to find the words to make Darlene understand. It was nowhere near as simple or as easy as she tried to make things seem. "I'd just hurt him, Darlene, and I can't bear that thought."

Darlene sighed deeply. "He's stronger than you think, and so are you. He won't just turn away from you. Aiden is going to fight until you accept his love." Silently she prayed he had the strength to go the distance.

Darlene took several moments deciding how to express her thoughts. "Cass, maybe you should go talk to someone professional. Some people find it helpful to discuss things with a therapist."

Biting her lip, Cassandra fought not to lash out at her friend's efforts to help. "No," she said firmly. "I don't need to be dissected by some stranger." She remained silent for several minutes then quickly changed the subject.

"I have some ideas for a new story," Cassandra finally stated. They spent the next hour hashing out plot details, all personal conversation put on a back burner. When the heat finally became too much they headed home.

* * * * *

Mike's death had not only released Cassandra from his psychological torment, but also provided her with a cash windfall from his life insurance. The money had purchased a comfortable home, and furnishings. The money earned from her books paid the monthly bills. While not living in the lap of luxury, they did all right.

The four-bedroom house provided enough room for her to have both an office, and a home gym. When physically tense, Cassandra would punish her body with a strenuous workout. Over the weekend she spent many hours in the small room, high-energy music playing at a deafening level.

Sweat sluiced over her body as she kept tempo on the stair stepper with the Def Leppard song, "Pour Some Sugar on Me". The loud music and strenuous physical demands on her body kept her from thinking about anything else. After a long, cool shower she collapsed in bed.

It didn't work. After several hours of staring at the ceiling, Cassandra cursed her well-intended plans. She spent the early morning hours Monday wandering around the house restlessly, wondering how to keep Aiden at a distance while still maintaining their friendship, and how to justify her feelings for Travis.

She felt like screaming in frustration. Her mind told her to remember the lessons of the past. Her body told her to think of the pleasure that would come from giving herself to Aiden. She knew from being held in his arms that they fit together perfectly. Instinctively she knew he would make her feel so good.

Just thinking of being in his arms brought warmth to her body. She longed to taste his lips, and feel his response. Her hands longed to play over the muscles of his chest and back. She imagined following the soft trail of hair below his navel. They would move together in bed as well as they did on the dance floor. Nothing would compare to the sensation of his big cock filling her empty body.

Violently she closed the door on her thoughts. Why was she tormenting herself with something she would never have? If she was going to be awake then she might as well work.

Cassandra moved into her office and booted up the computer. After logging onto the e-book website she opened her digital bookshelf. Darlene had placed several stories there for her research.

The first story she read was about a set of twins in love with the same woman. At first the woman had been unaware that it was two different men she was dating. She became confused when it seemed that her lover had two different personalities, and styles of making love.

Eventually she discovered their duplicity, and left them both. The brothers came together in an attempt to win her back. Together they seduced her, resulting in a ménage. In the end she kept both men in her heart and bed.

Reading the explicit scenes of passionate sex had her labia swollen, throbbing, and saturated with hot juices. She found it amazing that reading the story could make her so hot.

The next set of books she read involved three brothers. One found the love of his life, but he shared her with the others, bringing them all closer. The writer used many different sex toys with the characters, providing explicit details of their functions and desired effects.

The story had her glancing over at the box Darlene had brought. If she was truly going to write an explicit book, then she'd have to research. The toys would be a good place to start, but she went for the books first.

Chapter Seven

Cassandra was shocked by her state of arousal. If Aiden had been anywhere nearby she would have simply stripped him naked, and taken him with fierce need. It was a good thing she was alone. She'd have to be very careful about reading the erotic books.

She was particularly surprised to be so turned on by scenes involving anal sex, and ménage à trois. She'd never known such activities would interest her. Her sexuality had been buried so deep for so long. How could reading fictitious sexual encounters bring her unknown desires out?

Cassandra's mind got away from her. She pictured acting out some of the scenes with Aiden. Imagining having a butt plug vibrating in her ass while he took her pussy with long thrusts of his cock drove her crazy. She knew on some deep level that it would be incredible.

The alarm clock in her bedroom beeped shrilly. With a reluctant sigh she made her way down the hall. After silencing the infernal machine she woke Sam for school.

Cassandra remained very distracted as they shared a breakfast of cold cereal, fruit, and yogurt. As soon as she dropped her daughter at school, she returned to her office, famished for the next story. Reading about two big, dark-haired cousins hit a little too close to home. In the story the men came together to share a ménage with one of their wives for her birthday.

As she read the story, Cassandra substituted Aiden and Travis for the characters in the book. Her mind vividly played the scene out with the two of them coming to her. She could almost feel the incredible sensation of being pleasured by both men simultaneously.

Her pussy throbbed with need. Looking down, Cassandra realized that not only had she soaked her panties, but a large dark spot warmed the crotch of her jeans. Her nipples stood hard and aroused beneath her silky bra.

Deciding to read some more of the stories on her electronic bookshelf had not been a very bright idea. Reading explicit sexual encounters did nothing but increase her mounting tension. After changing her panties for the second time, Cassandra finally gave up.

One lusty scene in particular where the dominating man was preparing his submissive partner for anal intercourse had Cassandra's pussy throbbing painfully. The man first used his fingers to lubricate, stretch, and prepare the small hole for his cock. After inserting a thick butt plug he roughly fucked her pussy. Later in the story he slowly fucked the woman's ass.

Thinking of the possibilities brought both fear and a tingle of excitement. Could she enjoy pleasure that came with the bite of pain? She wasn't sure, but intrigued.

Another story depicting a woman's fears during her first ménage left Cassandra shaking with need. Having two men thrusting into her body sounded so decadent, wild. Would Aiden share her with another man? Her visual images brought a fresh flood of juices gushing from her slit.

Looking over websites which sold sex toys, Cassandra learned of the uses for the different devices. She could not imagine how people could invent such imaginative toys. Removing the box from under the desk she sorted through it again. She might as well kill two birds with one stone, perform some research and ease the demands of her throbbing body. Her pussy pulsed just from her looking at the various toys.

Opening all the packages and inserting the required batteries took quite some time. She turned on each vibrating device to study its function. Picking up a tube of lubricating gel,

Cassandra selected two devices. Reading the packages again she determined the blue snake was a flexible probe for g-spot or anal stimulation.

The other device which caught her attention was an eight-inch-long purple vibrator that could be made to rotate, vibrate, pulsate, or all three at once. It was formed from three graduated ovals with nubs on the last one. The package boasted six speed settings, and a glow in the dark controller.

She locked the office door before stripping off her clothes, then moved to the plush couch and contemplated the toys. Stroking her palms over her swollen nipples increased the ache in her pussy. Spreading her legs she looked at her swollen labia dripping with her cream. The musky smell of her arousal filled the air. As she teased her nipples with her fingers, Cassandra watched in amazement as more cream poured from her vagina.

Gingerly at first, she ran a finger over her passion-swollen lips, spreading her slick cream. When her finger was saturated, Cassandra gently thrust it into her pussy. A primal moan escaped her lips as her finger brushed over her g-spot. Finding that sweet bundle of nerves was something she'd learned to do during her reading. Soon she had two fingers thrusting in and out of her clenching pussy.

Turning the purple vibrator to its lowest setting she stroked it over her drenched slit. After circling her swollen clit several times, Cassandra drove the shaft into her pussy. A few deep thrusts had her hips surging with each penetration caressing her sensitive vaginal walls.

Adjusting the controls to add in rotation she moaned deeply, the vibrating head repeatedly swirling over and against her cervix. Plucking at first one sensitive nipple, then the other sent fire spreading into her already overheated pussy.

Closing her eyes, Cassandra again pictured Aiden thrusting deeply into her moist flesh. Moving the vibrations up a notch, she felt juices saturating her slit, soaking her thighs. Wet slurping noises and the scent of sex filled the air.

Cassandra felt her climax hovering on the edge, but was unable to push her body over into the release she needed. Leaving the vibrator rotating against her g-spot she squirted some gel over the blue snake's head. She draped one leg over the back of the couch, and turned onto her side. Arching her back she reached around, and guided the slender probe into her tight back channel. Her muscles tightened over the dual invaders as hot bursts of pleasure-pain spread through her ass.

"Oooooh, yesssssssssss."

Afraid to move, she took deep breaths and focused her mind on relaxing the tight tissues. Eventually her muscles eased, and she began to truly enjoy the feel of the slim device against her extremely sensitive nerve endings. With her thumb she triggered the controls for the snake sending vibrations through her tight passage. She began a synchronized thrusting with both devices. With wild pants she flew over the edge into a pulsing, wet, intense orgasm.

The deep contractions continued endlessly. Their force caused the probe to be pushed out of her ass. Slowly removing the big vibrator, Cassandra stroked her fingers over her swollen pussy in a soothing motion, bringing her down from the intense heights of orgasm. Curled up on the coach she gasped for each breath as her body began to recover and cool down. *Wow!*

Aftershocks of sensations fluttered through both canals. Cassandra decided that exploring anal sex could be delightful. Although, considering the small size of the snake left her fearful of having a man's cock in that slender channel. The sensitive tissues there continued to endlessly throb from the shallow, vibrating invasion. Umm, writing explicit erotic books was going to be a thrilling adventure.

She jumped up suddenly, startled by the shrill ringing of the telephone. Snatching up the handset she felt guilt and embarrassment take over her emotions. Of course, the person on the phone couldn't know what she'd been doing. *Okay, get a grip.*

The unmistakable huskiness of her voice shocked her as she rasped out a breathless, "Hello." She almost didn't recognize the sound as having come from her. After several moments there had been no response, so she repeated the greeting.

"Cass?"

Her heart stopped hearing the rich, resonant sound of Aiden's familiar voice, then restarted at an irregular beat. Realizing she hadn't responded she finally managed to reply, "Yes."

"Oh God, Cass. You're driving me crazy. I need you so much." They were both silent for several long, drawn-out moments. The unmistakable sound of a zipper opening filled the gap in conversation. Aiden took his rock-hard cock into his hand and began stroking its smooth length.

"Damn it. I'm sorry, Cass. I won't push. I just wanted to make sure you're all right, that we're all right."

Cassandra found it hard to speak as her heart leapt up into her throat. She felt embarrassed, and strangely titillated that he seemed to know what she had done.

"Aiden." His name was whispered on a sated sigh.

He cursed violently under his breath. He could tell by the sound that she had found release by herself, again. "You should've let me help you, Cass. I'd never hurt you. I can make you feel so good."

In a husky voice, she started to explain about the new ménage book Darlene wanted, the box of research material, and her recent reading. Aiden felt his blood heat up to a nearly volcanic level.

He continued long, slow strokes over the satiny smooth skin of his cock. Closing his eyes he imagined that Cass was stroking him. He pictured her stretching her rosy lips over his shaft, milking him until his hot semen jetted into her throat.

When he spoke again his own voice had turned even huskier. "I won't be back until Thursday. Arrange for Sam to go over to a friend's house for the weekend, baby. We need to talk. I'll be over Friday night around eight. We'll skip the club this week."

"Oh God, I'm so embarrassed," she croaked out miserably.

"Don't be, baby. Just promise to let me help you next time. It'll be so much better. I promise." He was quiet again for a moment. "I'll talk to you Friday, Cass."

After hanging up the phone Aiden knew he would never be able to relax now. He pictured Cass spread open for him, crying out his name when he thrust into her pussy. His own release came within moments.

He spent the next several days thinking about both Cass, and Sam. He had to make her see that they were a family, that he loved them both. He always had, and always would. They belonged together.

* * * * *

Cassandra was happily surprised to find that she had slept well since talking to Aiden. Telling him about the new book, toys, and research she was conducting had been a relief. She had found release for the tension in her body. And knowing that they would talk about the mounting sexual tension between them allowed her to relax her mind.

First thing she did was make plans for Sam. On Friday morning she dropped her off at her friend's house before school. Cassandra had thought about talking to Becky, the other girl's mother. They had become friendly over the past few years, but were not very close. Thankfully she changed her mind before her mouth had a chance to say anything embarrassing.

During the drive home she decided on calling Darlene. Who better to talk about sex with than the publisher of romance and erotic e-books? Feeling happy with this decision, her mood lightened. She would have faith in Aiden, and pray that having sex with him would strengthen their relationship. She would deny her strong feelings for Travis. Hell, she would have enough trouble handling one man, two were unthinkable.

Darlene had listened quietly to her fears, concerns, and desires. Her friend was able to read between the lines to what she wasn't saying.

"You are the biggest nitwit I've ever known," Darlene stated with a chuckle. "After reading your books, I just can't believe you haven't had sex in so long. I don't think it would be possible for a saint to abstain for seven years."

Chuckling softly, Darlene continued. "I know you're an enlightened woman, but having a relationship with only an inanimate object can't be very healthy."

Cassandra gasped, "Darlene," dragging out the word.

"Honey, if you didn't want to hear the truth you should've called someone else." She gave that comment a moment to sink in.

"In all seriousness now, Aiden is a good man. He has always been there for you and Sam. I think you should trust him, and I know that you want him. If so, then fuck him."

Darlene could only laugh again at Cassandra's shocked gasp.

"The real question you have to answer is do you love him?"

Cassandra nervously pushed her hair behind her ears. When she spoke her voice was very quiet, but confident. "I love him with all my heart." *But I love Travis too.* She wouldn't speak that thought out loud.

"I knew that too," Darlene said. "I just wasn't sure if you did. In that case, marry him."

Darlene heard the yearning in her friend's reply. "If he would have such a neurotic mess as me, I would. But, then there's Travis. I don't know what to do about my attraction to him. I don't want to come between them."

With a deep sigh Darlene said, "Well, for heaven's sake, at least fuck those boys. Oh, and I want explicit details." Her raucous laughter echoed over the phone line. "Hell, the experience should fuel your creativity for at least a hundred steamy books."

Chapter Eight

Having made her decision, Cassandra was a nervous ball of energy. Her closet became a riotous disaster as she randomly pulled out, and then discarded outfits. Her hair was tousled from repeatedly raking her fingers through the long tresses.

If she dressed up would it be too obvious? She wasn't sure she cared. Her only wish was to not make a complete and total fool of herself, and not be rejected.

Finally giving in to the nerves she called Darlene again. Cassandra didn't even take the time to say hello, but started firing off nervous questions upon hearing her friend's voice.

"Okay, if I dress up will I look naïve and obvious? You know I mostly wear jeans and T-shirts. Would it be ridiculous to wear a dress? And what about makeup? I never wear makeup."

Her voice was high and borderline shrill. "Damn it, Darlene. I'm not a high-class, sophisticated, polished woman. I'm the tomboy next door. I can't pull this off, and attract a man like Aiden." She barely took a breath. "I'm not good enough for him."

Taking a deep breath, Darlene said, "Slow down, honey. Breathe. Go open a bottle of wine. I'll call you back in a few minutes." She hung up without waiting for a reply.

Cassandra was so wound up that she broke the cork while opening the wine. Small brown pieces floated in the neck of the bottle. Deciding she didn't care, she poured a large glass and drank greedily. God, she had descended to the level of drinking in the morning.

"Okay, you can do this. A little liquid fortitude. Just have to be careful not to get drunk."

Staring at the ceiling she had to laugh at herself. "Now I'm worried about you, Cassandra. You're talking to yourself."

When the phone rang she shot out of the chair as if attached to a spring. She fumbled the receiver and anxiously questioned, "Darlene?"

"Listen to me, Cass. Go take a long hot bath, and use some scented oils. Wash your hair, and put on a robe. I set you up for an emergency house call with a stylist. His name is Andre. He and his team will take good care of you. Don't even continue thinking you are not good enough for Aiden. You are beautiful, sexy, and more than he deserves."

Yeah right, Cassandra thought. She must be out of her mind. Bolstering her courage she decided she had no other choice. She needed Aiden desperately. "Darlene, I don't know what to say. You are such a lifesaver."

"Remember that the next time I give you a deadline, honey. Now, don't drink more than two glasses of wine. Call me if you need me, Cass. And most of all, have fun, girl!"

"Thanks, Darlene. I will."

* * * * *

Within a few hours the house was descended upon by a pack of stylists and technicians. Cassandra sat while her hair was trimmed, dried, curled, fluffed, and sprayed. At the same time, a nail technician performed a manicure and pedicure, painting her nails a deep crimson color called "Seductress".

Andre was a hurricane of motion and chatter. He complimented her elegant facial structure and complexion. Then he told amusing stories about Darlene, while constantly offering Cassandra more wine.

When the first team was finished the next group advanced. Cassandra was given a facial massage, followed by intensive moisturizers, and finally, artfully applied, natural-looking makeup.

Once all the "groomers" were gone the couture divas put on a full-out fashion show. Cassandra must have tried on two dozen outfits before selecting a feminine dress that made her feel as if she were walking on air. It had a handkerchief hemline with a tiered and layered flowing skirt. The low neckline and spaghetti straps accentuated her full breasts. The pale blue silk chiffon was embellished with jewels and bugle beads in an elegant pattern.

Cassandra wore no bra because of the thin straps and open, plunging back. Her high, firm breasts filled out the bodice nicely. She wore light blue lace thong panties with a matching garter belt attached by satin straps to thigh-high stockings.

The outfit was accessorized by a pair of sexy silver sandals with a thin strap slide, and matching double ankle straps. When her house was finally empty, Cassandra added small diamond stud earrings, and a thin silver bracelet to complete the look.

Standing in front of the mirror, Cassandra was shocked by her transformation. She felt like Cinderella on the night of the ball. The comfortable, tomboy soccer mom was nowhere to be found. She had been replaced by an elegant, seductive woman. Never before had she felt so feminine and sexy. Just maybe she could pull this off.

The dress showed off her muscular arms and prominent collarbones. She worried briefly that she was looking too muscular from her kickboxing classes, workouts, and daily runs. Quickly she dismissed her concerns. The mirror did not lie. She looked incredible.

Using her digital camera, tripod, and manual exposure timer, Cassandra snapped several pictures. She downloaded the images onto her computer, and attached them to an e-mail thank-you note to Darlene.

Searching through her CDs, Cassandra tried to find the perfect one. She wanted something soft and sexy, maybe even a little racy. Pulling out *Damita Jo* she decided that it was perfect. Seductive, explicit, great beat, just what she needed.

After turning on the music, she lit several candles and sat down in the living room to wait for what she felt would most likely be one of the most important moments in her life.

* * * * *

Aiden was wiped out from barely sleeping for the past week. Add in the stress of travel and tension with Cass, and he was a wreck. No matter what, he would find a way to get through to her. He had to. There really was no other acceptable option.

This morning he had been full of confidence. Now that the evening was rapidly approaching a flicker of doubt had started to creep into his consciousness. He tried to keep his anxiety at bay by remembering that he knew Cass better than anyone.

After taking a shower he dressed in a cream-colored silk long-sleeved shirt, black wide-legged gabardine pants with double box pleats, and a black leather belt. Casual black leather loafers completed the ensemble.

By the time he pulled in the driveway, Aiden's hair was mussed from repeatedly dragging his hands through the thick strands. He felt a surge of panic seeing only soft, minimal lighting through the front windows. Maybe she had gone out to avoid having this conversation.

Stepping inside the front door he immediately noticed the Janet Jackson CD softly playing a seductive song. After closing the door he turned the deadbolt lock, and called out her name.

"In the living room," she replied in a deep, sultry tone.

He stubbed his toe on the entry table while trying to make his way through the lowly lit room. Biting back an expletive he strode into the living room. The minute he passed through the doorway he felt as if a vacuum had sucked all the oxygen from the room.

He couldn't breathe, couldn't think. He just stood there staring at Cass, the pain in his toe instantly forgotten. All that existed were the moment and his woman. He could not imagine anything half as beautiful as his woman. One look told Aiden that she had already decided to take their relationship to the next level. Talking was unnecessary.

Cassandra began to fidget under the unwavering intensity of his eyes. Oh God, she looked stupid. How could she have let Darlene truss her up like a pig for roasting? She dropped her eyes to the floor in utter embarrassment. Her arms crossed over her chest in defeat.

Watching Cass shutting down broke his trance. Aiden was across the room in two swift strides. He gently tilted her chin up and whispered in an astonished tone, "You take my breath away. I have never seen anyone half as beautiful, Cass. Please, don't shut me out now."

Taking her hands he spread her arms wide, then stepped back struggling to find words that would express his feelings. "You did this for me?" he asked, with awe and appreciation clear in his tone and expression. "Thank you."

Cassandra could not find her voice. She nodded shyly and gazed up at Aiden from under lush, dark lashes. The need for his approval was clear on her face.

"Baby, I know Mike did everything he could to break down your confidence. The things he told you never meant anything. They were lies. You are a vision of pure feminine beauty. You're perfect, Cass. Absolutely perfect."

Her quiet thank you let him know that she was not convinced. Taking her hand he said, "I guess I'll have to show you, because words just can't do justice to describing how beautiful you are."

Cassandra gasped as he folded her fingers over his firm erection. The heat radiating from his hard cock nearly burned her, but she did not try to pull away.

"I've never wanted any woman as much as I want you. No, not want. I need you, baby. I'm going to spend the rest of my life pleasuring you. Just relax, let me love you."

When she would have melted into his arms, Aiden held her back. "Hang on, baby. Let me look at you for another minute. I want to remember everything about the way you look tonight."

Taking his time, Aiden drank her in, greedily feasting on every wonderfully feminine curve. The dress barely covered her mound, while sheer layers revealed every shapely detail of her legs. The thin straps of the sandals caressed her slender ankles, and showed off sexy little crimson-painted toes.

A low growl of masculine approval came from deep in his throat as Aiden moved around behind her. The thin spaghetti straps extended in a crossing pattern down her delicately arched back. The material plunged all the way down to the top of her slender crack where it softly gathered in silky folds. Her tanned skin called out for his touch.

"So beautiful!" he praised.

With trembling fingers, Aiden traced the low edge of soft material. Gathering her cascading hair he moved it over her shoulder, out of the way. His lips placed searing kisses along her elegant neck. Then his tongue traced the curve of her ear, before descending to taste the pulse beating wildly in her throat.

"You taste so good. I want to lick every gorgeous inch of your body."

Reaching the tender curve where neck met shoulder, Aiden gently scraped his teeth over the sensitive flesh, then soothed away the small hurt with his tongue. His breath was a warm whisper caressing her ear. Her sudden intake of breath sent shivers of anticipation down his spine.

"You're like hot cinnamon, and sweet sugar on my tongue." He paused for a moment. "Are you sure, baby?" he questioned. Her huskily whispered affirmation nearly brought him to his knees.

Leaning back against his chest, Cassandra felt his hard cock pressing into the deep cleft of her ass. She could feel the throbbing heat through their layers of clothing. A reciprocal warmth flooded her pussy, the wet response quickly saturating her panties. "I want you inside me," she boldly whispered.

His tongue trailed down the path of crossing straps sending shuddering waves of heat through her. "Be patient, love. I've waited a long time for this. I'm going to lick and taste every inch of your body first. God, Cass. You go right to my head like fine wine."

Cassandra moaned and shifted against his body in anticipation. The dark, sexy words sent throbbing pulses through her superheated core. Her slow movements rolled his thick cock over her ass.

"Mmm. I bet you're ready for me, aren't you? Your sweet pussy must be throbbing, aching. Are you wet for me, Cass?"

Her only reply was a deep moan and an increase in the slow movements of her hips, driving his cock deeper into her crack. She ached to feel him buried deep inside her body.

He wanted to make this last. Pulling back from her heated movements, Aiden slowly worked his way down her back, teasing and tasting the satiny skin along the way. When he reached the material covering her ass, Aiden pulled it between his teeth, making way for his tongue. In a slow, sensual motion he slid his tongue down between her rounded cheeks. While he knelt behind Cass, one hand moved from her hip, sliding under the sheer material to caress the soft skin of her inner thigh.

"Aiden." His name was a moan of pleasure rolling over her lips. The feel of his hot tongue on her ass made her toes curl.

He cupped and kneaded one firm cheek before sliding his fingers to the saturated crotch of her panties. The soft caress over the silky material caused even more dampness to pool there. "Oh, baby. You're so ready for me. So hot and wet."

God, how would he survive this? He wanted to taste her, but knew that would be the end of him. Breathing in the aroma of her arousal was nearly enough to snap his control. Instead of giving in he stood once again, letting his fingers brush over her heated flesh in a featherlight caress. A taste from her sweet lips would have to be enough for now.

Aiden stood up quickly, giving himself a moment to calm down. Moving around her side, his cock dragged over her hip until Aiden held her firmly against the length of his body. "You fit my body so perfectly. I bet your pussy will fit my cock like a satin glove."

"Unh," she moaned. Cassandra was stunned by how his dark, sexual words affected her. She felt as if her entire body was melting, being reshaped by his hands. She needed more than words though.

He took her mouth in a kiss that started off sweet and sensual. When her lips opened on a sigh, Aiden dove into her mouth with a deep thrust of his nimble tongue, imitating how he would thrust his cock into her slick heat.

"So sweet, baby," he praised.

The kiss became a wild mating of intertwining tongues, driving their desires higher with each stroke. Cassandra forgot to breathe as she melted into his mouth. Why had she waited so long to come to the man she loved? Of their own volition her arms went around his neck, her fingers sinking into his wavy hair.

Warm hands moved up to cup her breasts. Massaging gave way to the rasp of his thumbs over her hardened nipples. Streamers of sensations shot straight from the sensitive peaks to her swollen clit. Cassandra became lost in his warm mouth and hands. Her breasts began to throb with the need to be kissed, suckled.

Dark, sensual words filled her mind. Not allowing herself a chance to think, she began speaking. "Aiden. I want...I need you inside me, f-fucking me, NOW!" She had never imagined wanting to speak such dark, crude, sexual words. Somehow it was freeing.

A low moan rumbled through his chest. "Slow down, baby. This is going to last all night. I've waited too damn long to rush anything now that I finally have you in my arms."

Giving herself to her overwhelming needs, Cassandra began working on the slippery buttons of his shirt with trembling fingers. His kisses had moved to her jaw, then her ear, and on to her neck. His cock pressed firmly against her lower abdomen.

The buttons were stubbornly keeping her from where she needed her hands. Overcome with frustration and the need to touch him, she firmly pulled on the material sending buttons scattering in different directions. As her hands sank into the muscular flesh of his chest she arched into his firm body.

She pulled the soft material down over his sculpted arms, trapping them behind his back in the still buttoned cuffs. Taking full advantage of his bared torso her hands lightly caressed the masculine flesh. He felt better than she'd ever dreamed. Her fingers spread over hard ridges of sinew, teased shallow indentations, loved every inch of his solid chest. She felt feverish, burning with need.

"You feel so good," she whispered.

Cassandra was unaware of her other whispered pleas and moans. All that existed was Aiden's wet tongue, and hard body. "Please, Aiden. Oh, yes. Please."

Not being able to touch her was more than Aiden could bear. He violently ripped the shirt in his efforts to free his hands. Her abandoned response was driving his control to the breaking point. In one swift motion he scooped her up into his arms and carried her into the bedroom.

Chapter Nine

Aiden slowly let Cass slide down his body in a long caress until her feet reached the ground. He knew her legs would be wobbly, and thoughtfully kept a supporting hand on her at all times.

Shifting into a calmer pace was the only way he would be able to make this last. "I want to see all of your beautiful body, Cass." Tenderly his big hands cupped her face. Trailing his fingers in a light caress past her jaw, down her neck, they finally reached her shoulders. He continued the smooth movement, picking up the thin straps of her dress with his index fingers along the way.

Slowly his hands slid down her slender arms, dragging the straps to her elbows. Aiden then brought both hands to her waist. Reversing direction, the tips of his fingers flowed up over her ribs, brushing the sides of her breasts, stopping at the top of the dress.

Holding the soft material between his fingers, the caress was again repeated in the opposite direction. As his hands flowed over Cass' sides, the dress slowly slid down revealing her breasts, inch by tantalizing inch. He alternated between watching her eyes and her body.

"So pretty, baby."

He massaged both firm, smooth globes with his palms while taking her mouth in a mind-blowing kiss. When she was sufficiently wrapped up in his mouth, his thumbs slowly circled her rosy areolas. Delicate, fraction by fraction, the circles became smaller until his thumbs rasped over the sensitive crests.

Her nipples were so responsive, beading up at his touch. Her soft moans and whimpers were driving him crazy. And the sweet taste of her skin, *wow*. He couldn't wait to lick and taste everything.

"Oh, yes," she moaned.

Pressing closer, she rode his thigh, grinding her pussy against his leg. He could feel the feverish heat rolling off her in waves. When he finally got his cock in her hot pussy she'd likely burn him alive.

Watching for her reaction he began to gently roll her nipples between his fingers. A low moan was building in her chest as he tormented her relentlessly. At the first flick of his warm tongue on one turgid peak, Cassandra's head fell backwards on a deep, rumbling moan of pleasure.

"You like that, baby? How does my tongue feel on your pretty little nipples?" Aiden began swirling his tongue around her nipple, watching as she arched her breasts closer. His tongue made quick circles around the soft flesh, flicking and teasing.

"Umm. I think you enjoy my tongue loving your nipple. Let's see how you like it when I suck you deep into my mouth."

The gentle suckling at her breast drove Cassandra to a mindless need. Twining her fingers in his hair she fought to hold his head even closer. She moaned, arched her back, and held him tightly against her breast while he sucked. When Aiden released the wet peak she whimpered in protest.

"Can't leave the other one neglected, now can we?"

He gave her no time to respond. The breath was stolen from her lungs at the feeling of his tongue laving her other nipple. His fingers never stopped kneading her breasts while he devoured her.

Aiden slowly dropped to his knees. His hands caressed from her ankles, along the outside of her legs to the hem of her dress, then back down again. On the next stroke he moved along the inside of her legs, took hold of the hemline, and pulled the dress over her hips. The soft material pooled around her feet unnoticed.

"Holy shit!"

For several long moments all he could do was to stare. He wanted to rip off her little thong panties and take her standing up, still wearing the garter belt and stockings.

"Give me strength," he pleaded.

His hands stroked up the inside of her legs again, this time stopping at her knees. Gently he lifted one leg, and pulled the sandal from her foot. He sat her foot against his thigh and stroked both hands to the top of the stocking. With deft motions of his fingers the clips were easily released. A slow caress rolled the stocking down over her long leg. Returning her foot to the floor he repeated the same steps with the other leg.

Hooking his thumbs under the elastic band of the garter belt, he slid the lacy material over her lower body. He did the same thing with the thong, drawing in a sharp breath at the first sight of her swollen, drenched pussy and the dark triangle of hair.

Protractedly his fingers slid through the dark, wet curls. In an attempt to slow down, Aiden bit the inside of his cheek, but the pain made no difference. He had to taste her sweet juices or die from the need.

His fingers gently spread her swollen, pink lips. In one fluid stroke his tongue slid over her slit, and upward to circle around her clit. Her sweet, spicy taste spread through his mouth, flooding his senses. A deep moan of masculine appreciation vibrated against her sensitive flesh. "You taste so sweet, baby."

She continued to plead. "Aiden. Oh, please. I need you." Her eyes were nearly black, dilated with passion.

Flicking his tongue over her clit he asked, "What do you need, Cass? What is it you want?" He wanted to hear her say the words.

Cassandra looked at him through a sensual haze. Her desire and need were clearly written on her expressive face. Okay, she could do this. She could seduce him with words. Hell, she was a romance writer after all.

"Mmm," she purred seductively. "I need you inside me. I need to feel your thick cock filling my hungry pussy. I need your lips on my nipples. I need to hold your firm ass in my hands while you come inside me." Hey, not bad for her first attempt. Cassandra felt very proud of herself.

Dark desire filled his melted chocolate eyes. The visual images she created sent tremors coursing through his body. He'd never seen this side of her.

Seeing and feeling his response made her bolder. "Aiden. I'm going crazy thinking about how it will feel to be impaled on your cock, again and again. Moving faster and deeper with every stroke. You'll be so slick from my cream when my muscles tighten on you, and your hot seed fills me. Please, Aiden. Fill me up," she ordered.

Cassandra never broke eye contact. Her words drove his burning needs higher. Aiden could almost feel the sensations she described.

"Damn, baby. You're killing me." He lifted her effortlessly into his arms. Placing her in the middle of the bed he stood still, looking down at her.

Finally, he moved to the foot of the bed and slowly crawled up between her thighs, gently spreading them wide as he moved closer. "I've wanted to fuck you since the first time I saw you, Cass. But first I'm going to eat your pussy until you come for me."

Seeing his face between her legs caused Cassandra to moan in frustration and need. His dark, wavy hair looked erotic next to her tanned flesh, hovering over her pussy. Hungry brown eyes devoured her.

One long finger slid slowly through her juices, parting her lips. "I want to watch you come for me, baby. I want to lick up all your sweet juices, and feel them slide down my throat."

She cried out as his finger thrust deep inside her aching flesh. Her hips bucked underneath him, her cream soaking his fingers.

"God, you're so tight." The walls of her vagina stretched as he sunk a second finger deep inside her hot pussy. He thrust in and out with his fingers while his tongue made lazy circles around her clit. She cried out again when he firmly sucked the sensitive nub between his lips. The muscles in her belly contracted while she whimpered with the fierce need to come.

She was so close. He knew it would not take much to push her over the edge into orgasm. Maintaining sucking pressure, his tongue firmly stroked the elongated button until she was rocking her hips against his face, eagerly fucking her hungry pussy against his mouth. She cried out with pleasure as he suckled and nibbled her, then speared his tongue inside her hot, wet pussy.

Frantically her hands dug into his hair, mindlessly pulling him closer. The slurping and sucking sounds as he eagerly lapped at her were driving them both mad. She jerked beneath him, breathing in great sobbing pants.

Pinning her down with his elbows, Aiden continued the unfaltering strokes that sent her soaring to heights she'd never before experienced. He nipped her clit gently with his teeth. His sultry whisper held her poised on a high peak.

"Come for me now, Cass. You taste so good."

"I...I can't," she sobbed.

"Yes, you can. You have to let go for me, baby. Let go of that tight control. Just feel, baby. Come for me," he demanded.

Aiden felt like shouting out in triumph the moment she finally let go of the last of her self-imposed tight reins of control. The strong sexual nature she fought so hard to keep hidden surged forward. Strangled cries of ecstasy pierced the room as wave after wave of pleasure shattered through Cass. Her strong muscles clamped down on his fingers, sucking them in deeper. He continued sucking, licking, and thrusting as she exploded.

His long fingers gently stroked over her folds, gentling Cass, bringing her down slowly, tenderly. Aiden waited for her harsh breathing to ease before covering her body with his own.

With fierce need, his mouth clamped over hers. His mouth and chin glistened with her cream. Cassandra could taste her own juices on his lips and tongue. Their mingled exotic taste excited her in a whole new way. Leaving all inhibitions behind, she forcefully grabbed his face, ending the searing kiss. "If you don't fuck me right now, I'll scream."

His laugh was dark, sensual. "Oh, baby. I'm going to fuck you *until* you scream." He sucked her bottom lip between his teeth, gently nipping the generous curve.

He was awed by the depth of passion and sensuality she had kept tamped down for so long. "Damn, baby. I wish you could see how beautiful you look when I take you, when you come for me."

He caught sight of their reflection in the mirrored closet door, giving him an idea. The dark smile that claimed his mouth made Cassandra worry what he was thinking. "Umm, what do you have in mind?" she questioned cautiously.

Without answering he climbed from the bed. Aiden stared into her eyes as he slowly removed his pants and boxers. He kicked them off, standing before her in all his naked glory.

He was so beautiful. His cock was thick, long, and incredibly engorged. The tip curved up slightly, the perfect angle to hit her sweet spot while he thrust into her pussy. It stood out proudly from his lean body, surrounded by a dark nest of pubic hair. Unconsciously she licked her bottom lip while wondering how he would taste. She smiled when his cock jerked in response.

Aiden's eyes followed the glistening movements of her tongue. He nearly ejaculated just watching that primal, hungry gesture. It would feel so good to have her rosy lips sliding over his throbbing cock, but neither of them was ready for that.

He turned to her closet and picked out a pair of black spiked heels. When he turned back to the bed he held out his hand to her. "Come here, baby."

Taking his hand she rose from the bed on slightly wobbly legs. He positioned her facing toward the mirrored doors. Aiden knelt down and gently fitted the shoes on her feet, then pulled a chair over from the vanity table, sitting it in front of Cass.

"Aiden?"

He moved around behind her and whispered, "Spread your legs wide for me, baby." He rewarded her compliance with a soft kiss on her nape. "Good girl. Keep your eyes open, baby. I want you to see how beautiful you look while I take your sweet body."

His deeply tanned hands snaked around her sides to massage her swollen breasts, looking exotic compared to the pearly skin. She watched in fascination as her breasts rose toward his caressing fingers. She could feel the ache in her nipples — hard, swollen, begging to be sucked.

Tilting her head to the side she provided his mouth easier access to her neck, then leaned back against his strong chest. Her eyes remained opened, watching the couple in the mirror. It was the most incredibly sensual experience. She was being cherished by Aiden's mouth and hands as she looked on.

"You are so damn sexy," he whispered against her ear. He traced the outline of the supple lobe before lightly scraping his teeth over the sensitive flesh. "Hmmm," he purred with satisfaction as she trembled in his arms.

His cock throbbed against her buttocks, pushing against the deep cleft. Cassandra was overwhelmed with the need to feel him buried deep inside her pussy. *Okay, you can do this. You are a wanton sex goddess. Make him lose control.*

Cassandra began to roll her hips with a sensual sway, caressing his cock with her ass cheeks. She reached around their bodies and firmly massaged his firm male buttocks with her fingers, pulling him closer. Keeping eye contact in the mirror she moved her tongue over her lips in a slow, sexy motion. "Mmm. You're making me so hot, Aiden. I can't wait to feel your cock slide so deep into me."

Wow, did she just say that? She almost shouted out in triumph at the dark, heated look which crossed his handsome face. It was obvious he couldn't believe she'd said it either.

Holding her hips, Aiden bent her slightly at the waist. "Hold onto the chair, Cass." His voice was dark and strained with need, stroking over her nerve endings. He urged her legs wider apart with his hands between her thighs. Bending down he ran his hands over the length of her long, luscious legs.

"Damn, baby. Your legs go on forever. I can't wait to have them wrapped around me as I drive my cock into you." A calloused finger circled around her tight, puckered anus before sliding further to stroke her clit. The caress was repeated several times as he spread her cream over her aching body.

The tight, dark little hole called out to him. Aiden wanted to thrust his cock into her firm ass, but she would have to be prepared for that first. He couldn't stand the thought of hurting Cass.

With his hand, Aiden guided his cock between her legs to stroke along the wet slit. The engorged, plum-shaped head looked sinful peeking out between her spread legs. Her hot juices coated him, searing his flesh. Springy pubic hairs teased his silky shaft.

The wild goddess came roaring to life once again. "Oh, yes. Fuck me…now."

Her hand slipped between her legs, capturing his cock as she tilted her hips back toward Aiden. The motions sent her knuckles firmly sliding over her swollen clit. After stroking them both several times she guided his straining head to the dripping mouth of her pussy.

Aiden grabbed her hand, stilling her motions. "Whoa. Hold on, baby. I have to get a condom first."

He tried to pull back, but Cass did not release her possessive grip on his shaft. She felt desperate, frenzied. There was no way she'd let him step away now.

"No. I only want to feel you, Aiden. I'm on the pill for irregular periods." She moaned in frustration. "What are you waiting for? Just fuck me, now!"

He stood still, watching her eyes. She needed him. What was he waiting for? She was wet and open and ready, but he had to be sure. "Tell me you want this, baby."

"Damn it, Aiden. I need you now. Do I have to worry about something?"

His response surprised her.

"I've never had sex without a condom. I'm clean." The burning intensity of his dark, smoldering eyes made her shudder.

"Good. This will be a first for both of us then."

He couldn't believe it. He was about to have sex with Cass. Just Cass. There would be nothing between them. Just their bodies joined completely together. He looked up at the ceiling for a moment, saying a silent prayer. *Thank you.*

The trust implicit in coming together so completely hung heavy in the air. He felt like he'd just been given the most precious gift in the world. He stared at their bodies in the mirror as she guided him into her tight pussy while pushing her hips back, driving him deep inside.

"Oh, shit!" he gasped.

Flexing his knees Aiden drove himself forward, watching his cock slowly disappear inside Cass. He grabbed her hips to hold her still, waiting for her tight vaginal muscles to relax. The hot walls of her pussy held him in a vise-like grip.

He slowly pulled back until only the tip was held tightly within her body. He groaned and shuddered as her tight, wet walls clasped the thick head of his cock. The intense, burning heat of her tight pussy enveloped him as if she'd been made just for him.

Aiden watched her eyes as he drove forward a little deeper. He began a slow rhythm as they both watched, transfixed by the joining of their bodies. In and out, again and again. Her tight pussy gripped him firmer than a fist, stretching wide around his cock.

"Watch, baby. Watch me fuck your tight pussy."

The sensations were incredible. He could feel every bit of her near volcanic heat scorching him, placing her brand on his flesh. He belonged only to her now, forever.

The friction of her soft vaginal walls took his breath away. There was nothing to dull the sensations. He'd never felt anything so good in his life. It was like coming home. After several thrusts, Cassandra began to move her hips in counterpoint.

"Damn it, Aiden. Stop holding back. I need all of you."
Wow. You go girl, you wild and wanton sex goddess.

A primal, animalistic groan rumbled over Aiden's lips as his control snapped, driving forward with savage need. "Don't worry. You'll get every inch," he purred as he angled his hips, driving forward as Cassandra thrust back. Her eyes snapping shut as she cried out.

Aiden fiercely growled, "No! Keep your eyes open, Cass. I want you to watch us become one."

Forcing her eyes open she shifted her gaze from his to where their bodies joined together seamlessly. She clenched her vaginal muscles, milking his cock. She was rewarded by another deep growl.

"Fuck. Now, Cass. Come for me now."

She watched in the mirror as their sweat-covered bodies slapped together with a wet noise. Her nostrils flared, drinking in the mingled scents of their sex. She cried out as his hard thrusts sent his tight balls slapping against her pussy, stimulating her clit.

Aiden's face contorted as his cock began to throb frantically, sending her over the edge into ecstasy. With a final deep thrust their eyes locked together as their bodies throbbed in release, merging together, becoming one.

Strangled sounds escaped her throat. She screamed his name as bright light washed over her weakened body. Only his hands gripping her hips kept her standing. She was trembling, her thighs shaking from her explosive orgasm.

Hot jets of cum hit her womb as their bodies convulsed. He moaned and pushed into her one final time, holding himself deep as her spasming pussy milked his orgasm from his throbbing cock.

Looking in the mirror she studied her image. Her hair looked wild and sexy. Her face was flushed, cheeks pink, lips swollen from his kisses. Her wide eyes revealed a happily satiated woman. Her arms and legs trembled as he held her against his big body. Damn, she really looked like the wild, wanton sex goddess she'd tried to portray.

Chapter Ten

Aiden gently carried Cass to the bed and laid her down. Holding her close he moved the damp hair away from her face. His trembling hand stroked over her arms and back in soothing motions.

With a shaky voice he asked, "Are you all right, Cass?" The tender, loving look in his eyes tore at her heart, breaking away more of her barriers. "God, baby. I wasn't too rough, was I?"

"Aiden." Reaching up she stroked her fingers gently over his face. The love in his eyes was reflected back in her own. "You were wonderful. I never—I mean…um. That was my first time that, um, that I didn't bring my orgasm about by myself." Her pretty face flushed in embarrassment.

Amazingly, Aiden felt his cock snapping back to attention. Even though he had just spent himself in Cass, he was ready for her again. How could it be that no one had ever tapped into her deep well of passion before?

"You never had an orgasm during sex before?" he asked. "How could someone as responsive as you not have reached orgasm?" He shook his head in wonder. A surge of male pride washed through him. She was certainly good for his ego.

Her fingers drew lazy circles over his chest. "Well, um. Bryce and I were both virgins. Neither of us knew what we were doing. Mike, well…" She couldn't believe she had just made those statements like it was nothing.

"Hmm," he mumbled. "Well, I plan on watching you come several times a day, every day, for about the next fifty years." He moved over top of her, taking her mouth in a toe-curling kiss.

She whimpered into his mouth, reveling in the feeling of his strong, hard body pressed so tightly against her. Feeling his hard cock press against her abdomen, Cassandra questioned, "Already?"

"Oh yeah, baby. Again and again. I'll never get enough of your sweet little body." Bending his head down, Aiden flicked his tongue teasingly over a taut pink nipple.

Fire surged through her body from just that quick, simple lick. She groaned inwardly. *Damn, girl, you're in trouble now.*

He worked his way down her body with his mouth, licking, sucking, nipping on her flesh. He felt drunk with her taste, a mouthwatering combination of spice, sugar, and sex. He became lost in the high of having her in his arms.

Aiden tongued her navel sending electric sensations through her abdomen. Oh, the way he looked at her body. It was as if she were the most beautiful woman in the world. His eyes roamed hungrily over every inch of her, like a man starved for the sight of a woman. As if he would eat her alive. And he treated her like a precious treasure.

Aiden rose from the bed and disappeared into the hallway. Confusion filtered through Cassandra. Why had he left her? She'd thought he was ready to make love again?

A few moments later he walked back into the room with the box of toys from her office. His face held a wicked grin, which sent wild shudders through her body.

"Aiden? What um…what're you doing?"

Setting the box down on the nightstand he began sorting through its contents. "I'm helping with your research, baby."

Panic flooded Cassandra as he studied the various devices. Seeing the fear in her eyes, Aiden paused. "It's okay, Cass. I'd never hurt you." Never breaking eye contact he asked, "Do you trust me?"

She nodded her head, and attempted to relax her body. Fear quickly turned to anticipation. Aiden stared at her for several moments before returning to the box. He leaned over, placing a black satin blindfold over her eyes.

"Aiden!"

"Shh. I want you to use your other senses. Trust me, baby. It will feel wonderful." He waited until she laid her head back against the pillows before continuing.

"Good girl," he praised. The mattress dipped down as he sat on the edge of the bed. Her anticipation built as she waited to feel his hands on her body.

Looking over her sumptuous body, Aiden felt a desperate compulsion to use the leather restraints. Nothing was more beautiful than a woman restrained, spread open, trusting in him to ensure her pleasure. That wasn't a possibility with Cass though. She'd been abandoned too many times, scarred too deeply. She wouldn't allow herself to trust anyone to the degree necessary for bondage, yet.

"Just relax and let me love your body, Cass. Keep your hands at your sides. Let me pleasure you."

Cassandra gasped when something soft tickled her ear. Soft, light caresses floated over her face, tickling her lips and cheeks. Searching her memory for the contents of the box she remembered seeing a lush, pink feather. She lay quietly, anticipating his next movements.

Soon the feather moved over her jaw, under her chin, and along her neck. The light caresses sensitized her skin, bringing every nerve ending to life. Slowly, it teased down her arms to her hand where the sensitive skin between her fingers received lingering caresses. Soon the feather was sliding over her prominent collarbones, then down the valley between her breasts.

The decadent touches made her feel cherished, warm and incredibly sensual. As the feather circled her breast she arched in response, seeking a firmer touch. At the same time the feather slid over one nipple, the other received a hot, wet lick drawing a deep moan from her throat.

She felt a cool breeze flow over the wet peak just before hearing his exhaled breath. It took every ounce of will she had to keep from touching him. "Aiden. Oh God. I can't stand it. Touch me, please," she begged.

"Mmm. Not yet, baby. I want your whole body on edge first." He continued teasing with the feather for what seemed to be an eternity. Cass giggled as it traced down her ribs, and over her abdomen. It came breathtakingly close to her mound before skirting around her hips to her legs. The feather stroking over her fevered flesh felt divine. Like a million tiny fingers softly caressing.

A great deal of attention was devoted to both legs, but especially the sensitive arch of her feet. As the feather finally began to move up the inside of her legs, Cassandra held her breath. She was finding anticipation to be a powerful aphrodisiac. Her pussy was dripping steamy juices over her thighs, saturating the sheets. Just before the feather touched the crease of her thigh his breath whispered through her dark, curly pubic hair.

"Unh," she moaned. Cassandra found she was unable to form words or sentences, which was an entirely foreign state. Never before had she been unable to verbalize her thoughts and feelings. Streamers of sensation surged through her body as the feather glided over her labia. She became overwhelmed with the sensual caresses when Aiden gently parted folds of flesh, and teased her clit with the lightest of touches. Her hips bucked up toward the feather, seeking more.

She whimpered as it was removed from her body. The sheets made a rustling sound near her head, and she turned toward the sound as it retreated lower on the bed. Aiden's hand snaked under her lower back wringing a cry from her lips.

"Lift up your hips, baby," he instructed.

When she complied two pillows were placed under her ass, angling her pelvis upward, making her more accessible to his touch. The feather soon returned to caressing her inner thighs and labia. Then the soft sensations moved lower until the feather was playing around her anus.

She inhaled sharply at the intense, forbidden sensation. At first Cassandra was shocked, but soon she gave herself over to the naughty caress.

Aiden watched closely for her reactions. When her body relaxed he began to trail his finger over the tiny puckered hole. With each stroke he increased the pressure. Using a generous amount of lubricating gel on his finger he began to slowly penetrate her anus. Her sharp moans delighted him.

After her initial stiffening response he felt Cass slowly relax her muscles. When his finger was inside her tight channel to the first knuckle, Aiden began to wiggle the digit in a circular motion.

The sensation was strange at first, but not unpleasant. "Ohhh. More please, Aiden," Cassandra begged. She began to rock her hips against his finger.

"You like that, don't you, baby." Slowly Aiden used his finger to work lubrication into the tight hole. He had to take slow, cleansing breaths to calm himself once his finger was buried in her tight channel. "God, Cass. You are so tight. I can't wait to fuck your gorgeous ass."

His dark words sent heat coursing through her. "Yes, Aiden. Please, I need you in me."

A second finger joined the first, sending searing pleasure-pain spreading outward from her ass. Aiden held his fingers still while her sensitive tissues became accustomed to the added girth. When her muscles relaxed again he began slow movements, continually adding more lubrication.

His fingers fucked her ass while his tongue slid over her clit in a matching rhythm. Soon she was thrusting her hips against his fingers, seeking a deeper penetration.

Aiden picked up a butt plug he'd placed on the bed. He coated the rigid device with lubrication. He continued licking her clit as he spread his fingers, stretching her tight tissues. Finally he removed his fingers, and began slowly rocking the plug into place.

"Aiden?" Her hands tightly clutched the sheet.

"Shh. It's okay, baby." He fucked her shallowly with the plug until it moved easily. "That's it, baby." He watched the deep, rapid rise and fall of her chest with each breath, thrusting out her breasts. On her next exhalation he pushed in the plug up to the flared base.

Cassandra's cry was more pleasure than pain. The feel of his tongue gently laving her clit kept the pain in the background until it faded away. Slowly it turned into blistering sensation.

Aiden sank two fingers of his other hand into her dripping pussy. As he thrust his fingers, he sucked her clit again. Soon she was bucking against his hand and mouth, calling out his name. She hurtled into orgasm as his teeth closed lightly over the aching nub. He continued his ministrations as she rode wave after wave of sensation. The intensity of the orgasm was frightening. She felt like she'd break into a million pieces. It was the most intense thing she'd ever felt.

Aiden brought her back to earth slowly. Sighing deeply, Cassandra sunk sleepily into the mattress feeling like a boneless mass. Never would she have thought that so much pleasure could be possible. If she'd had enough strength, she would have kicked herself for waiting so long to be with Aiden. He was such an incredibly passionate, caring lover.

"God, baby. I just can't get enough of you," he whispered against her ear, sending shivers down her spine. Once again he began slowly loving her body with his mouth. "You are so damn responsive."

Listening to his praise, Cassandra felt the sex goddess awaken within her once again. *Oh boy, here we go.* "You're not so bad yourself, lover. I want your big cock inside me."

Aiden gasped at the shiver her words sent through his body. "Hmm. I think someone still wants to play." He slid the head of his cock over her sopping wet slit, and then pulled the blindfold off to see her expression.

"You've left me very wet, Aiden. I think you should finish what you've started."

One eyebrow arched up high on his forehead. "You're going to be the death of me, baby." He watched the emotions play across her features for several moments. "Where do you want me, Cass?"

A wicked smile crossed her face. "Hmm, let me think about this." He continued to teasingly slide through her juices, coating his cock. "I think maybe there," she said.

"Where?" he teased. He wanted to hear her say the words.

"I want you in my pussy," she lustily declared.

Aiden quickly picked up the game. He pushed only the bulbous head into her hot opening. Once again he raised his eyebrow. "Here? Are you sure?" He couldn't suppress his laughter at the impatience in her voice.

"Yessss. Oh, Aiden, please." She arched her hips, trying to take him deeper.

"Well, if you're sure," he teased. His own impatience quickly got the best of him. Aiden drove forward, sheathing himself to the hilt in one smooth thrust, then held still inside her warmth. With the butt plug firmly in place she was even tighter than before. "Umm. Maybe you're right."

"Oh God, yesssss. Aiden, fuck me," she pleaded.

He could no longer hold himself back. "Your wish is my command." Aiden began a slow, steady thrusting along with a passionate kiss. Soon their movements became more urgent. Her legs wrapped tightly around his waist felt so right. Using her muscular thighs she pulled him deeper, heels pressed tightly against his ass.

Between ragged breaths, Cassandra said, "Oh…yes…feels sooo good…sooo full." With the pillows underneath her ass tilting her pelvis forward, each motion stimulated her g-spot, his pelvis grinding against her clit.

Her nails sank deeply into his shoulders as she held on with ferocious intensity. The world spun away from Cassandra, every thought and feeling focused on her lower torso. With each deep thrust she felt him fill her more completely, all the way up into her chest. Her whole body tensed and convulsed as she rocketed into pure ecstasy. Primal sounds were forced from her throat as her orgasm shattered her world.

As her vagina clamped forcefully on his cock, Aiden's own release was milked from his body. His legendary staying power melted away. He kept pumping until her movements stopped, then collapsed on top of Cass. It took every remaining ounce of strength in his body to finally roll to his side, gently removing the plug from her ass. Before drifting into a deep, contented sleep, he tucked her in close against his side.

Chapter Eleven

Cassandra woke feeling more relaxed and sated than she had at anytime since childhood. Memories of making love with Aiden multiple times during the night spread warmth through her abdomen. She could feel the heat of his body under her hands.

She allowed the lingering smell of sex to permeate her senses. As her eyes slowly opened she was staring at a blurry, blunt object. Blinking several times her eyes finally began to focus. Her head rested on his abdomen, his erect cock jutting toward her face, the one-eyed monster staring at her.

Throughout the night she had wondered how he would taste. Aiden had kept her from exploring him the way she'd wanted. Her newfound alter ego, the wanton sex goddess, leapt with joy. Deliciously wicked ideas began to take shape in her mind. She'd always been told turnabout was fair play.

Being careful not to wake Aiden she gently secured him to the bed with the leather restraints. She placed several items on the side of the bed before returning to her waking position. She started by gently expelling her breath over his cock. His reflexive jerk assured her that it must feel good.

She was very naïve about how to pleasure a man. Most of her knowledge came from her recent reading. Cassandra had never before desired to perform fellatio. Her feelings for Aiden ran so deep that she wanted to give him this pleasure, and she longed to share this experience with him.

Deciding to follow her instincts, she started by tracing the small slit in the tip of his cock with her tongue. She was intrigued by how silky the warm skin over his steely shaft felt. Soon she was twirling her tongue around the exotically shaped crown. His salty, masculine taste had her juices flowing from her slit. His taste excited her, and she moaned softly.

She quickly became consumed with discovering this new delight so magnificently stretched out before her. She noticed that with each stroke his cock swelled and jerked toward the warmth of her mouth. She began to feel sexually powerful as she watched him helplessly respond. Quickly she learned that the ridge and just below it were very sensitive, especially the v-shaped area. It was such an intensely intimate act, taking him into her mouth. She felt closer to Aiden than ever before, eager to take everything he had to give.

* * * * *

Aiden dreamed his cock was being slowly devoured. It was not a new dream. Many mornings he woke up with a hard-on after having visions of Cass' warm mouth swallowing him, her lips stretching around his girth. He struggled to stay asleep and enjoy the dream as long as possible.

The more intense the dream became, the more alert Aiden became. When his eyes finally opened he couldn't believe what he was seeing. Cass lay curled around his body slowly sucking his cock. Her emerald eyes sparkled with passion.

For some reason he could not move. He kept trying to move his hands toward the long caramel tresses fanned out over his abdomen. He became fully alert with the realization that she had tied him to the bed.

"Oh shit. Cass...baby. What're you doing?" He strained against the restraints uselessly. He was both shocked and delighted with this new twist to her normally sedate sexuality.

"Mmmmmm. Good mornin'. Just relax, babe. It's my turn now," calmly stated the sex goddess. Her words echoed statements he had made during the night.

She began to tongue him eagerly, enjoying each throb and jerking motion. Maintaining eye contact over the length of his torso, Cassandra slowly slid his cock as far into her mouth as she could. His moans of pleasure fueled her needs and desire to love him in this way.

Between gasped breaths he tried to form words. "Cass…baby…stop…oh God…yes…please."

She laughed around his swollen flesh, sending erotic vibrations through his shaft. "Hmm. Which is it? Stop, or yes please?"

Her tongue trailed down the length of his shaft and slid lower, down to his scrotum. Gently she took first one then the other globe into her mouth, suckling and swirling her tongue insatiably.

Very quickly Aiden became lost in the sensation of having Cass so unselfishly pleasuring him. It was what he had always dreamed of, but never really thought would become reality. He felt his love for her growing stronger by the second.

"Oh, God. Let me go, Cass. I need to touch you, baby," he pleaded.

Cassandra hummed in response while sucking both testes, sending vibrations surging through Aiden.

"Damn it, Cass. Mmmm…ooooh. I can't take it, baby."

Releasing his scrotum, she trailed her tongue down over the soft flesh between his balls and anus then made light circles around the tight, puckered hole. He moaned as her finger began to press into the tight channel.

"Yes, you can take it. Just like I did." Her laughter sounded slightly wicked. "You taste so good. I've never done this before, Aiden. It's my turn to touch and taste you." She paused, and stared into his eyes longingly. "I'll stop if you want, but I am really enjoying this."

Her obvious pleasure rocked Aiden to his core. "Damn, baby. I've created a sex monster," he teased. "Don't stop if you're enjoying it, baby. It feels so good."

All other conscious thought left his mind as she took his cock in her warm mouth again. She let him slide slowly in and out as her head bobbed up and down. With each stroke her tongue rasped over the sensitive flesh below the head. One of her hands tightened around the wet base, stroking close to his balls.

Cassandra alternated her ministrations between the head of his cock and his balls with no clear pattern, keeping him off balance. His sounds of pleasure drove her enjoyment higher. She would never have imagined enjoying such an intimate experience. Soon she found herself fantasizing about how it would feel when he came in her mouth.

Aiden lost control and began fucking her mouth, groaning her name. He fought to keep his eyes open to enjoy the vision of Cass, clearly loving eating him alive. His scrotum pulled up tightly against the base of his cock.

"Cass. I'm gonna come, baby," he warned, giving her a chance to release him first. Her reaction shocked Aiden beyond belief.

Reaching down between his legs she took the tissue that connected his scrotum to his body firmly between two fingers and pulled downward. This light tugging on his vas deferens would delay his climax. Aiden was amazed that she would know that trick.

Seeing the shock play across his features she had to laugh. "I've been learning quite a lot through my recent research, babe. I'm not quite so innocent anymore. I could probably amaze you with my recent fantasies."

Returning to her task, Cassandra began creating slurping sounds as she sucked him with more vigor, his cock becoming saturated in her saliva. Then once again she began sucking on his balls.

She ran her fingers through her own juices, and brought them to his anus. Turnabout and all that. She teased the small opening with small circles before slowly pushing inside again. Immediately his body clamped down on the invading digit.

Hearing his moans of pleasure let her know she should continue. Cassandra began with one pinky, not wanting to hurt

Aiden. Returning to her pussy she continued to generously coat her fingers in the juices. Using more lubrication she gently thrust her finger into the tight hole as he gasped, sputtering meaningless words.

Following his prior example she waited patiently for him to relax. When he finally did she began to wiggle her finger. Slowly she advanced further into the narrow canal until finding the walnut shape of his prostate. A wickedly knowing grin spread across her lips, which were stretched around his cock. With her other hand she again gently tugged his scrotum back down.

Close at hand were the supplies she'd laid out before beginning. Using the tube of lubrication she prepared a tapered butt plug. Choosing comfort over finesse, Cassandra put the tip of the tube against his anus and shot a cold stream of the gel past the tight ring.

"Oh shit," he gasped. "Cass?" He began struggling against the restraints again.

"Hmm. Just relax, Aiden. I think you're gonna like this." Placing the narrow tip of the plug against the hole she laughed as his eyes widened with sudden knowledge, fear, and desire.

Oh God, she wouldn't.

No sooner had the thought crossed his mind when her emerald eyes told him exactly what she intended. With a slow motion the plug began sliding in and out of his anus. With each stroke the plug slid a little further inside.

He gasped and sputtered between moans as his narrow ass was penetrated by the plug, which grew wider the more deeply it was inserted. He'd never experienced anal stimulation before, and the sensitive nerve endings sent sensations surging along his spine, straight into his cock. His balls pulled up tighter against his body.

The final inch of the plug brought searing fire through his ass as it passed the tight ring with a pop. Once seated in place his muscles began to relax, and become accustomed to the device. Aiden released a breath he hadn't realized he was holding.

Shudders racked his body as she once again gently tugged his scrotum away from his body. *How the hell long would she attempt to hold his release back?* If this was the result of her research he'd have to consider doing some reading too.

Slowly she soothed away the pain with her tongue laving his cock. He allowed himself to relax as she worked over his sensitive shaft with her all too skilled tongue, cupping his balls gently.

Deliberately, she incrementally increased her sucking. It did not take long before he was panting again, fucking her mouth deeply. She used her teeth to scrape at his sensitive skin with just enough pressure to make sure he felt every sensation. He brokenly pleaded and begged her.

"Oh, baby, suck me. Yeah. Suck me harder. Oooh, that's so good."

With a wicked smile she flipped a small switch in the end of the plug, sending powerful vibrations through his ass. Aiden's eyes widened and he gave up his last thin grasp of control. He cried out her name.

"Oh, God yes...suck me...suck me hard, baby," Aiden gasped. "I'm gonna come."

Cassandra sucked his hard flesh in as deeply as she could. Coaxing her throat to relax let her draw him slightly deeper until the soft head bobbed against the back of her throat. His deep primal growl had her juices sluicing down her thighs.

She sucked him harder and faster, pumping with one hand, feeling his balls draw up tightly in her other. The first hot jets of semen to hit her throat made her gag, but Cassandra would not give in to the sensation. Her desire to share this with him allowed her to push past the natural reflex. She forcefully swallowed, while continuing to suck and slide her mouth over his cock. The salty taste of his cum on her tongue had a tidal wave of juices pouring from her aching pussy.

His cock pulsed against the back of her throat as he poured his release into her. Her moans of pleasure sent vibrations through his shaft, increasing his shattering release, drawing it out impossibly longer.

As Aiden's movements slowed, so did hers. She continued to suck until she'd milked every drop of salty fluid from his cock, then proceeded to clean him with light licks. Aiden panted, struggling to gain control over his breathing.

The plug was still sending strong vibrations through his body, keeping his cock hard. His release had been incredible, but not nearly enough. Her loving act only renewed his needs. She turned off the vibrations, and slowly removed the plug. The slick glide of the device made his cock jerk. He still felt like the plug was vibrating in his ass after it was removed.

Slowly she moved around the bed untying the restraints. He watched her closely. As soon as she untied the last one, Aiden grabbed her, flipping her over onto her back. No one had ever loved his cock with such passion.

"Holy hell. There are no words, Cass. That was indescribable." It was the best blowjob he'd ever received.

His fingers slid over the soaked lips of her pussy. "Aw fuck. You loved it too, didn't you, baby?" he asked. "How have I ever survived without you?" It was more a statement than a question, but she responded anyway.

"I don't know how either of us has survived," she stated. Her eyes were darkened with love and desire. "But I'm really glad we finally had this 'talk', babe."

A devilish smile lit his face, showcasing his deep dimples. "Who said we're done talking?"

Chapter Twelve

"I may just have to start reading some of your 'research' materials. Is that where you got those ideas?" he asked.

Cassandra laughed huskily. "Umm, some did come from my research, but the rest was instinct."

After a searing kiss, Aiden flipped her over onto her belly. Pulling up on her hips he positioned her on her hands and knees, then slid his cock between her legs, teasing her wet slit. Cassandra thrust her hips back against his warm body. She never had submissive tendencies before, but the naughty position struck her interest. She knew that by putting that plug in his ass she was asking for him to fuck her there.

Aiden teased her mercilessly with his cock, stroking over and around her clit. Pressing against her ass with one hand, he stroked her nipples with the other. Gently pushing her shoulders down toward the bed raised her ass up higher. He urged her legs wider apart with his knees.

Aiden continued to stroke his erection over her slit until his cock was dripping with her juices. Spreading her cheeks wide he saw her pink anus opening up for him. The plug he'd used on her had done its job.

"Oh, Cass. I'm gonna fuck your sweet ass." With his thumb he stroked down the deep crevice. When he pressed the wide tip against her tight hole she pushed her hips against his hand.

"Umm. I'm gonna make this so good for you, baby." After several easy strokes with his thumb, Aiden spread more of her juices over his shaft. "Tell me if it hurts, baby, and I'll stop right away."

She moaned as he pressed the thick tip of his cock against her back entrance. "Oh please, Aiden. Yes."

He held his cock against the well-lubricated hole, applying steady pressure with the bulbous head, slowly inching inside as she pushed back lustily. He slowly worked the tip past the tight ring. "Damn, baby. You are so tight." Aiden took great care to move slowly, allowing her tight muscles time to adjust to his invasion.

It was too slow for Cassandra. She wanted to feel him thrusting into her ass. Her nerve endings tingled, sending waves of pleasure through her body. "Damn it, Aiden, fuck me," she growled, pushing her hips back fiercely.

Aiden tightly grabbed her hips to slow her motions. "Shit, baby. Slow down."

"No! I want you buried in me, now." Taking her weight on her shoulders she reached between her legs, and grabbed hold of his thighs. With more strength than she knew she possessed, Cassandra pulled him closer while thrusting back against his cock. The fierce motion sheathed him to the hilt in her ass.

Her scream scared him. He held rigidly still. "Oh my God. Are you okay, baby?" Aiden gasped and panted trying to catch his breath. "Talk to me, Cass."

"No, I'm not okay. Fuck me, Aiden."

When he began slow thrusts and they were still not enough, she braced herself against the headboard, then began slamming her ass against his pelvis. The thick invasion of his cock inside her tight channel made her feel as if she were being split in two.

"Yes. Ah, harder. Please," she begged repeatedly as the burning pressure grew within her.

It was all Aiden could take. His fragile restraint and control broke upon hearing her pleas. He fucked her ass for all he was worth, but his renewed thrusts only drove her needs higher. She pounded back against him as every muscle in her body tightened, drawing his cock deeper.

Feeling his own release hurtling forward, Aiden held her hip firmly with one hand. The other slid over her abdomen, and down to her clit. With firm strokes he felt her orgasm build, her ass tightening around his cock. He fought to hold back until she shattered around him, triggering his own climax. The tight milking contractions of her ass drew his cum from his body as he screamed out her name.

Cassandra finally felt the burning pressure inside her ass rupture, releasing molten streaks of lava shooting through her body. Her sensitive tissues clench tightly against his thick cock. She screamed as hot waves of painful pleasure flooded her senses.

Cassandra panted, burying her face in the pillow, biting the soft surface. Her release seemed to explode everywhere, not just her ass. The intensity of her orgasm was shocking. Tears streamed from her eyes as muffled, racking sobs escaped her tightly clenched teeth.

Aiden withdrew quickly, then turned her toward him. "Shit, Cass. Did I hurt you?" He held her cradled in his arms. "I'm sorry, baby."

It took her several moments to catch her breath and be able to respond. "You didn't hurt me, Aiden. It was incredible. I've never experienced anything so intense." She kissed the corner of his mouth. "I can't describe how breathtakingly beautiful that was."

Lying on the bed, he slowly tried to recover from the most mind-blowing sex he'd ever experienced. She was the most remarkable woman. Cass' breathing slowed as she headed toward sleep. He knew the sweat coating her body would soon begin to itch, making her uncomfortable.

She muttered a protest as Aiden gathered her into his arms, and lifted her from the warm bed. "Let me take care of you now, Cass. You'll rest much better after a warm shower."

Setting her down on the closed toilet lid he turned on the shower, and adjusted the temperature. Picking her up again he carried her into the large stall, pulling the glass doors closed. Feeling weak and sated himself, Aiden held her against the shower wall with the weight of his body.

He washed her tenderly with a generous amount of lather. Once they were both clean he turned off the water, and pulled soft, thick towels from the rack. Wrapping one around his hips, Aiden dried her satiny skin, then carried her back to bed.

After drying himself he joined her, spooning her body against the length of his own. Within moments they both slipped deeply into sleep.

* * * * *

Cassandra had lost all track of time. The insistent grumbling of her stomach pulled her out of the last cloaking layers of sleep. How long had it been since they'd eaten?

Aiden grumbled in protest when she tried to move from his embrace. His arms tightened around her, pulling her closer against his body.

"Aiden, I'm starving." She worked at releasing his grasp. "If I don't go get something to eat soon, I'll have to eat you."

"Umm," he purred against her ear. "Sounds good to me."

She couldn't help but smile. "Aiden," she scolded. "Let me go and I'll make us some big, thick burgers," Cass said, tempting his hunger.

His stomach began to angrily rumble out its protest. Just the thought of a thick hamburger brought him fully awake. "Okay, baby. Come on, I'll help."

She moved around the kitchen in the nude without giving it a thought. Normally her nudity would embarrass her, but she felt comfortable. Looking over at Aiden she saw his cock lying flaccidly between his legs. She smiled at the knowledge that she'd worn him out, and pleased him.

"Keep looking at me like that and all you're going to get to eat is me," he only half-jokingly threatened.

Throwing back her head she laughed with delight. "Aiden, you can't tempt me with that limp noodle. It'll be a long time before you're able to do anything other than talk."

Her laughter was music to his ears. He was so turned on by her sense of humor. His cock began to rise in response. "Wanna bet," he challenged.

She looked over at him and gasped at the sight of his cock slowly rising to attention. "You're insatiable," she said with a whimper.

"Better hurry with those burgers before I have to show you just how insatiable I can be, baby."

* * * * *

After filling their bellies they fell back into the bed. Cassandra loved the feeling of warmth and safety that came from being sheltered within his arms. She needed to use the bathroom, but was reluctant to move.

Finally rising from the bed she took the plugs with her. With each movement, Cassandra felt the soreness in her ass. She cleaned everything up, brushed her teeth, washed her face, and combed her tangled hair. Then she spotted her pink razor.

"Aiden," she called out, walking back into the bedroom. "I read a lot during my research about women shaving their pubic hair." She stood in quite contemplation for a moment. "It's suppose to make you, er, more sensitive. What do you think?"

"Hmmm," he mumbled sleepily. "It's sexy as hell, but you might want to think twice about that, baby." He turned on his side to face Cass. "It can be really itchy when the hair grows back, and you can get razor rash. It's better to wax."

"Oh." After returning the implement to the bathroom she slowly walked back into the bedroom. For some reason she was feeling suddenly shy and nervous.

Noticing her hesitation, Aiden patted the bed next to him. "Come back to bed, Cass."

She went readily into his open arms. His chocolate brown eyes clearly revealed his deep emotions. Sleepily he tucked her back against his body. Snuggling close she sighed contentedly. Just before drifting off to sleep she whispered, "I love you!"

Sleep was no longer an option. Her whispered words of love kept repeating through his mind. Hope surged through his heart. Did she really mean what she'd said, or was it just happily sated post-coital pillow talk.

Could she possibly give her love to him so easily? His confused thoughts continued to circle around the issue. When he finally fell asleep, Aiden felt his body suffused with joy and a tentative hope for the future.

* * * * *

Light streamed past the edges of the curtains when Cassandra next woke. She felt pleasantly full and horny. As her senses became fully alert she looked up into Aiden's smiling face as he slowly thrust his cock into her. There was something different in his eyes that she couldn't quite place.

"Good mornin', baby," he whispered. He groaned after completing several more slow thrusts. "I can't think of a better way to wake up, can you?" he asked.

He took her with a sweet tenderness that made her heart ache. This was decidedly different from the rest of the weekend. Emotions raged through her as he slowly made love to her body.

Shit, that had to be it. Aiden was no longer fucking her. They were now making love. When had this change started? Panic caused her heart to seize in her chest, sending her pulse racing. Had Aiden fallen in love with her? How was she supposed to handle the emotions she felt practically oozing from every fiber of his being. She'd end up hurting him now for sure.

Feeling her tense beneath him, Aiden froze. "What's the matter, Cass? Are you too sore?" Concern was etched across his features.

She screamed with frustration in her mind. Shit, what the hell was she supposed to say? *Come on sex goddess, wake up. I need some help here.* Giving herself a mental shake, Cassandra fought to relax her body.

"Umm. Feels good. I've never been woken up quite this way before." Watching as the concern was replaced with a smile, relief washed through her. She could do this as long as she kept the goddess firmly in place.

The slow coupling was torture. Why couldn't he have been happy to fuck? Why the hell did he have to bring love into things? Yes she loved him, but this was different.

Finally she gave herself over to her body, shielding his heart behind lust. *Come on goddess, do your damn job.* Digging her nails into his ass cheeks, she pulled Aiden hard against her heated flesh. "Oh, yes. Faster, I need you harder," she pleaded.

Her words and actions swept away his resolve, changing things once again. He began fucking her, hard and deep. This she could handle. Wrapping her legs around his waist, Cassandra drove his lust higher. "Oh God, yes," she gasped. Then she gave herself over to the orgasm building within her body.

His thrusts grew even harder, faster as hunger raced through him. She cried out, shuddering and bucking underneath him as he drove deep and hard, over and over again. He angled then twisted his hips, grinding against her, his cock stroking her sweet spot. He smiled with pure male pride as she gasped and bucked against him, her pussy clenching his cock tightly.

"Oooh, I'm gonna come. I want to feel your seed filling me," she begged.

Her words sent him spiraling over the edge. He shouted her name as he came, filling her spasming pussy with hot jets of semen. They climaxed together moments before Aiden collapsed on top of her.

"Oh shit," he gasped. "Damn, baby. I wanted to go slow," he complained. "You take all my control away."

There was her answer. She could control what happened with sex. Anytime he became too tender and loving she would bring on the powerful goddess to chase away the unwanted emotions.

Lying under Aiden, she worried about the future. How long could she pull this off before he ended up leaving her alone once again? Everyone left her eventually. When they turned loving it was the kiss of death for their relationship. Already she mourned the loss of the man she loved so deeply.

Her thoughts turned to Travis, leaving her feeling guilty. It almost felt as if she was cheating on him, which was ridiculous. Yes, she had strong feelings for Travis. Possibly as strong as what she felt for Aiden, but she'd made her choice. She would not let regret tarnish what she had with Aiden.

When she was sure he was deeply asleep, Cassandra untangled herself from his body. The cold had seeped back into her. It had felt wonderful for a few days to let the warmth back in, but she knew that could never last.

She showered and dressed on automatic pilot. After preparing a light lunch she went to wake Aiden. Sam would be home soon. Cassandra did not want her daughter to become confused or hopeful.

She managed to get him out of the house just in time. Becky pulled up with the girls not twenty minutes later. It had been just enough time to make the bed, and put away the candles and toys. Everything, including her emotions, was back in order by the time Sam entered the front door.

Chapter Thirteen

Aiden actually whistled while he walked into work early Monday morning. The weekend had been the most incredible experience of his life. Love and happiness flowed through his veins. He laughed seeing Cindy's mouth hang open as he walked past her desk. Served her right to get a little shock. Today she would not be able to bring him down from his high.

Out of habit he slid his cell phone out of his pocket, and tossed it into the desk drawer with his keys. The device, which was normally a nuisance, had been blissfully silent since Friday.

It didn't take Cindy long to recover. She strolled into the office, closing the door behind her. Plopping down into a chair she could not hide her shit-eating grin.

"Details, boss. I want lots of delicious details."

Aiden laughed deeply, throwing back his head. "Details of what?" he innocently asked.

She shook a finger at him. "You know exactly what I'm talking about, Aiden. There's only one thing in this world that could make you look like that, and her name is Cassandra McCarthy."

"Umm, I suppose you're right. No details though, I'll do you one better. Take the day off, Cin. I have no intention of accomplishing anything. You might as well enjoy the day too."

Cindy just stared at him for several minutes with a strange expression on her face. Finally she shook her head. "No thanks, boss. I think I'll stick around to see what other interesting developments happen today."

"Fine, Cin. Do whatever you want," he said in a chipper tone. Nothing was going to make a dent in his happiness. When he was finally alone, Aiden allowed visions of the weekend to play delightfully through his mind. Ignoring the office phone, he sat doodling on a pad of paper.

* * * * *

A gentle breeze swept across the soft, powdery sands. Seagulls took flight, squawking out their protest as Cassandra walked along the beach. The sun shone down brightly from a nearly cloudless sky. Between her bare toes the sand felt refreshingly cool, slightly damp.

Taking walks on the beach allowed Cassandra to think and to clear her mind. The gentle roar of waves as they crashed into the shore brought her relaxation. Once in a while she'd stop to pick up a pretty shell that caught her attention.

Thankfully her little piece of paradise was far removed from the tourist-ridden area of hotels and noisy vacationers. Many of the homes around her were empty now, used only seasonally. At times she could take a walk and never see another person.

Movement in the sand dunes caught her attention. She could not tell if it was an animal or a person. Of course, if it was an animal it must be hurt to be thrashing around in the sand dunes.

Moving cautiously, Cassandra froze as she heard a deep moan. What the heck? Was someone sleeping out here on the beach? The shimmering glow cast by the sun revealed a dark shape within the shadowed valley of sand.

The closer she moved, the clearer the image became. Someone was moving around on a blanket, moaning. Maybe they were sick, or injured.

"Oh yes…fuck me."

The words were carried to her on the gulf breeze. She moved into the minimal cover provided by a group of palm trees. She could now hear ragged breathing, low pants, and moans of ecstasy. Oh shit, someone was fucking on her beach in broad daylight.

Something kept her feet rooted in place while her mind yelled that she should leave. She should not be watching this couple have sex, but her feet just would not obey. It made no sense why she would want to watch strangers fuck. It was perverted, certainly it must be morally wrong, maybe even criminal.

Damn, she was some kind of peeping Tom. Or maybe it's a peeping Jane since she's a woman. Of course, it didn't matter what you called it. She felt demented, dirty...and turned on beyond belief.

The erotic scene before her sent her pulse pounding through her veins, roaring in her ears. The muffled moans sent fingers of need raging through her body. She had never watched anyone have sex before, except in movies. This was real, live and in person, buck-naked wild sex. And it was making her extremely horny.

The woman's ankles were locked over a firm male ass. Her large breasts jiggled as the man slammed into her body. Swim trunks lay pooled around his knees as he forcefully thrust against her. Cassandra could even hear the distinct sound of flesh pounding against flesh.

Her nipples hardened, her breasts swelled, and heat pooled against her suddenly throbbing pussy. Oh, she was really sick. She was watching two strangers fuck on the beach, and it was making her wet. The woman whimpered, and Cassandra wanted to echo the sounds. She shared the woman's aching need to come.

"Oh yes...fuck me hard," the woman panted. "Harder...oh yeah."

Cassandra had to stifle her own groan. She was hot, wet, aching, and completely empty. Running her fingernails over her taut nipples, she bit her lip in an effort to remain quiet. The scene before her was so carnal and erotic.

The man began thrusting faster. Leaning forward he took one of the woman's puckered nipples into his mouth. Her answering moan of pleasure sent more moisture flowing between Cassandra's legs. She slipped her other hand below the waistband of her shorts, matching the couple's rhythm as she stroked her engorged clit.

Her fingers quickly became coated in hot juices. The sensual sounds coming from the blanket had her driving two fingers into her pussy. Her thumb continued circling the sensitive, throbbing nub. She only managed not to cry out by biting her lower lip again.

Weren't they worried about being seen? Um, but was that part of the thrill, the potential danger of being caught. Somehow they did not look too concerned about that possibility. Hell, they weren't even trying to be quiet.

Oh God, she should not be doing this. She certainly should not be enjoying herself. The sex goddess inside her broke free, demanding she find release. Cassandra focused on her own body. Her hips thrust forward, fucking her fingers. She rode her fingers hard, stimulating her g-spot with each upward thrust.

The couple's moans drove her need higher. Her movements matched the rhythm set by the man. Whatever force had brought her latent sexuality to life was driving her insane. She would never have pictured herself standing on the beach watching someone fuck, while masturbating.

She leaned back against the trunk of a tall palm for support feeling every muscle in her body begin to tighten. She was so close. Every fiber of her being was on point, ready to explode.

"Oh fuck...damn, baby. I'm gonna come. Come with me. I'm...oh, yeah...oh fuck...fuck."

Cassandra was assaulted by wave after wave of blinding ecstasy. The salty taste of blood mingled with her saliva as she bit her lip harder. Oh God, she'd just fingered herself to orgasm while watching a strange couple fuck.

The couple lay back on the blanket, fighting to regain control of their breathing. Cassandra leaned against the tree doing the same. Her legs felt weak and wobbly as she tried to quietly slink away undiscovered.

* * * * *

Finding release at her own hand was decidedly unsatisfying. Cassandra craved something more. Pacing the house with restless need she could only think of Aiden. She needed his cock, now.

The wanton sex goddess came up with a delicious idea. After changing into a slinky little red sundress with white Hawaiian flowers, and a pair of strappy sandals she quickly drove to the offices of Danbury Industries.

Cindy gave her a puzzled look as she approached the woman's desk. "Cass, what are you doing here? Is something wrong?" With a frown Cindy stared at her for several moments. "You look different."

"Hmm, is he in?" she asked, inclining her head toward the closed door.

"Yeah. Ah, what are you up to, Cass?"

They spent the next ten minutes involved in some serious getting acquainted girl talk. Cassandra was surprised by some of Cindy's comments. They had never really taken the time to get to become friends before. She decided to work on changing that, making a real effort to bond with the other woman.

Without giving much detail, Cassandra told the other woman that she was planning to bring a certain cocky alpha male down a notch or two. It was definitely time for Aiden to get a little taste of what it felt like to be taken by surprise and left a speechless lump.

By the time they finished talking, Cindy wore a devilish grin. "Oh to be a fly on the wall. I would love to see what you have planned and his reaction, but I think I'll just disappear for a while." Taking her purse from a desk drawer, Cindy paused before heading down the hallway. "Oh, by the way. Thanks, Cass. He should be in a great mood when I get back." She walked away wearing a broad grin.

Taking great care, Cassandra opened the door quietly. Once inside she leaned against it taking deep fortifying breaths. Aiden sat staring at his computer, deep in concentration until the lock clicked into place with a loud metallic sound.

His head snapped up. "Hey, baby."

His bright smile washed away her nervousness.

"What a great surprise." His gaze slid over her like a caress. "You look fabulous. What's the occasion?"

Moving slowly she put more sway than normal into her hips. "I'm hungry." Her voice came out sultry. The pink tip of her tongue slid in a seductive arc over bright red lips, leaving a glistening shine.

Aiden became slightly wary, fidgeting in his chair. "Um, okay. How about I take you out to lunch?" Confusion swept over him. What exactly was going on? He'd never seen Cass act so blatantly sexual.

Oh, and the little excuse for a dress she wore. *Wow!* He stripped her naked in his mind. Damn, now he was getting hungry, and not for food.

Unbound thick strands of dark hair fell over her shoulders. He itched to slide the silky tendrils through his fingers. The jeweled caramel strands were shot through with tantalizing streaks of gold, amber, and garnet.

He slid his chair back as she came around the corner of his desk. Moving to stand between his knees, her slender fingers trailed down his cheek. If he wasn't reading her wrong, the look on her face said "fuck me".

"Um, so what are you in the mood for, baby? I could go for some Chinese."

A wicked smile lit her full lips, accentuated by the bright lipstick. "Hmm, Chinese is all right, but I'd rather eat you." Her fingers caressed down his chest seductively.

Aiden quickly fell under the spell she cast. His cock woke up, and pressed painfully against his trousers. "H-here?" he stammered lamely.

"Here and now, Aiden. I can't wait to have that big, tasty cock in my mouth." Bracing her hands on the arms of the chair she slowly sunk to her knees. Finding his cock hard and ready, she hummed in approval. "Yes, I think this will satisfy my hunger just fine." Leaning forward she pressed her lips against the large bulge, and exhaled.

Aiden watched in amazement. Her hot breath spread through his entire body. Wow, he had unleashed one hell of a sexual vixen over the weekend. She was an entirely different woman. Gone was the soccer mom. This woman was a naughty, provocative minx.

With a few deft tugs and pulls she freed his tumescent shaft. "Umm, this will do just fine," she murmured.

Full, red lips opened to kiss the tip of his cock. Aiden leaned back in the chair deciding that he might as well relax and enjoy this erotic little treat.

Taking hold of his hips, she pulled him closer to the edge of the chair, while dragging his pants down his thighs. With her tongue, she traced the curves of his head before teasing the slit. He moaned deeply as her lush lips spread over his cock, sucking him deep inside the warm cavern.

"Oh yeah, baby. Damn, that feels so good."

One hand massaged his scrotum. The other stroked the base of his shaft. Her hot tongue traced the throbbing veins, and then made intriguing patterns along the cock. Pre-cum glistened on the tip, and she greedily licked it up.

"Oh yeah! Suck me, baby. Suck me hard," he gasped.

With one smooth movement she sheathed his cock in her mouth. Relaxing her throat she sucked again until the head bobbed against the back of her throat. Her hair spread out over his thighs in a cool caress.

Aiden twined his fingers into the beautiful strands keeping her close. Letting instinct take over, his hips began thrusting forward, fucking her sweet mouth.

With each thrust her talented tongue stroked the underside of his shaft. Her fingers massaging his scrotum moved lower, sliding over his perineum. Beads of sweat broke out across his brow as heat blazed through his body.

His deep, rumbling moans drove her to increase her pace. This was for her, and she had a goal in mind.

The ringing phone failed to cut through Aiden's dazed pleasure. Without missing a stroke, Cassandra snatched up the handset, and held it to his ear. It was the voice of George Danbury, CEO of Danbury Industries, which finally broke through the sensual haze fogging his brain.

"McCarthy? What the hell? Are you there?"

Fighting to focus his thoughts, Aiden mumbled, "Yes, sir. I'm here."

Biting his tongue, he just managed to keep from moaning into the phone as a wet finger circled his anus. Blinking furiously did not change the picture before him. The top of the sundress hung around Cass' waist. Letting his cock pop out of her mouth, she leaned forward and encased his shaft in the deep valley between her flushed breasts.

Pink lacquered fingernails stood out against the pale flesh being pressed together in her tanned hands. Moving up and down, she licked the tip of his cock each time it appeared between the full globes. His hips surged forward of their own volition as he fucked her ripe breasts.

George Danbury was speaking very loudly now. "What the hell's wrong with you, McCarthy? Are you sick or something?"

Latching onto the provided excuse, Aiden stuttered out a response. "I…um, yes…so hot…sweating."

The CEO's voice softened. "Well damn, son, go home then. Can't have you making the rest of the staff sick. Call me when you are back on your feet. We need to move on that security program."

Aiden could not suppress the moan this time as once again she sucked his cock deep into her hot mouth. A wet finger returned to his anus, circling lazily before plunging inside the narrow opening.

"Try some zinc," recommended Danbury.

The sight of her red, swollen lips stretched around his shaft was more than Aiden could take. She let him slide from her warm mouth, then pursed her full lips over the tip, sucking hard against the narrow slit.

Aiden felt his toes curl as she worked to draw out his seed. Every fiber of his being tightened, and his eyes rolled back in his head. He struggled to get Danbury off the phone before her hot little mouth sent him into heart failure.

"Thank you, sir," he gasped out. "I'll be fine," he said, before practically throwing the handset into the cradle. Lightning traveled his spine as she sucked his cock harder, her finger stroking within the hot channel of his ass.

His balls tightened up against his body moments before cum exploded from his cock. He stared in amazement as Cass greedily slurped up his seed, swallowing his head down the back of her throat. She licked up every last drop she'd milked from him, a satisfied smile stretched across her swollen lips.

Aiden lay back in his chair fighting for breath, sweat trickling down his face while Cass calmly straightened her dress. Leaning in she gave his quivering abdomen a quick kiss.

"Thanks, babe. That was just what I needed." She turned and walked quietly out the door.

"Holy shit," he muttered, his mind reeling.

Cindy was just returning to her desk as Cassandra left the office. "He should be real nice the rest of the day, Cin. If not, just let me know."

The two women shared a quick, knowing smile.

Chapter Fourteen

Sleep eluded Cassandra that night so she worked, pushing thoughts of Aiden to the background. The plot and characters for her new book were beginning to slowly take shape. It would be the story of a sexually powerful woman striving to keep her lover in the neat little niche she'd made for him.

The ménage à trois would be what trapped her. She would fall in love with the two men who unselfishly saw to her every desire. The main character would have to make some tough choices. Almost as tough as she'd made in picking one man. Thoughts of Travis still gnawed at her insides, but she kept them tightly locked away.

After dropping Sam off at school she moved outside to work. Sitting on the front porch, Cassandra wrote out plot twists and turns on her notebook computer. It had turned into a glorious day, and working in the warm sunshine helped fuel her imagination.

In her mind the confident male heroes were beginning to look more and more like a certain pair of men she knew. Like Aiden and Travis, the two men freely gave of themselves without question. It took the female heroine some time to realize that they never asked for anything in return, just gave their support and love unselfishly.

Finally closing the notebook, she set it aside to think about the characters and her own life. She had to make sure the main male characters did not come off as being weak, and that the woman didn't take too long to open her eyes. She puzzled out the story, while sipping from a cold glass of sweet tea.

Cassandra closed her eyes trying to visualize the characters, while letting the condensation on the glass drip between her breasts. The cool liquid helped keep her from sweating. She held the glass to the pulse in her neck sending cool sensations through her overheated body.

The sound of a car door closing nearby pulled her from her thoughts, and she rubbed her eyes to clear her vision. She had to be asleep, dreaming of the smiling man walking up the path. Her mind screamed that there was no way he was actually there, that she could be actually seeing him.

Thoughts and emotions swam wildly around her. In a haze she slowly stood, staring at the unbelievable aberration. It just was not possible. Her focus narrowed, time distorted. Everything moved in slow motion.

His shoulders were broader than she remembered. He appeared slightly taller too. Heavenly dark blond strands of hair still hung rakishly over his forehead, refusing to be tamed. Piercing, brilliant blue eyes penetrated her being.

"Cassie."

When he spoke, Cassandra trembled. The resplendent sound of his voice wrapped around her heart, squeezing painfully. Deeply buried memories flooded her senses. Smells and sounds she knew were not real, but their memory assaulted her anyway. The agony of long ago betrayal sent shattering waves of pain tearing through her soul.

Her fingers tightened around the glass in her hand as she was overcome with emotion. The painfully tight, white-knuckled grasp she held on the glass went unnoticed. Every thought, every sense focused on him. She cried out briefly when the glass shattered, driving small shards deep into her palm and fingers. Blood dripped down her hand, splattering her legs and feet.

"Oh shit!" he gasped.

The words did not penetrate the unreality that had taken over her mind, body and soul. The dream apparition rushed up the steps. His words swam around her head as he tried to pry open the death grip her fingers held on one remaining large piece of glass.

She had to hold onto something as the world tilted around her. Her field of vision narrowed down to a rapidly closing tunnel. Darkness closed in around the edges of her vision and mind. He appeared so far away, his words making no sense, sounding warped. Distantly, Cassandra felt herself falling as everything tilted and dimmed around her. Her last coherent thought as blackness closed over her was of Aiden. She needed Aiden.

* * * * *

Deep pain coursed through her chest. Something was grinding against her breastbone, making her breath catch. A strong male voice commanded her to open her eyes. No, she didn't want to wake up. She attempted to shake her head, but the small motions made her stomach do wild flip-flops.

The painful grinding on her chest came again. She tried to raise a hand to swat away whatever was there, but her hands wouldn't respond. Panic and fear coursed through Cassandra. She could not move.

Forcing her eyes to open she stared up into the blurry image of several people staring down at her. The room was extremely brightly lit, making her eyes begin to water. At least the grinding stopped. Distantly she heard a voice. The words did not make much sense.

"Miss McCarthy, you're at County Hospital. I'm Doctor Preston. Everything's going to be all right now. Your hand is going to require some stitches, but will heal nicely. There's no tendon damage, thankfully."

Her hand? What was wrong with her hand? She needed to sleep. Cassandra allowed herself to be swept back into the darkness.

* * * * *

The horribly strong scent of ammonia assaulted her nose. Cassandra tried to bat away the offensive object, but it was firmly held close to her face. She coughed and gagged as her mind fought to focus.

Slowly her surroundings began to crystallize around her. Ugly mint green walls, and a white curtain appeared before her watery eyes. "Where the hell am I?" she croaked in an unfamiliar, raspy voice.

"County hospital," a woman's voice replied curtly.

Her head swam as she turned toward the sound. A nurse stood before her in a pair of light blue surgical scrubs. Much to Cassandra's relief the large woman finally moved the offending capsule away.

"Do you remember what happened?" the nurse questioned.

She struggled to determine the last things she remembered. "I...I was sitting on my front porch in the middle of a daydream before everything went black."

Raising the head of the bed, the nurse held a glass of water to her parched lips. Cassandra drank greedily until the glass was removed.

"Do you know what day it is?"

Cassandra struggled to focus her thoughts, "Uh, Tuesday...I think."

Male shouts and the sounds of a struggle erupted outside the curtain. His voice cut through her confusion. Cassandra groaned. "Oh shit, he's really here," she stated to no one in particular.

"Umm, and mad as a hornet," the nurse mumbled before drawing the curtain open to reveal Bryce being held back by a security guard. "It's okay, Frank. He can come in now."

Relief crossed his features as Bryce shook off the other man and rushed forward.

Cassandra raised her right hand to her mouth, and cried out in pain. She looked at the bandaged appendage with confusion furrowing her brow.

The nurse gently took her elbow, guiding her to rest her hand on her lap. "You cut that one up pretty bad. You'll have to learn to be a lefty for a while."

The mentioned left hand was taken into Bryce's firm grasp. He sat on a stool next to the bed. Concern and fear were clearly apparent in his stormy blue eyes. "You scared me to death, Cassie," he stated.

"No one calls me Cassie anymore," she mumbled lamely. "I've grown up." Tentatively she raised her trembling, bandaged hand up to his face and lightly pressed her fingers into his cheek. His flesh felt firm, real. She stared at him with an amazed expression. "You're really here."

Oh, God. Why now? I waited so long for him to come back. Why now when it's way too late? It had been too late for several years. Pain, hurt, and confusion each warred for control of her frazzled emotions.

Cassandra's mind whirled as she gently dropped her hand back onto her lap. "Wh-where…why now?" she asked. "It's been seven years, Bryce." Her voice sounded very far away, even to her own ears.

His voice had turned husky, "I know." He dropped his gaze. "I never should have stayed away so long."

Oh, how she had missed that voice, the dark sultry quality and smooth cadence of words. She'd dreamed of his sexy voice, his handsome face for so long. Then she'd moved on.

Steeling her nerves, Cassandra's voice became cold. "Why are you here, Bryce?" Her thoughts focused on her daughter. She had to protect Samantha from the pain and confusion his sudden arrival would cause.

"Cassie, not a day has gone by that I haven't thought about you," he sighed deeply. "I had to make something of myself before I could come back. I tracked you down through a private investigator." His thumb rubbed lightly over the pulse point in her wrist, while he kept her hand captured in his own.

She felt herself falling into the bright blue depths of his eyes, just like when she was a teenager. He could still draw her in so easily. Breaking eye contact she looked down at his hands.

Before he would continue, Bryce gently lifted her chin and waited for her to look into his hypnotizing gaze again. "I came back for you, Cassie."

Oh God, no. How could he do this to her? To just show up out of the blue after all this time. It was too much to take. What the hell did he expect? That she'd just fall back into his arms.

Her shocked system could not handle this overload of emotion. For so long she'd kept all emotions safely tamped down, locked away. In a few short moments, Bryce threatened everything she had worked so hard to build over the past seven years. She felt her hard-won independence and confidence waver.

Looking up, she opened her mouth then closed it again without saying a word. What the hell could she say to him?

"Don't push me away, Cassie," he pleaded in a tentative tone. "Please, I need you so much."

He needed her? How could he say that? How could he expect her to fill that need? Where the hell was he when she'd needed him? When their daughter needed him?

* * * * *

Aiden spent the day looking at engagement ring designs on the internet. He tried to slow down and take things easily, but his raging emotions would not let that happen. He wanted his ring on Cassandra's finger. She was his woman now.

A sharp knock on the door drew him from his thoughts. "Come in," he called cheerily. He knew it wouldn't be Cindy since she had an appointment with the dentist.

The office receptionist stood there looking worried, chewing on her bottom lip.

"Hi, Karen. What's up?" he questioned.

"Aiden, I've been getting frantic phone calls from Meadowlawn Elementary school, and Travis Lundy. You haven't been answering either your cell or office phone."

She looked down at the slip of paper clutched in her hand for the names. "Cassandra McCarthy did not show up at the school to pick up your niece, Samantha. The school called her first, tried to get you, and then reached Mr. Lundy, who is frantic. He wants you to call him immediately. There appears to be   some   emergency."

Aiden was on his feet instantly. He pulled open the drawer and flipped open his cell phone. The battery was dead. "Damn." He slammed it down and snatched up the office phone. "Thanks, Karen," he said dismissively while dialing. His hands were shaking so badly it took three tries to get the number right.

His heart stopped, and the blood froze in his veins. There was not much that would keep Cass from picking up Sam. Heck, she was the most reliable mother he'd ever met. That little girl was the center of her world. Panic took his breath away.

Travis picked up on the first ring, "Aiden, where the fuck have you been?" he questioned.

"Never mind. What the hell's going on?" he asked. Rolling his eyes heavenward, he sent up a silent prayer.

"Apparently, Cass never showed up to pick Sam up from school. They tried to get you before finally calling me. I asked them to keep Sam while I figure out what happened to Cass." He paused briefly then took a deep breath.

Fear held Aiden's heart in a vise. "Travis?"

"Her Mustang is in the garage, the front door is unlocked, but she's nowhere to be found."

Aiden could tell the other man was holding back something. "And?" he questioned.

Travis sighed deeply. His voice trembled with raw emotion when he spoke again. "There's blood on the front porch, and down the walkway. It stops at the road. I don't know what the hell's going on."

Gravity took hold of Aiden as his legs became weak. He plopped down hard in the chair. His world had just been ripped away leaving only fear and confusion.

"Her purse is on the hall table. Cell phone's inside." Travis took a shaky breath. "I've called the police, Aiden. They're on the way."

"I'll be right there," Aiden mumbled before hanging up. He called Darlene and arranged for her to pick up Sam, and take her home until they found Cass. Sam would be afraid and need her friend, Jessie.

Aiden drove like a bat out of hell, ignoring most traffic signs and lights. He made record time getting to the house. Seeing flashing red lights cut through the normally serene neighborhood made the situation a reality. Something had happened to Cass. Fear seized his heart, constricting his chest like a tight fist.

When he pulled up near the house, Aiden sat in the car for a moment. Once he finally began moving he felt better, until he saw all the blood. Fat, dark red drops were everywhere. Yellow crime scene tape surrounded the yard, keeping onlookers at a distance. The earth kept shifting below his feet as Aiden walked in a shaky stupor. His legs threatened to give out at any moment.

As he neared the driveway, Aiden spotted Travis talking to several grim-looking police officers. He made his way toward the group in a trance. A burly cop tried to stop him, but Aiden just shoved him away.

Travis' voice seemed to come from far away. "It's okay. He's her brother-in-law. Aiden is the closest family she's got." Travis took his arm, steadying Aiden.

"There's so much blood," he croaked out in a weak, foreign voice.

A senior officer turned his attention to Aiden. "No. It's really not as bad as it looks." He frowned and looked down at his notebook. "Mr. McCarthy, have you heard from your sister-in-law today?"

"I…um, no. My cell phone's dead, and I was ignoring my office phone." Tremors racked his body while he stared at the blood. "Have…have you found her?" he asked.

"She's not on the premises," the man stated in a cold, detached tone.

Fury raged through his veins. He needed to strike out at someone, anyone. "Well, then don't you think you should fucking do something other than stand around?"

Turning away from Aiden, the officer addressed Travis. "Mr. Lundy, maybe you should take your friend for a walk to cool off, get his head together."

Travis nodded, but he was in very much the same state as Aiden. He had no idea how he was still standing, or keeping the fear that was ripping through his body contained.

Chapter Fifteen

Sitting on the passenger seat of Travis' truck, Aiden felt numb. Travis prattled on endlessly, and kept forcing a bottle of water into his hands. Obediently he drank, but he didn't even feel the water slide down his throat.

Time moved ponderously. He distantly observed the movements of the police officers around the property. To Aiden they appeared to be making a big show at doing nothing.

A suddenly raised voice caught his attention. A uniformed officer called out, "Captain Ramsey," holding a cellular phone up in the air.

Aiden was the first to reach the man, with the Captain not far behind. "Miss McCarthy showed up at County with a hand wound. She's fine, just getting stitched up."

Relief surged through his body in waves, waking up his deadened nerves. His entire body tingled with new energy. Turning on his heel, Aiden raced toward his car. He stopped short when the Captain stepped in front of him, blocking his way.

"I think you should ride with your friend. We'll provide an escort to ensure you make it to the hospital safely."

Aiden considered just jumping in his car and speeding away, but if he ended up in an accident he couldn't help Cass. "Fine," he stated.

The short drive to the hospital was nerve-racking. At least they'd said she was all right. He couldn't imagine what had happened. When they arrived at the emergency room Aiden had to fight with the clerk to let him inside.

"Miss McCarthy already has a visitor, sir. You'll just have to wait."

Travis intervened before Aiden could lose his temper. "Look, um, Miss James," he said after glancing at her name tag. "Mr. McCarthy is family. Whoever is back there isn't."

Finally they were admitted to the treatment area, where they were led to a curtained-off cubicle. He had to battle again with a nurse to be allowed into the area where they had Cass.

When the nurse finally pulled back the curtain, Aiden rushed forward talking a mile a minute. "Oh my God, Cass. Are you all right? The school called, and I saw all the blood. Scared the shit out of me." He gently picked her up off the stretcher, cradling her against his chest.

He stroked his hands over her hair, arms, and back. Tucking her head under his chin, Aiden pressed kisses over the top of her head. It felt so good to hold her in his arms. He'd been so afraid that he'd lost her. "I love you, baby," he whispered.

His attention remained focused on Cass until the man sitting next to the bed cleared his throat. Looking over he stared into eyes the same blue as Sam's. His heart clutched painfully. He knew immediately that this was Sam's father, Cass' first love. Their facial features were very similar.

He noticed Travis standing rigidly at the end of the bed. His entire body was tensed, ready for battle. The look on his face was pure rage and hatred.

Fighting to ignore the other men, Aiden asked, "What the hell happened, Cass? There was so much blood everywhere."

With her good hand she tenderly stroked his face. "It's okay, Aiden. I cut my hand on a glass. Bryce drove me here." She paused for a moment. "I tried to call, but got your voicemail."

Fuck. What a dumbass. How could he have let his cell phone battery die? "I'm sorry, baby. I should've been there for you," he whispered.

Pain etched deep lines across his forehead. She gently soothed her good hand across his brow. "I'm fine, Aiden. Everything's okay. You can breathe now."

Cassandra's heart clenched as she watched the depth of love, concern, fear, and pain that played across his face. She felt bad that he had been so worried. Looking over she saw the same pain and anger coursing through Travis. She wanted to go to him and soothe the large man, but Aiden was not about to let her go.

The nurse walked in and frowned at Aiden. "Could you please put my patient down so I can go over instructions with her?" She waited impatiently, tapping her foot on the floor. Looking at the other men she gave them a sharp look.

"Don't be starting any trouble in my ER, boys." Her tone and fierce look let them know there would be hell to pay. As soon as Aiden sat Cass down on the stretcher, the nurse forcefully nudged him out of the way.

She spent several minutes taking Cass' blood pressure and pulse, writing everything down on a clipboard. Instructions for cleaning and bandaging the wound were rattled off quickly. Cass was to return in five days to have the stitches removed. If any infection was found she was to return immediately. She was given a prescription for pain medication.

After she signed several papers an orderly approached with a wheelchair, and stood nearby waiting.

"Is that really necessary?" Cassandra asked the woman.

"You've been given some strong pain medications, Miss McCarthy. It will be several hours before you're steady on your feet again." Taking Cassandra firmly by the biceps the nurse assisted her into the chair.

Cassandra wanted to scream. Aiden walked at one side of the chair with Travis, Bryce walked at the other. All of them wore fierce scowls on their handsome faces. She could picture the scene to come as the men fought over who would take her home. "Aiden, did you bring your car?"

"No. Travis drove me over in the Beast. The police wouldn't let me drive."

"The police?" she gasped.

Aiden lightly punched Travis in the arm. "Yeah! Um, Travis freaked and called the police when he saw all the blood. They roped off the yard with crime scene tape. The whole neighborhood is waiting to see what's going on."

She groaned deep in her throat. "Great! Travis, would you and Aiden bring the truck up on the ramp. I need a moment with Bryce before you take me home." Cassandra gave Travis an imploring look.

"No problem, sugar. Come on, Aiden," he said, dragging him away by his arm. Once they were out of earshot he said, "You need to trust in her, Aiden."

Pushing off Travis' grip, Aiden grumbled, "It's not her I don't trust."

* * * * *

Silently Cassandra thanked Travis for taking his time in returning. Bryce bent down so she would not have to stare up at him. "We need to talk, Cassie."

"I know, but not right now, Bryce. This has waited seven years, it can wait another day. Call me tomorrow afternoon and we'll work something out. Right now I can't think straight."

It was painful to look into his eyes. She'd dreamed of him returning for so long before giving up hope. Now her life had changed. What was she suppose to do with Bryce now?

He'd said that he'd come back for her. How could he think she could ever trust or love him again? He'd walked out on her while she was pregnant, not to be heard from for seven years. What did he expect to happen now?

"What is he to you, Cassie?"

She didn't have to ask who he was talking about. "It's complicated, Bryce. I'd really rather not discuss Aiden right now."

He stared deep into her eyes for a moment as regret and something that looked like pain crossed his features. "He's your lover."

It was more a statement of fact than question so she remained silent. Thankfully Travis pulled up, effectively ending their conversation. Aiden quickly jumped from the truck to help her from the wheelchair. Just before the door closed behind them she heard Bryce say, "I'll call you tomorrow, Cassie."

* * * * *

A tense silence hung in the air between the three of them. When they got to the house, Travis left to go fill the prescription, leaving her alone with Aiden.

Cass' normally expressive eyes and features were closed off. She was keeping her feelings and emotions held close to the vest. She did not say a word, just remained focused on her thoughts.

After calling Darlene so Sam could talk to her mother, they arranged for her to spend several days with their friends. Cass would need the time to recuperate.

Aiden had insisted on carrying her into the house, and took her straight to the bedroom. He'd fussed over her for several minutes, fluffing pillows. He set a carafe of ice water and a glass close by on the nightstand. His nervous actions made her feel jumpy.

"Aiden, please stop. I need you. Would you just come here and hold me?"

Without a word he climbed on the bed next to Cassandra, pulling her into his arms. He held her with a tenderness that touched her heart.

"I feel so sleepy," she said while trying to stifle a yawn.

"The nurse said you'd probably sleep a lot for a few days, Cass."

"Mmm, I feel like I could sleep for a week."

He gave her a gentle squeeze. "Go ahead. I'll still be here watching over you."

"You're so good to me, Aiden. What would I do without you?"

"Let's not find out." He remained quiet for several moments. "I was so afraid, Cass. I didn't know what the hell was going on, and then Travis found all that blood." He shivered at the memory. "I was afraid I'd lost you."

Cassandra didn't say anything, just snuggled closer against the shelter of his body.

"What happened, Cass? Why did he show up now?"

She told Aiden about standing on the porch in total shock as her past sauntered up the walkway. How her emotions were all twisted and tied up in knots. Holding nothing back she told him what Bryce had said, and that they had arranged to talk the next day.

Aiden felt as if his entire life hung in suspension, waiting to see what she would do. Would she go back to her first love? Would she stay with him? Hearing her breathing deepen with sleep he knew it would be some time before he got any answers.

He held her close while she slept. With his fingers he traced random caresses over her face and neck, reassured that she was safe and in his arms. The question was for how much longer? Would the fragile new relationship they had started survive the return of Sam's father?

* * * * *

Aiden woke a few hours later to the sound of soft whimpers. Cass' body was rigid against his side. He knew it had to be bad for her to cry out. The tough woman next to him had a high threshold for pain. She never even took Novocain for dental procedures. She hated to feel altered in any way, or to take medications. She was often reluctant to take even aspirin.

"Cass? What's wrong? Are you hurting, baby?"

Her jaw was held so tightly clenched that all she could manage were moans and one word at a time.

"Unh...Aiden...throbbing...bad..."

He quickly jumped from the bed to retrieve the pain pills. "Damn it, Cass. You should've woken me up. You're too damn independent and stubborn."

Supporting her head and neck with one arm, Aiden placed a white pill on her tongue. He held a glass of water to her lips while she took several gasping sips. Before lowering her back to the pillows he stroked her forehead soothingly.

"I hate...to take pills," she choked out. "They make me...too dopey."

Aiden climbed back onto the bed and began massaging her taut muscles. The concern reflected in the warmth of his brown eyes touched her heart. It seemed to take forever for the medication to take effect. Gradually she began to relax by small degrees. His caresses became lighter until he absently stroked his fingers over her ear and neck.

The tenderness of the light, instinctive touches penetrated past her barriers. The movements were so natural, reassuring, and loving. She was certain they were given unselfishly to provide her the comfort of his presence.

As the pain receded further the delicate fondling brought his absolute love through to Cassandra. More than words, his touch let her know how much he cared, and that he would always be there.

I'm not alone anymore.

The feelings of safety, protection, and love overwhelmed her. She found that the light caresses brought incredible desire to her hazy brain. Perhaps it was the medication's effects that allowed her to lower her guard enough to perceive his feelings. Each soft, lingering touch made passion course through her veins.

"Aiden." His name was barely a whisper in the darkened room.

"Are you okay, Cass? Is the pain still bad?" he questioned.

"Aiden, I want you. No, I need you." She fought for words to express her longing. "I want you to make love to me."

He stared down into her eyes, his own longing clearly written on his face. "Not while you're in pain, Cass. You need to rest. I don't want to hurt you."

"Aiden, I ache. I need you to take away the emptiness. Please!" She smiled up at him seductively. "Are you really going to deny me what I need, Aiden? You could never hurt me even if you tried."

His voice took on a feral tone as Aiden was overcome with the need to show her just what she needed. "Oh, I'll give you what you need, Cass. Don't doubt that for a minute."

He made love to her with a sweet, aching tenderness. His feelings were reflected in every touch of their bodies. As he thrust slowly, carefully into Cassandra, she was filled with his love. The last of her barriers fell, allowing her to give herself to him completely, without reservation.

Aiden held back his release until she began to tighten around him, tremors rocking her body. They came together, joining more than their bodies. Cassandra gave Aiden her heart and soul, as well as her passion. She gave herself to him, feeling almost complete for the first time she could remember.

But in the back of her mind she knew that there was still something missing. As she fell asleep that thought haunted her.

Chapter Sixteen

Over the next several days, Darlene stopped by with Jessie and Sam for brief visits after school. The girls brought her cards and pictures they'd made. Travis also stopped by several times a day to check on her. Aiden rarely left her side and if so, only for brief periods.

For the most part she lay in a lounger on the deck, taking frequent naps. She was not sure if this was the result of the medications, or just overall fatigue. By the fourth day her hand had finally stopped throbbing, and she began to regain her strength.

Aiden had kept Bryce at bay during his daily phone calls. Finally giving in he handed Cass the cordless phone, then went into the kitchen to give her some privacy.

Hearing Bryce's voice brought back echoes of the past. His voice was still the same, but its effect on her had changed. Although the sound brought old memories to the surface, it no longer pulled on her heart. She loved Aiden now.

The conversation was brief. Bryce expressed concern over her well-being and set up a time to talk that afternoon. Tension hung in the air as she and Aiden waited to hear why he had come looking for her after such a long time.

When Bryce arrived, he came bearing gifts. Flowers and candy, how trite. Aiden walked him out onto the deck then went inside to pace the floors.

Smiling brightly, Bryce leaned in to kiss Cassandra. Pain crossed his features when she turned her cheek to receive a chaste peck. The gesture spoke volumes.

They talked for over two hours, and even took a walk on the beach. Bryce told her about his four years in college. A sharp pang of jealousy struck Cassandra while he spoke of that time. It had always been her dream to attend college, not Bryce's. He had lived her dream while she struggled to survive and care for their child.

It took all of her self-control to remain calm when he talked about the company he'd formed for book distribution. It had started his first year of college through his own search for a less expensive source of text books. The dot com book business had taken off like a rocket right from the start. His pride was evident as he spoke of the success of his company, and all he'd accomplished in the past seven years.

"It's primarily internet-based, but I've expanded over the past year. We distribute all formats and genre of books. We also find out-of-print and rare editions for our customers."

Cassandra wanted to resort to some childish response. She itched to put her thumbs in her ears, waggle her fingers, and make mocking sounds. Instead she attempted a cheery response.

"That's great, Bryce. I'm very happy for you." Her tension only mounted the longer they talked. His lingering looks, full of longing and regret, made her uncomfortable. What did he want? Would he try to get visitation with Samantha? He hadn't even mentioned their child, or asked about her yet.

"I've always kept an eye out for anything you may have written. I was surprised when I never saw anything written under your name." He paused briefly before continuing.

"I first learned of your new last name, and the Lacy Harte pseudonym from the investigator I hired to find you. I didn't know you had married, or been published under that name."

She could see the unasked questions in his eyes, but remained silent, letting him finish his story.

"I now have copies of all your published works, and e-books. You really became an excellent writer, Cassie." His pride in her small accomplishments was clear. "I have to say, it came as a shock to read the romances. I saw so much of our time together, and myself in your words."

Cassandra nodded her head in acknowledgement. "Like most writers, I draw on my past experiences." She said nothing more on the subject, but waited silently for him to continue.

Bryce stopped walking and turned her to face him. He held both her hands in his own and watched her eyes. "I struggled to become a man who deserved someone like you. I wanted to be someone you could be proud of. I wish we could have a happy ending like in your stories."

He struggled for several moments. When he spoke again, his voice was thick with emotion. "Cassie, I love you so much. I want you in my life again. You're the best thing that ever happened to me, driving me to become a better person. Everything I've accomplished was for you."

Feeling drained both mentally and physically, Cassandra encouraged him to sit with her. The sun was just setting, turning everything deep shades of orange and red. It should have been a romantic scene, which made it all the more tragically sad.

She fought with her emotions, both new and old. She had once loved the boy Bryce had been, but she did not even know the man he'd become. His touch no longer affected her the way it once had, the way Aiden's did every day. Taking a deep breath she proceeded cautiously.

"Bryce, I have a different life now. I fought and struggled to survive, and made it through some very difficult times. I've grown into a different person, just as you have. I'm glad that I inspired you to succeed." She squeezed his hand gently.

His eyes became stormy. "I hear a 'but' in there," Bryce stated.

She sighed deeply before continuing. "The feelings I had for you were all destroyed long ago. When you disappeared my world shattered." It was difficult to maintain eye contact. His emotions were so close to the surface. Cassandra no longer felt the desire to melt away into the dazzling blue depths of his eyes. She just wanted to get this over with.

"Bryce, I'd always have doubts. In the back of my mind I would always be wondering when you would disappear again. I just can't live like that."

It was obvious in his expression that she was crushing his hopes and dreams. Cassandra gently stroked his cheek before continuing. "My daughter is a very big part of my life, and you never even mentioned her. Aiden is also very important to me. I love him, and I'm committed to him." He turned away from her and stared out at the ocean blindly for several moments. When he finally turned back she saw that his eyes still held a small shimmer of hope.

"Can't we spend so time together, see if there's still anything between us."

She shook her head sadly. "Bryce, if you'd come back during the first year it might have been possible. Too much has changed now. Spending time together would not lessen my feelings for Aiden." She squeezed his hands gently. "I'm sorry."

Relief surged through her. Bryce was not here to make any kind of claim on their daughter. He never even mentioned Sam. While that hurt, she would rather have it be that way. She did not want Sam's heart torn apart by the man who had so severely hurt her.

With nothing more remaining to be said between them, Cassandra rose. Obviously Sam would never be anything to Bryce. How could he expect her to want to try when their child didn't even enter into his mind?

They walked back to the house in silence. She acknowledged Travis, but did not see Aiden. "I'll be back in a few minutes after I walk Bryce out."

When they got to his car, Bryce handed her a piece of paper with his home and email addresses, and phone number. "If you ever change your mind…if you ever need anything."

Impulsively, Cassandra pulled him into a hug. She held onto Bryce for several moments before rising up on her toes to lightly brush a kiss across his lips. "Goodbye, Bryce. I hope you find happiness."

She remained focused on Bryce until he got in the car and drove away before turning to walk back inside. She was happy to finally have closure on that part of her life.

* * * * *

"You look really tired, Cass. Why don't you go lay down," Travis said when she walked in the door. "Do you want me to get you a pain pill?"

Sinking down onto the couch she shook her head. "I'm fine, Travis, thanks." She looked around for a moment. "Where's Aiden?"

Travis kept his features bland as he spoke. "He needed to run some errands." He walked over to her and extended a hand. "Come on, I'll tuck you into bed and make sure you're comfortable."

Cassandra was effortlessly pulled to her feet. "I need to talk to Aiden first."

Travis sighed deeply. "He won't be back for several days. Another company trip to Knoxville. You're going to need to give him some time, Cass. He's hurting right now." Travis pulled her into a hug. "Come on, sugar."

If Aiden had been anywhere near, Travis would've beaten the crap out of him for walking away from Cass. She had been through too much. His heart ached with the need to provide comfort.

She did not have enough energy to resist Travis' greater strength guiding her to the bedroom. "Why is Aiden hurting? I don't understand, Travis."

"Shh. It's okay. He just wants to make things easier on you, sugar. Aiden is giving you some space. And he doesn't want to hear about you and Bryce." Travis thought about how bleak and filled with pain Aiden's eyes had been. The brown pools had been so dark, they had looked almost black.

Cassandra violently shook her head. "Travis? What are you talking about? I sent Bryce away." She struggled against his embrace. "I have to go to Aiden, now."

Travis just shook his head. "Give him some time, Cass. He's gone home. Monday afternoon he leaves on a business trip."

"Damn it! He turned and ran away? Funny, I never saw Aiden as a coward. Why couldn't he face me and hear what I had to say? Why couldn't he have a little bit of faith in me?" Punching her pillow, Cassandra let her fury rise. "I'm gonna kick his ass when I find him. Doesn't he know me at all?"

The thought froze her heart. After everything they had shared he knew so little about her. "Like I would go back to Bryce just because he showed up out of the blue."

Travis turned to leave. "I'll try to call him…"

"No." Her sharp reply stopped Travis cold. "Don't call, don't tell him anything. I'll handle Aiden myself." Pulling up the covers she sank down into the warmth of the bed. "Go home, Travis. I'll call you if I need anything."

He stood at the door for a moment watching her as she struggled to find comfort in the empty bed. He would stay and watch over her until Aiden came to his senses. If he didn't, well, then all bets were off.

* * * * *

Cassandra lay in bed pretending to sleep, thinking about how insane the week had been. First, she and Aiden had started a relationship. She'd had sex for the first time in seven years. Absolutely incredible, totally hot, and wonderfully mind-blowing sex. Then Bryce had stepped out of the past, and she'd ended up in the emergency room getting stitched up. Now Aiden had turned and walked away from her without a word.

She really needed Aiden right now. It had been so painful to talk with Bryce and find out that he had given no thought to their daughter. He had no idea what a bright, beautiful girl she was, and no desire to find out.

God, how had she ever thought she loved such an unfeeling man? Memories of the past assaulted Cassandra with a vengeance. She had been blinded by love, never seeing the truth of their one-sided relationship. She had prayed for Bryce to come back, right up until the day Aiden had walked into her life.

She wanted to be held tightly in his arms and let him soothe away the old hurts. She needed Aiden to make love to her throughout the night. How could he not know how she felt about him?

Standing in the doorway, Travis heard her sobs. Her pain was tearing a hole in his heart. He could not just stand by and watch her suffer. Striding into the room, he scooped her up against his chest. "It's all right, Cass. I'm here." His hands stroked gently over her hair.

"I need him…need to be held," she cried. "How could he not be here when…when I need him so much?" Cold shivers racked her body.

"Shh. I'm here, Cass. I'll hold you, and take away the pain. I'm strong, sugar. Give it to me."

Her arms were so cold. Travis climbed into the bed, and covered them both with the comforter. He caressed her hair, arms, and back tenderly. It felt so right.

There was nothing sexual in his touch. He wanted only to comfort, and ease her pain. He didn't sleep, just held her close through the night providing what shelter he could.

* * * * *

Turning off his cellular phone, Aiden crammed the offensive device into the console of his car. "Hold my calls," he said with a wild laugh. There was no one he wanted to talk to, not that it mattered anymore. The most important person in his life was going back to her first love.

Thankfully he hadn't proposed yet. Now that would have been really embarrassing. Seeing Cass hold onto Bryce Martin so tightly had been more than he could take. They had held hands while walking on the beach, stared into each other's eyes. He certainly couldn't wait around for her to come back in the house, and tell him how deliriously happy she was. That was too much.

Really, who could blame her? The man was Sam's father. He was her first love. Of course she would take him back, no matter how out of character that would be for her.

Aiden had waited so long for her to finally see him as a man, not just a friend. Once she did, he thought he'd died and gone to heaven. For years he had dreamed of finding a woman even half as responsive and sexually adventurous. He'd been in love with Cass before they ever made love. Now he had fallen totally ass over teakettle. She was his perfect match. They belonged together. How was he supposed to go back to living without her now?

For all of about two seconds he considered going to Tammy. No, a meaningless fuck with her would not ease the ache he felt. He had learned that already. Anyone else would just be a pathetic substitute now that he'd had Cass, been touched by her love.

Briefly he considered calling Travis to make sure she was all right. He quickly dismissed that idea, not wanting to hear details of the happy reunion.

He would have never imagined strong, independent Cass falling back into the arms of a man who had so severely hurt her. Hell, at times she was downright pigheaded. She never thought of asking for help. Even when it was offered, she normally turned it down flat.

Aiden vividly remembered finding her in a lake of water, working on a plumbing problem. Water had been spraying out from the bathroom cabinet. Cass was soaked, and cursing a mile a minute as she brandished a wrench roughly the size of her forearm. She'd looked so incredibly sexy, all wet and pissed off.

When Aiden had tried to help she'd pushed him out of the way. "I don't need a man to fix things for me. I'm perfectly capable of taking care of my home."

She had done just that too. He'd watched as Cass battled the recalcitrant pipes. Her fierce determination and indomitable spirit touched his heart. There were so many times he wanted to race to her rescue. Normally he found himself sitting back and watching her conquer any obstacle she faced with aplomb.

I love Cass so much. How am I supposed to just be a friend again?

After driving around aimlessly for several hours, Aiden went home to his empty condo. He spent the night tossing and turning, trying not to think about how much he had lost in the blink of a blue eye.

Chapter Seventeen

It amazed Cassandra how much stronger she felt the next day, regardless of the sleepless night. Knowing Sam would be coming home brightened her spirits.

She could still smell Travis on her clothes, and skin. After a long shower she pulled on a silky robe before heading into the kitchen. Somehow she was not surprised to find he hadn't left. She walked into the kitchen and did a double take, at first thinking he was Aiden. They looked too much alike.

Shirtless and barefoot, he stood facing the stove wearing only a pair of tight jeans. His black hair was pleasantly rumpled from sleep. Muscles rippled over his wide back with each small movement. The faded denim hung low on narrow hips, molding to the firm curves of his buttocks. Damn if he didn't have the most magnificent ass.

Travis was slightly taller and wider than Aiden, but from behind it was difficult to detect the subtle differences. She stood still, drinking in the leashed masculine power which radiated around him. That was one hot hunk of man standing in her kitchen.

Unbidden images of his naked, sinewy body glistening with a fine sheen of sweat as he fucked her invaded Cassandra's mind. She pictured his face above her own, contorted with deep pleasure. Would he be as insatiable as Aiden? Would he prefer slow and easy lovemaking, or hard and fast fucking? It would certainly be fun to find out.

Her attraction to him must be due to his striking resemblance to Aiden. How else could she be attracted to one man when so totally in love with another?

The recent research she had been performing came to mind. She remembered the ménage à trois scenes, and how she had pictured the characters being Aiden and Travis. Sharing in a ménage with two such sexually confident alpha males would be explosive. What a wonderful fantasy.

Two delectable hunks in her bed satisfying her every desire. Two mouths devouring her breasts, four sets of hands loving her body. Two long, thick cocks sending her into one shattering orgasm after another. She really needed to be at her computer capturing the glorious images with words.

She also needed to check the thermostat. It was certainly hot inside. Heat suffused her body, and her pussy began to throb. Hot juices coated her slit, and dampened her panties. Each breath she took had the silky material of her robe caressing her taut nipples. Damn her out of control hormones.

Forcefully, she shook off her lascivious thoughts. Taking a deep breath, Cassandra walked further into the room and headed for the coffeepot. She poured a cup of the dark, aromatic brew and deeply inhaled the wonderful scent, sighing with pleasure. *Thank you, God, for creating coffee.*

"Mornin', Cass. How are you feeling today?" His voice was husky with sleep, and utterly appealing.

Somebody, give me strength. "Good morning, Travis. I feel much better today, thanks." Just being near the sexy man was waking up her dull morning senses without the benefit of a caffeine fix.

He turned toward her, and Cassandra's mouth nearly dropped open. The button of his jeans was undone. *Oh shit!* She wasn't sure why, but she'd always found that totally erotic. All a girl would have to do is give a little tug on his zipper and…

She couldn't keep her eyes from following the narrow trail of dark hair along the open waist of his pants until it disappeared under the material. *The happy trail. Someone sign me up for the next trip. Oh yeah, definitely time to adjust the thermostat.*

He moved over to the toaster, standing only inches away. Mmm, he smelled so good. Earthy, clean, and totally male. His scent was not unlike Aiden's, but distinctive nonetheless. She gripped her coffee mug tightly to keep from reaching out to stroke her fingers down his abdomen. She quivered with tension, ached with desire.

Travis' voice cut through the fog of her thoughts. "You seem a little tense this morning."

Tense? Who wouldn't be tense around a half-naked, hot, sexy man like Travis? "I'm just tired." She couldn't keep her eyes off his phenomenal body. Her own body was rigid with the sexual tension crackling in the air.

"Are you hungry?"

Unconsciously she licked her lips. "Starving," she purred.

Travis struggled to control his unruly response to Cass. He wanted nothing more than to strip her naked, and thrust his cock into her pussy. Being so close to all that silky, bronzed skin but not touching was enough to drive away all his good intentions. He wanted to back her up against the counter and drive his aching cock between her luscious legs.

Fuck. His own thoughts were likely to drive him crazy.

Cass was Aiden's woman. What the hell was wrong with him? But damn, she was looking at him as if she'd like to sink her teeth into his flesh. The spark of desire in that heated, sparkling emerald gaze was nearly enough to melt a man. If she made a move on him, would he be able to stop her, turn her away?

"Damn, Cass. What's up with the hungry eyes? See something you want?" He left it up to her to decide if he was talking about the breakfast he'd prepared or something else entirely.

Oh, yeah! I want. Give it to me, stud.

She wasn't sure how to deal with the unexpected sparks that flew between them. The hot look that swirled through his eyes caused her to quiver, tightening her abdominal muscles.

She stepped back slightly and shook her head. What the heck was wrong with her? She was turning into a nympho or something.

How was she supposed to respond? Was he offering what she thought, or just joking?

Thankfully she was saved from responding when Darlene and the girls burst through the front door. Sam's shriek of joy cut through the sexual tension. "Mom, you're up."

Sam launched herself into Cassandra's arms. She caught her daughter easily, while keeping her bandaged hand safely out of harm's way. Hugging Sam close she said, "Now that's a greeting worth waking up for."

Travis cooked breakfast for everyone while the girls all sat and talked. It was still early, so after eating they headed out to the beach for a walk before school. Sam and Jessie wanted to collect shells for a secret arts and crafts project.

The tension between Cassandra and Travis was palpable. In frustration, Darlene sought to break the silence. "So, what are you going to do about Aiden?" she asked.

Cassandra did not respond or acknowledge the question. She mulled over the options in her mind. Just when Darlene was ready to try another tactic, Cassandra sighed deeply.

"I've been thinking about it all night. There is only one thing I can think of to get through that thick skull of his." They stopped walking, both of them waiting for her to continue.

"I planned to go talk to him this morning at the office, but I don't think talk is going to be enough." Of course, talk was only a small part of her plans. What she had in mind was daring, adventurous, and would put her in a vulnerable position. If it meant getting her man though, Cassandra would do whatever was necessary.

"I need to work out the details first. It's not something I'll be able to accomplish alone." She turned to Travis. "I'll need your help, but it's not going to be easy." She searched his eyes, finding both jealousy and acceptance.

"I want to spend some time concentrating on Sam for the next few days." She turned to Darlene. "Can she stay with you over the weekend while I set my plan in motion?"

Reaching out, Darlene gave her hand a reassuring squeeze. "You know we love to have Sam with us. She is like a sister to Jess."

They started walking again to keep the girls within sight. "Thanks, Darlene. Travis, we'll put my plan into effect Friday night. Aiden is going to get quite a surprise when he gets home from that trip." A wicked gleam lit her eyes. Yes, it was going to be quite the surprise. And hopefully a temptation he could not resist.

* * * * *

After her shower, Cassandra dressed in her typical jeans and T-shirt. She put her hair up in a ponytail for the drive to Aiden's office. Opening the garage door she stared in at her baby for a few minutes. The beauty of her little pony car never failed to move her. Girls can have toys too!

The sexy little Saleen Mustang had cost a great deal. The price did not matter though. It was her one indulgence. Aiden and Travis called it the "land shark". It did kind of resemble a shark with the dark, shadow grey metallic paint, and the gill-like louvered side scoops. The leather seats, roll bar, and convertible top were all black. Titanium rims with five thick spokes adorned the wheels. They had been a fortune, but were worth every penny. From the rearview mirror hung a sexy silver faerie, riding on a rose quartz crystal.

Getting in the car, Cassandra triggered the button to bring the power top down. Turning the key in the ignition she melted at the throaty sounds of the large 425-horsepower engine.

Popping in the new CD by Pink, Cassandra cranked up the volume on the stereo and sang along with the bawdy rocker. The singer was such an incredibly wild woman. She was a blatantly sexual, tough-as-nails woman who was not about to conform to anyone's idea of who she should be.

Cassandra wished she could be so free, but she was a "soccer mom". Her biggest deviation from conformity was driving the sexy Mustang instead of a Volvo or mini-van. After all, she was a young single woman, not just a mother. That's where she drew the line though. Giving free rein to her wild side would be going just a little too far. She had to set a proper example for her daughter.

She took a deep, relaxing breath. Life just didn't get any better than riding in her pony car. She had nicknamed the car Don, short for Adonis. If anything could justify the name it was that hot little muscle car.

Driving the responsive sports car always put her in a good mood. Men hooted, hollered, honked, and whistled as she drove down the road. Bumper to bumper, the car screamed power and sex. Unfortunately, it had also landed her several speeding tickets. Like right now when she was delayed getting to the office while she flirted her way out of getting another.

Parking as far away from other cars as possible made for a long walk into the building, but the effort was worthwhile. By the time she entered the lobby, Cassandra was feeling hot and bothered. Thankfully the air conditioning seemed to be running at full blast.

Cindy greeted her with a wide grin. "Damn, girl. He's in a foul mood. Are you sure you want to go in there?" she teased.

Cassandra winked at the other woman. "Sorry, Cin. I'm the reason for his temper." They shared a conspiratorial grin. "How bad is he this morning?"

"Hmm, let's put it this way. He can't leave for the airport soon enough for me. The man about tore my head off this morning for bringing him a cup of coffee."

"Ouch. Well, you might want to take your lunch break early. I have a feeling my visit is not going to improve the situation."

Taking her advice, Cindy took out her purse. "This is perfect. By the time I get back he will already have left. Thanks, Cass."

Entering his office, Cassandra pushed the door shut behind her, not noticing when it did not close all the way. She stood still for a moment, steeling herself.

"I would have never thought you were a coward before yesterday," she calmly stated.

Startled, Aiden spit an impressive stream of coffee across his desk. "Cass. What are you doing here?" There was no welcoming smile on his lips.

Ignoring his question she posed one of her own. "Why did you leave without talking to me yesterday?"

He stood stiffly behind the desk. "What's there to talk about? Your long-lost first love is back. You two got nice and cozy real quick-like, so I got out of the way. Didn't take a brain surgeon to see what was happening."

None of the normal expressiveness was visible in those dark chocolate eyes. Just a blank expression that revealed nothing. Crap. Moving closer, she reached out a hand toward him, but he pulled back from her touch. "Aiden...let me explain." She watched him as he paced the floor behind his desk. "Bryce is…"

He spoke right over her words. "Explain what, Cass? That pretty boy's back, but we can still be friends?" His hands slammed down on the desk. Keeping that barrier between them, he continued. "Look, I scratched an itch for you. No big deal, right. Just a simple fuck."

Cassandra was dumbfounded. How could he call what they shared just scratching an itch? Just a simple fuck? Oh God. The arrogant, don't-need-anybody look on his face made her cringe.

Even though her face drained of all color she saw red. She was also paralyzed by shock, barely able to form a response. "How dare you?" Anger, pain, and fear all vibrated through her body. Her heart stuttered, then beat so fast she wondered if it would explode.

Aiden continued to dig himself even deeper. "You know, I'm not sure why I lusted after you for three years. It's not like you're incredible in the sack. And it's not like it meant anything. Hell, it wasn't love, just casual sex." If only he could convince himself of that.

Cassandra stood shaking violently. Her fragile, rebuilt heart shattered. She had thought he was special, different. In the end it was the same old thing. Fuck her then dump her quick. Never love her. Strike out at her to hide your own pain and inadequacies. When she spoke the words barely came out as a whisper, "You bastard."

"That's just about enough," Travis growled from the doorway, spitting out the words. Neither of them had noticed him standing there. He felt mad enough to spit nails.

Regardless of the half-hour head start he had given Cass, she was still there. And what the hell was Aiden doing? Rage rolled off Travis in waves. He would kill him before watching him tear Cass to shreds. The idiot didn't even know he was in love with her. Or maybe he was just not man enough to face it.

Cass stood facing Aiden, aching with the pain that shuddered through her at his words, and devastated by the hurt she glimpsed in his eyes. Tears streamed down her pale cheeks. Still her head was held high, her pride evident in her stance. How could one woman be so fragile, but so strong all at the same time?

Travis wanted to comfort her, pull her into his arms, but first he had to put Aiden in his place. He ran a hand roughly through his hair. He'd never been angrier in his life.

"Look, Travis. This is none of your business. She got what she wanted. We both had some fun. Now she's off to her true love." Aiden looked toward Cass again. "Sorry, hon. I'm not the kind to still be friends."

Chapter Eighteen

Cassandra flinched. Hadn't the damn man been listening to a word she'd said? Her eyes blurred, and burned with tears. Hot, primal rage swept through her body. Before she knew it she'd moved forward, raised her good hand, and slapped Aiden.

The strength of the blow snapped his head to the side, and the red angry handprint she left behind on his cheek stood out lividly against the pallor of his face. Her hand stung from the force of the blow.

"God, how could I have been so stupid?" Her voice was eerily calm. "I should have remembered the lessons I learned in the past." She avoided Travis' outstretched arm as she moved toward the door.

When she turned back all emotions were gone. Her tears had dried up. "I should have known there was no way you hadn't been affected by your controlling, masochistic bastard of a father. Hell, Mike should have taught me that lesson." She shuddered at speaking her dead husband's name out loud. "You have no heart or soul, just like your brother."

Her laugh bordered on being hysterical. "I know your reputation. I was just another woman, just another fuck, another notch on your bedpost. Well, fine, no problem."

Travis tried to block out the words that were too hurtful to hear. "You don't mean that, Cass. He may be stupid, but he's not cruel like Mike was."

Aiden turned on him. "Shut up, Travis. Don't try to help me. I can fuck things up enough on my own," Aiden growled.

She ignored Aiden. "No, he's worse than Mike. I made a huge mistake. I protected my heart from Mike, but I let myself fall in love with his brother. Guess I'll have to write that off as a learning experience. I'll never give my heart to another man again." A shrill laugh escaped her lips.

Not that she had a heart left anyway. Damn thing got stomped into the ground too many times. Nothing left but scar tissue. She walked from the office and never looked back.

"Know what, Aiden? You're even dumber than a box of rocks. To think I used to believe you were so frickin' smart. Mr. MIT grad, super computer genius. Your heart must be made out of microchips." Travis stood staring at Aiden. "Aren't you going after her?"

Aiden considered taking out his anger on Travis. They hadn't had a good knockdown drag-out fight since puberty. His blood was so boiling hot that he couldn't think straight. Hell, Travis still held a defensive stance, his weight on the balls of his feet, ready for action.

"What would be the point?"

"Sit down and I'll enlighten you." Travis waited for Aiden to comply. He'd thought about going after Cass himself, but first he had to make Aiden see what he'd just done.

"After you left yesterday, Cass sent pretty boy packing. She told him there was no way she could ever trust or love him again. She also told him she was in love with someone else." He paused briefly for effect. "Gee, I wonder who that could be."

Aiden dropped his head into his hands. *Oh God.* Why hadn't he given her the benefit of the doubt? Why hadn't he trusted her? Had he really just said those things to Cass? How could he hurt her like that? Damn, she was right. He was just like Mike.

Travis' words began to hit home. "She said what?"

"You dumbass. She told him that she is in love with and committed to you. If you didn't have your head so far up your ass, you'd have seen that. It's clear to anyone with a pair of eyes."

He stood, pacing. "I've got to cancel my trip…"

"No." Travis' words were final. "You go on your trip. Try to find your brains while you're gone. I'll talk to Cass. You've hurt her enough."

Aiden stared at Travis for several minutes. Tapping into their deep bond, he searched for Travis' feelings. He had always sensed that he had desired Cass. Was it more than that?

"Travis?" No matter how hard he tried to hide his inner turmoil, Aiden felt it. "You've fallen for her."

He turned back, and faced Aiden from the doorway. He would give him one chance. "When you come back you have twenty-four hours to stake a claim. After that all bets are off, and I make her mine." Travis would not just take her to bed. He would make her a permanent part of his life.

"I always knew you had the hots for Cass. Why do you think I told everyone she was off-limits?"

"That's another place where you're wrong. I don't want to just get her into bed. When I go to her, it will be for keeps. I'll show her the way she deserves to be treated by a real man. You might want to consider that on your trip."

* * * * *

Travis gave her some time to herself before going back to the house. He sat down next to her on the deck. "Tell me your plan, Cass."

Snorting in disgust she said, "Doesn't matter anymore."

Turning her to face him, Travis took her face in his hands. "It does matter, Cass." He sighed in frustration. "Aiden is an ass, but I am not. If your plan does not work in waking him up, I'll still be here."

He looked deeply into her eyes for understanding. "Do you know what I'm saying, Cass?"

Not trusting herself to speak she shook her head.

"Aiden may not be smart enough to love you, and make you his own. I'm not that stupid. I've hid my feelings because of Aiden, but if he doesn't step up to the plate…well, then it's my turn at bat." Understanding flashed across her green eyes, along with a little bit of hope.

"I won't play games or wait forever. If Aiden turns away, I want you to be a permanent part of my life. I'll teach you how good love can be, sugar."

The endearment, softly spoken in that sultry voice sent her pulse racing. Emotions overwhelmed Cassandra. She loved Aiden, but had always harbored feelings for Travis. He had just offered her the world on a silver platter. Leaning into his strong body she rested her head against his chest, and listened to his heart beat wildly.

"How did I ever get lucky enough to find two such extraordinary men?" It was more statement than question, so he remained silent. Cassandra gave a few small details of what she'd planned along with her fears and apprehension.

Travis sat listening quietly. Tension strummed through every muscle in his big body. "You are so incredible and adventurous. I don't think he will, but I pray Aiden walks away."

* * * * *

Time passed quickly, and Friday arrived before Cassandra was ready. She had yet to fill Travis in on all the details of her plan. It would only work with his cooperation, and there was no one else she could trust as unconditionally. Still doubts plagued her. Would he be willing and able to carry out her idea?

After dropping Sam off at school, Cassandra began gathering the things she would need. Everything went into an overnight bag. If Travis agreed she wouldn't be home again during the weekend.

The tension between them had not lessened. She chose not to say anything when he continued to stay at her house. Having Travis nearby felt good. Every night he held her while she slept. His presence was reassuring, and Sam was absolutely smitten. She flirted with him shamelessly and quickly had the big man wrapped around her little finger.

Sitting on the deck steps she watched him walking up the beach. Why did all the men in her life have to be so hard to resist? She wanted to strip off his clothes and touch every inch of his remarkable body. She knew he wouldn't turn her down, but she wouldn't try. Her heart belonged to Aiden, although Travis had captured a portion of her love over the past week.

He came and sat down next to her. Taking her hand in his much larger one, Travis interlaced their fingers. "So, what's the whole plan?"

He sat quietly listening to her detail what she had in mind. His expression gave away nothing of his feelings. She expressed her concerns over their attraction, and how hard her plan would be for both of them. Cassandra waited for him to say something, anything. She resisted the urge to break the silence. When he finally did she shook nervously.

"Are you sure you will be able to go through with this?" Travis asked. His dark chocolate eyes were serious.

"Yes. It's the only way to prove to Aiden that I trust and love him completely." Looking into his eyes she finally felt reassured. "You are the only two men on earth I could ever trust enough to even consider this."

Cass' words touched him deeply. Her confidence and trust in him were staggering. They had become very close, but it was hard for him to believe she could go through with her adventurous plan.

She was the most extraordinary woman he had ever known. If Aiden weren't his best friend…then nothing would stop Travis from claiming her. He was absolutely green with envy. Aiden didn't deserve her.

"Will Cindy be okay with this? I don't want to cause any problems for your relationship." Concern darkened her eyes.

"Cass, it's not like that with us. We are close friends with benefits, nothing more. We don't hold each other's hearts. We are convenient and safe." He shrugged his shoulders. "It's not like with you and Aiden. He's always made it very well-known how possessive he feels about you. How much he loves you."

Leaning her head against his firm biceps, Cassandra sighed deeply. Travis' words had just changed her perspective on many things having to do with the group. It also cleared up some questions she'd never been comfortable enough to voice.

Travis pulled her up close against his side, draping his arm over her shoulders. It was going to be nearly impossible for him to walk away from her tonight, but he would do as she asked.

* * * * *

Time had slowed down to nearly a crawl for Travis. Aiden's flight was not due in until seven o'clock. The afternoon stretched out before them endlessly. Cass looked exhausted, drained. Her anxiety was wearing on his nerves.

"Why don't you try to rest, Cass? You're going to need your strength tonight." Of course, he didn't know where he was going to find the strength to survive the night.

"I'm too restless to sleep," she said while pacing the living room. "I'll sleep later. I always seem to sleep better when I'm being held."

The temptation was too great. He reached out and took her hand. "Come on, sugar. You're making me crazy."

Travis led her into the bedroom and pulled her onto the bed. Lying on his back he nestled her up against his side, gently tucking her head into his shoulder. His chin rested on her crown. She felt so perfect there.

Once again he was glad his job had flexibility, and that he could do so much from home on his laptop. While it had been a tough task, he had actually managed to get work time in while she rested. He would not have been able to spend this time with Cass if he had to punch a clock. "Now rest," he commanded.

With great effort, Travis fought to control his reactions. He concentrated on making every breath slow and even. He struggled to keep his heart from racing. It felt so good to hold her in his arms. His nostrils flared, taking in her scent. She smelled like clean air after a summer rain shower.

As her breathing deepened and slowed with sleep, Travis became lost in thought. His erection jutted up hard as a steel beam. Cass' plan would be the ultimate test of his self-control.

In her sleep she moved closer. One slender thigh slid over his. Her arm draped over his abdomen, perilously close to his throbbing cock. He bit the inside of his cheek to keep from flipping her onto her back, and taking what she unknowingly offered.

He groaned as she rubbed her face against his chest. The hand on his abdomen slid lower, cupping his erection. Travis moved with lightning speed. He grabbed her hand and tucked it safely under his arm, pinning it to his side. Would he be able to restrain himself when she lay helpless before him?

As soon as she woke up, Travis rolled away from her and leapt from the bed. He mumbled some excuse about having to take care of some things. She wasn't buying it. She had seen the bulge in his pants.

Doubt invaded her mind. Was she asking more of Travis than he could give? Looking at the clock she realized that it would not be long now before she found out.

* * * * *

After showering she stood in front of the bathroom mirror, wrapped in a fluffy peach towel. The door was open slightly to let some of the steam escape. With great patience, Cassandra combed out endless miles of silken hair. Not for the first time, she considered how much easier it would be to handle if shorter, but quickly dismissed the thought. She liked her wavy hair long. The heavy strands felt good against her bare skin.

Staring into the mirror she searched her eyes for the courage to go through with her plans. Having Travis nearby would help. He was so protective and caring. She cherished the new closeness they shared.

Motion drew attention to the portion of the bedroom she could see in the mirror. Travis moved through the room picking up clothes, stacking them in a laundry basket. He didn't seem to notice her watching. *Wow! Hot, sexy, and he does laundry.* What more could a woman want?

More than anything she wanted to go to Travis, strip off his clothes, trip him then beat him to the floor. A tingling awareness spread through her body. Her nipples poked out against the damp towel. The mounting sexual tension was unbearable. They both needed release.

With all her concentration, Cassandra willed Travis to see her. She felt his stillness before realizing that he had finally noticed her reflection. Barely looking in the mirror from under heavy-lidded eyes she slowly opened the towel, dropping it to the floor.

Knowing that she held his undivided attention, Cassandra let her head fall back, her eyes to close. Travis would not touch her, but she would be his hands. She would share herself with him the only way possible.

Long, slender fingers trailed seductively over every curve, dip, valley, and crevice. A great deal of attention was lavished over her full, high breasts. She massaged the firm globes, rolling the taut nipples between her fingers. Immediate streamers of sensation raced to her pussy. Just knowing he was watching made her feel sexy, wanton.

Using her hands, Cassandra saw her body in a whole new light through Travis' eyes. Fingers glided easily over still damp flesh. Tingles ran up and down her spine as she slid her palm gently across her belly. Her skin was soft, the trail of her fingers radiating waves of heat. She let her fingers comb through the springy hair over her mound.

Sliding lower, she parted her delicate, swollen outer folds. The skin felt slick and hot, juices pooled at her vaginal opening. She caught some of the thick fluid on her fingers and spread it upward, around the hood of her clit, the sensitive nub standing out boldly. Oh, that felt good.

She could feel Travis' eyes in every touch. It was his fingers circling her clit, sinking into her pussy. The sensitive walls clung to the two fingers penetrating the warm cavern. She imagined his cock thrusting between her spread legs.

Pulling over the high, padded vanity stool she climbed up, spreading her legs wide before the mirror. Propping her feet on the vanity gave a clear view of her sopping pussy to her phantom lover.

Adding a third finger she increased the pace of her thrusts. Flicking her wrist sent them over her g-spot, echoing motions Travis might use. With her other hand, Cassandra lavished attention on her hardened nipples.

Barely peeking out below her lashes she saw that Travis sat on the bed, magnificent cock in hand, stroking in the rhythm she set. Every muscle, nerve, and molecule of her body was pulsing on the edge of cresting a tumultuous wave.

The heady sensations racking her body were impossible to ignore. There would be no holding back, she would give Travis everything. Her back arched, and she cried out involuntarily. Tension coiled as she rose higher on the wave, then suddenly plunged over into sweet oblivion. The walls of her pussy tightened, pulsing over her fingers.

No sooner had the initial waves subsided when she began feeling soft aftershocks pulse along her clit. The soft sounds of Travis' ragged breathing barely cut through the post-coital fog surrounding Cassandra.

His release was dramatic when viewed indirectly through the thick veil of eyelashes. Strong jets of milky seed arced impressively from his shaft, coating Travis' abdomen and chest. Cassandra wished she could go to him and lick up the salty cum, take his essence into her mouth. She licked her lips, imagining his taste.

Chapter Nineteen

Having a key did not make going into Aiden's condo without his consent seem any less like breaking and entering. Travis used a flashlight to navigate the hallways. They did not want to leave lights turned on that would give away their presence.

Once in the bedroom they turned on the bedside lamp while they got everything set. They moved around in silence, but she could not help wondering what was going through Travis' mind.

Neither of them had talked about what they had shared earlier. Cassandra was relatively certain he thought she'd not been aware of his presence. It had been one of the most blatantly sexual acts in which she had ever partaken, leaving her feeling closer than ever to Travis.

After getting everything in place he once again questioned, "Are you sure about this?"

Cassandra put a hand on his arm. "Relax, Travis. I'm sure."

"Okay." His nervousness only served to fuel her anxiety.

Travis looked at his watch for about the millionth time. "Well, his plane should be on the ground by now. I guess we better get you settled."

She nodded her head and went into the bathroom to get undressed. Not that it would make much difference. Travis would see her anyway, already had, but it would not be fair to undress in front of him.

Taking a deep breath she tried to still the fine trembling in her hands. After taking off her clothes she put on black thigh-high stockings, a red silk garter belt, and four-inch black stiletto heels.

Looking over herself in the mirror with a critical eye, Cassandra sighed. She was wet from anticipation already. Damn. Waxing her pussy had probably been a bad idea. Her state of arousal would be immediately apparent to Travis. Her labia glistened with her juices.

All right, come on wanton, wild sex goddess. A little help here.

Tamping down her apprehension, Cassandra held her head high as she walked out into the bedroom. Travis had just finished turning down the bed, and lighting several candles. He turned at the sound of the opening door. His sharply inhaled breath drew her attention. She stopped walking and stood facing him.

Travis felt his heart lodge in his throat. He struggled to breathe past the blockage. Cass was resplendent. The heels accentuated her long, sleek legs, drawing the eye. The lacy garter belt graced divinely curved hips.

Her bare pussy left her swollen, soft pink lips open before his eyes. Cream enticingly coated her naked flesh. Sometime during the afternoon she had waxed. Damn, that was so hot. Engorged, her clit beckoned to Travis. He wanted nothing more than to fall down on his knees and lick up her hot juices.

Sparkling candlelight reflected over her soft skin. His eyes followed her slim torso up to full, pert breasts. A muscle in his jaw twitched upon seeing the firmness of the turgid peaks. Waves of caramel brown hair floated over toned arms and slender shoulders. Her lips held a deep burgundy blush, and were slightly parted. She was truly a goddess, and she was as turned on as he had quickly become. His dick was so hard that he could pound nails with it.

He struggled for something to say. There were no words. He wanted to lay her down on the bed and spend the rest of his life loving every delectable inch of her body.

Looking at Travis she saw raw, undisguised need practically shooting out of his eyes, heating her flesh. Primal hunger rolled off him in waves, making her pulse race as fire spread from her core. She wanted to tear open his clothes and fuck him hard. Fierce need had her struggling for breath and control.

Cassandra finally got her mind to connect with her body. The sex goddess prodded, *Come on, girl. Get your ass moving.* She walked quickly to the big bed and stretched out spread-eagle on the black satin sheets. "I'm ready, Travis."

The double meaning of her words slammed into his abdomen like a fist. The air was thicker than molasses, making it hard to breathe. Time lost all meaning as he made his way around the bed securing her with the restraints. He took great care to ensure they were not too tight against her tender flesh.

When she was in position he stood at the foot of the bed in a state of suspended animation. Desire darkened his warm tawny eyes. The massive bulge in his pants throbbed visibly against thick denim jeans. He couldn't pull his eyes away from the incredible woman laid out before him.

"I...I need...Travis?" Her voice was thick and husky with passion. "I can't stay here alone, restrained. Please stay. Talk to me until Aiden gets here."

His hand rose slightly before dropping back down at his side, trembling. He spoke through clenched teeth. "Fuck. I...I can't, Cass." He dropped his gaze to the floor. "Seeing you open, wet and vulnerable like that... It's killing me. I'm not strong enough."

Cassandra felt her juices pouring from her slit, dripping down to her anus. The bed would be soaked before long. "Travis, don't leave me here like this alone. I can't stand it." Futilely she tugged on the restraints.

When their eyes met he felt the heat of her gaze. Unable to stop himself, Travis let his eyes drink in the breathtaking sight of her stunning beauty. When he saw how wet she was his breath hitched in his chest. He wanted her more than he'd ever wanted any woman. He could smell the musky scent of her arousal rising around them.

"Have you changed your mind?" he asked.

"No. I just need you to stay with me." She looked into his eyes imploringly. "Please, Travis. I know it's asking a lot."

He turned from the bed. If he looked at her any longer he would not be able to control himself. "You have no idea how hard this is for me." He walked to the patio doors and stepped outside, taking big, gulping breaths of air.

Leaving the doors slightly open he sat off to the side where he could not see her. "I'll stay out here and talk to you. My control is on a very short leash right now, so don't say anything. Your voice is too damn seductive."

Her ability to move was severely impeded by the restraints. Still, soft sounds of flesh moving over satin reached Travis as she writhed restlessly.

"Aiden has no idea what an incredibly lucky man he is, Cass. You are an exceptionally beautiful, giving woman. I hope he appreciates how much courage and trust this required." Travis would move heaven and earth to find such an amazing woman for himself. Then he would see to it that she never wanted for anything, and never left his side. If only Cass was his woman. She wouldn't have to go through this. He would make sure she did not doubt his love.

He talked for most of the next hour, reassuring her with his voice. It was exasperating to know that on the other side of the glass doors helplessly lay the most amazing woman he'd ever known. Unbidden images of Cass assaulted his mind. Travis knew that her dazzling beauty and strength would forever haunt him. All other women would be held up to her in comparison, and likely be found lacking.

Cassandra felt she would go insane with the need to be touched. Travis' deep velvety voice washed over her, sending heat rippling through her body. His words were supportive, but filled with longing. It took all her love for Aiden to keep from calling him back into the room and begging him to touch her.

She was so confused by her desires. Having seen his dark eyes filled with passion let her know she was not alone. It wasn't just a mutual sexual attraction that sparked between them. She could see both lust and love shining in his chocolate eyes. Travis was just as conflicted over the fire that arced between them. Images of the two men loving her body came to her mind. She knew there was no sense in hoping for something that would never happen, not even in her wildest dreams.

The cold conditioned air circulated by the ceiling fan did not touch the heat raging like a fever through her flesh. One touch and she would shatter. Anticipation and Travis' steady flow of words made her squirm.

Finally, hearing the sound of Aiden entering the condo brought Travis the knowledge that he would soon be released from his torment. It also brought extreme feelings of jealousy and envy. Why couldn't he have found her first?

"Good luck, sugar. You know where to come if it doesn't work out." The words were barely a whisper. He softly closed the sliding door, but waited to make sure everything was okay before leaving. She was in such a vulnerable position. He wanted to be there if she needed him, or if Aiden was still being stupid.

Cassandra cringed at the anguish held within the softly spoken words that she was certain he'd not meant for her to hear. She lay wondering how long it would take before Aiden finally came into the bedroom. Seconds became hours, but all she could do was wait.

* * * * *

Seeing all the people crowded around the baggage carousel, Aiden was grateful that he had not checked any luggage. The two small bags he had taken were easy to carry on the plane.

He could not remember a time when he had ever felt so utterly depleted. Emotionally he felt raw, physically he felt spent. First thing in the morning he would go and talk to Cass. He'd been so cruel.

The cab ride home only increased his weariness, but it was worth the discomfort to keep his Mercedes safely parked in the garage at home instead of in an airport lot for four days. Sweat poured off his body as the ineffectual air conditioner only pushed the stifling hot air around. The poor state of the vehicles shocks pounded his weakened body into the thin seat.

The whole trip had been sheer agony. He'd thought about canceling, backing out of his duties. Heck, it would have been easy to call in sick. In the end he'd done the right thing, honored his commitment.

It felt disconcerting to be out of touch for such an extended period of time. He had left his cell phone in the console of his car. Without it, none of his friends had been able to reach him. He usually never went more than a few hours at a time without talking to either Travis or Cass. It felt as if he were adrift at sea without an anchor.

Oh, how he'd missed the sultry, near breathless sound of her voice. Her melodic laughter and incandescent smile. She brought a sparkling exuberance for life to everything she touched.

As he walked toward his condo, Aiden considered how badly he had managed to screw things up with her. Why the hell had he waited three long years only to turn and walk away? He should have trusted in her. If she gave him another chance he wouldn't waste it this time. He'd grab hold of her, and never let go.

The darkened condo felt empty, desolate. Aiden dropped his bags in the entryway. He would unpack tomorrow if he found the ambition. While heading into the small kitchen he froze for a moment, hearing a strange sound. When everything remained quiet he brushed it off as imagination. The condo was as empty now as always.

Dropping some ice in a glass he poured in a generous amount of Chivas. Leaning against the counter, Aiden drank deeply, relishing the powerful burn of the amber liquid as it seared along his throat. Fingers of heat spread out from his abdomen, relaxing his weary body. He downed the drink then loosened his tie before pouring a refill.

He'd thought he would feel relieved to be home, instead of sequestered in the impersonal hotel room. It was disheartening to realize that his empty condo, though comfortable, did not feel any more like a home than the rented room had. The only place he truly felt at home was with Cass.

He was tired, but not ready for bed. Aiden carried the bottle with him into the living room where he sprawled out in the big leather recliner. Flipping through channels on the TV, he scarcely paid attention to the images flickering across the screen.

Briefly he considered calling Cass, but in the end decided it would be better to talk in person. Hearing her voice would not help him sleep. He thought about calling Travis then changed his mind. It was Friday night and Travis would be with the rest of their friends at the club.

Oh, what the heck. Grabbing up the cordless phone he dialed Travis' cell phone. Being back, Aiden had to know what was going on. Plus it would be good to check in.

The second drink sat untouched in the living room. He listened to the ringing as he headed down the hallway. A hot shower would clear his head, help him to think.

"Hello." Travis' voice was a whisper he barely heard.

"Hey, Travis. What's going on? I just got back."

"Ah, can't talk, man. Call me tomorrow." Travis hung up before Aiden could say anything else. That was really strange. Why the hell would he whisper? And Travis certainly was not at the club or he would have heard the music.

As he neared the bedroom door, Aiden knew something was not right. It was his habit to leave the door open. Soft light flickered on the carpet from under the closed door. No lights had been on when he'd left the other day.

He knew it wouldn't be difficult for someone to get in through the sliding glass doors from the patio. Great, he was being robbed. Putting his ear to the door, Aiden listened for any indication of intruders, but heard nothing.

Making barely a whisper of sound he turned the doorknob and moved quickly into the room. He stood crouched over, ready for anything, scanning the empty room with his eyes. Seeing the candles burning on the dresser explained the flicker of light.

"Aiden."

His name was a sensual whisper filled with need.

Rising to his full height he turned to the bed. What he saw took away his ability to speak, leaving him mute. He just stood there and stared, mouth hanging wide open.

Chapter Twenty

"Welcome home. How was your trip?" Nervous laughter escaped her lips.

Moving in a mystified haze, he slowly approached the foot of the bed. Shocked, tawny eyes moved slowly over her body, taking in every detail. Soft candlelight licked over her naked flesh. The garter belt, hose, and heels were sexy as hell. Juices soaked her bare pussy, and the sheets under her fine ass.

"Oh, fuck." It was the most erotic, sexy, sensual display Aiden had ever seen. "Damn, Cass."

Her thighs were spread wide, leaving her glistening, naked pussy open to his penetrating gaze. His hungry eyes feasted on her, drinking in every open, vulnerable inch of flesh.

She whimpered, staring helplessly up at him. "Aiden..."

She watched his eyes move over her swollen, aching breasts, lingering on her pebbled nipples. Then his focus moved lower, over her trembling abdomen, before finally fixating again on the slick folds between her legs. The expression in his eyes was raw, naked hunger. She pulled on the restraints, arching toward him.

His erection was full and aching, pressed painfully against his pants. His hands were sweaty, and a fine line of perspiration broke out over his brow. He'd never been so turned on in his entire life. "Mine," he rasped possessively.

Tracing his hand slowly over one restrained ankle, Aiden froze as his mind began to make connections. Restraining herself to the bed was a physical impossibility. Someone had tied her naked body to his bed, and whoever it was had made her wet. That thought brought a murderous rage with it. He would kill the person who had dared to touch his woman. "Who the hell restrained you, baby?"

Cassandra did not know about Travis' declaration to Aiden, otherwise she would have protected his identity. "There's only one other person in the world I'd trust to help me with something like this." She watched his face, worried about the fury that shadowed his expression. "Travis helped me and then waited outside so I wouldn't be alone."

Reaching the sliding door in a few quick strides, Aiden brutally yanked it back, banging it against the jamb. Travis stood in the darkness, making no attempt to cover his huge boner.

Anger rolled off Aiden in palpable waves.

"I only did what she asked, Aiden. I stayed to make sure she was okay."

"You son of a bitch. You've got a boner the size of Texas, and she's soaking wet. How could you touch her? You know she's mine," he growled.

Travis stood shaking his head. "You're so fucking blind. Don't you see what she did for you, how much it's costing her, costing me. You walked away from her once. Don't do it again, because this time I won't turn away."

"Aiden, Travis, come here NOW!" demanded Cass. Her tone left no room for argument. The fear in her sharply spoken words brought both men quickly to her side.

Passion and anger flickered across her wide eyes. "You moron. Travis was a perfect gentleman. He didn't touch me, Aiden, regardless of how much I wanted him to do just that." What was the problem anyway? She knew the rumors. Knew they had shared women before. He shouldn't be upset.

Her revelation had both men gaping. Well, good, she'd shocked the unflappable duo. In that moment she finally understood. She was trapped in a helpless situation. She loved Travis, and could no longer deny her feelings. Suddenly, she knew what to do. She needed them both. *Come on goddess, go for broke.*

"Don't just stand there with your tongues hanging uselessly out of your mouths. I need someone to lick my pussy."

Their matching stunned expressions drew a husky laugh of triumph from Cassandra. "Boys, I'm hornier than hell. Please, help me." She wriggled her hips as much as the restraints would allow, enticing her men. That was exactly what she needed, both of the men she loved.

Travis looked to Aiden for a clue as to what he should do. If he sent him packing he'd just have to deal with that. *Oh God, don't send me away,* he pleaded with his eyes.

Aiden was beyond shock. Cass wanted both of them. Oh, shit. It was more than he had ever dreamed she'd want, or accept. A slow smile spread across his lips, bringing out his deep dimples.

While he wanted her all to himself, Aiden could imagine nothing better than the two of them pleasuring Cass. He wanted to bring her that ultimate pleasure. Heck, he'd been considering it when she'd talked about her research. Pushing away his jealous feelings he decided to invite Travis to play.

"Damn, Travis. I can't believe you didn't even taste some of that sweet cream. You got her all hot, and left her lying in misery." He shook his head for emphasis. "Shame on you."

Travis just stood there with a wary expression on his face. Looking deeply into Cass' eyes, Aiden quietly asked, "Are you sure, baby? Is this what you really want?"

Her throaty whisper caused a reflexive jerk in both of the men's cocks. "I need both of you. Hurry, please."

Aiden put an arm around Travis' shoulders. "Aw, man. She tastes like exotic spices and sugar, all hot and sweet on your tongue." He gave Travis a little push toward the bed. "You got her horny, man, go take care of her."

When Travis spoke, his voice was a velvety caress, sending shivers of anticipation down her spine. "I could use some help, Aiden." They shared in a silent communication that she had always envied. Cassandra watched as the two men moved to opposite sides of the bed. Sitting next to her they stared down at her appreciatively for several moments, making her squirm.

"Mmm, I think I'll start with a kiss." Travis leaned forward, just close enough for their breath to mingle. His scent filled her nostrils — earthy, seductive, and bold.

The kiss started as a soft brushing of lips then gradually built in heat. She glanced over at Aiden for a reaction. He seemed to be caught up in watching them. Tentatively, she parted her lips slightly. It was all the invitation Travis needed. Slanting his lips across hers, his tongue plunged into her mouth. He greedily drank in her soft, pleasure-filled moans.

Longing to wrap her arms around him, Cassandra pulled against the restraints then whimpered softly. Aiden's eyes were filled with a combination of pride, lust, and love. Before she had realized that he had moved, Aiden's warm breath caressed her ear.

"Just relax and let us love you, baby. We won't do anything you don't want. Just let go and enjoy."

Cassandra let her body relax back into the mattress. Aiden's tongue trailed down her neck, teasing the tender area where it met her shoulder. She whimpered in protest as Travis ended their kiss, then echoed Aiden's movements.

The two men moved like mirror images. Four large, calloused hands roamed her body. Aiden's touch was firm, while Travis' was tender and tentative. Heat shot through her abdomen as each taut nipple was simultaneously laved by a warm tongue. Cassandra was overwhelmed with sensation. It all felt so electrifying.

Having two gloriously handsome men devour her breasts was maddening. Two distinct touches from two distinctly different tongues. The sheer excessive decadence was mind-numbing. Travis moaned against her nipple sending tremors straight to her clit.

"Damn, Cass, you are delicious!"

Aiden hummed his agreement against the other nipple.

Oh, she was so close already. Cassandra arched her back, pressing her swollen breasts closer to their hungry mouths. Her nipples were taken softly between their lips and sucked. Hands cupped and massaged the globes as the sucking pressure increased.

"Ohhh...yes, harder," she gasped as her body writhed.

They immediately obeyed, pulling her nipples taut then sucking in more of her breasts. Warm mouths open, their tongues licked and swirled around her nipples, teeth nipped, hands massaged.

She whimpered, moaned, and arched closer.

"Come for us, sugar."

Travis' sensual voice spread over her like hot butter, sending her over the edge. Heat exploded deep in the center of her body, surging upward over her breasts. Her pussy throbbed, pulsed, muscles tightened.

Their mouths worked in unison until her whole body was jolted with the vibrations of orgasm. Wave after wave took her under in a gentle release. Her cries hung in the air around them as her body shook.

Cassandra's breath came out in panting gasps. Their voices barely registered as the men continued to stroke and kiss her body. They whispered words of approval.

"Damn, Aiden. You didn't tell me she was so responsive. I've never seen a woman come just from having her breasts sucked before."

She could no longer differentiate which caress came from which man. It didn't matter anyway. All that mattered was the sweet sensations they provided.

"Mmm, just wait until you taste her sweet cream. Cass goes crazy over the feel of a firm tongue on her clit. And when you suck on it...umm. Right, baby?"

Having caught her breath finally, Cassandra struggled for a way to participate. Her options were limited by the restraints.

"Would you boys quit dawdling and someone lick my pussy already."

The husky sounds of masculine laughter filled her ears as they continued on their slow progression down her body. Cassandra thought she would go insane by the time they finally made it to her mound. At last she would have what she wanted, needed. Following their silent communications both men diverted around her core, trailing their tongues and hands over her legs.

Throaty moans of frustration escaped her lips. "Ah...boys, I think you missed a spot."

"You are such a smart-ass," Travis teased while kissing the erogenous zone behind her knee.

"Cass gets a little wild when you make her come. She loses all her inhibitions, lets her control slip, and abandons herself completely. Absolute and total surrender of her mind to the pleasures of her body. Isn't that right, baby?"

Soon tongues, lips, and hands were working their way up the inside of her thighs. *Oh, hell yeah.* Cassandra made little furtive noises in the back of her throat.

"God, I love the little squeaky sounds you make," Travis commented. "I can't wait to see what you do when I tongue-fuck your sweet pussy."

The little sounds increased as his dark, erotic words reached Cassandra.

"Thanks for inviting me to join in," Travis stated with a slight quiver to his voice.

Oh, that did it. Time for the sex goddess to play. "Excuse me. I need a little more attention. You two are all talk. How about some action?" If she had her hands free they would be fisted on her hips. She loved verbally bantering with them.

"Smart-ass," Aiden teased.

"Bite me," she hissed.

Male laughter was followed by her shrill shrieks as they followed her suggestion, playfully nipping at her sensitive inner thighs.

"Just wait until I get my hands free. You boys are going to suffer big-time..." Her words trailed off into mindless pleas as their tongues converged on her naked pussy. Cassandra could not breathe as one man lay over her abdomen and licked her clit while the other lay between her legs, thrusting his stiffened tongue into her pussy.

Travis' fingers felt thick as he separated the delicate folds of her sex. The taste of her juices on his tongue blew his mind. He groaned, pushing her legs wider apart, giving his tongue greater freedom to explore. Never before had he wanted to spend hours between a woman's legs. The smooth, soft flesh was hot and enticing.

"I can't believe you waxed," Aiden said. "It's so damn sexy, baby. And I bet you're more sensitive too."

A deep, passion-filled moan was her only response as he licked her clit. Strong, firm hands cupped her ass cheeks, tilting her pelvis toward their marauding tongues. Wet slurping, sucking sounds filled the room as the two men devoured Cassandra, hungrily lapping up her cream. The dual sensations were making her crazy.

Another set of fingers gently parted the pink folds covering her pussy, holding her open for two warm, wet tongues. They hungrily licked up every bit of her juices.

Cassandra now understood why people put mirrors on the ceiling above their beds. More than anything in the world she wanted to be able to watch. She wanted to see their expressions as their tongues feasted on her.

Thanks to the unique bond between the two men neither seemed to be bothered by their tongues making brief contact as they shared in her pleasure. She wondered if they would come together as naturally in other ways. It would be hot to witness a more intimate sharing. She would like to see Aiden and Travis also bring pleasure to each other.

A synchronized rhythm was quickly established. Her clit was sucked as a tongue thrust into her opening. Her clit was licked as the other tongue withdrew. Suck, thrust, lick, and withdraw. Again and again they repeated the maddening caresses until she screamed in mindless ecstasy.

"Oh, yes. Right there. Don't stop," she cried.

Her body convulsed as orgasm took over. The sensual assault never slowed, keeping her at a fever pitch. No sooner had the fierce waves of her climax subsided than the men built her up again, sending Cassandra hurtling into another wave of release.

Flickering aftershocks racked her body as the men soothed her with their hands. She did not even realize the restraints had been released as hands removed her shoes, rolled down the silk stockings, and slid off the garter belt.

She watched in fascination as the men removed their clothing, standing side by side next to the bed. Both men had sculpted, athletic bodies that Adonis would have envied. Aiden's long, thick cock waved toward her body. Travis' cock was fractionally shorter, but wider in girth. Both steely shafts sported thick veins which throbbed rapidly. The heads were plum-shaped, engorged with blood. All in all, two amazingly beautiful specimens.

"Damn, boys," she panted. "I need one of those hard cocks in my mouth. I want to taste one of those salty rods while the other fucks me senseless." *Look out, boys. The wanton sex goddess is on a roll.*

The men shared a look, competition gleaming in their eyes. They each knew what they wanted. "I get her mouth," Aiden stated, striking his claim.

"Good, because I need to fuck that sweet pussy," Travis countered. He moved to the nightstand, retrieving the foil packet he knew he'd find there.

"Wait," Cassandra blurted out. She quickly hopped up onto her hands and knees, facing Travis. "Let me," she said with a wicked smile. "I learned something interesting in my research that I'm dying to try."

Her excitement was contagious. Travis felt his cock jerk in response. It nearly shouted ooh, ooh, pick me, pick me. After opening the packet he handed the condom to Cass. She was positively thrumming with excitement.

"This is an old hooker's trick." Unrolling the condom slightly she placed it between her lips and teeth. Reaching out she pulled Travis closer, her fingers wrapped around the base of his shaft. As the head of his cock went past her lips she licked him through the condom. Slowly she took his length into her mouth, sheathing him as she took his cock deeper. Still, Cassandra had to use her hands to finish the job, unable to take his entire length into her throat.

Travis' breath came out with a hiss and deep moan. Aiden watched her actions with awe. "Shit, baby. That's hot as hell."

Cassandra remained where she was for a moment, wrapped up in tonguing his hard shaft. When she finally released him from her mouth she bounced up and down gleefully. "It worked. That's so much fun." She smacked her lips a few times, tasting latex. "Maybe a flavored condom would work better though."

Feeling wanton, she lay back on the bed spread-eagled. "Come on, boys. I need those cocks." A wild thrill surged through her as she replayed the words in her head. She had become a true wanton, wild woman. *Oh, hell yeah!*

Aiden knelt on the bed next to her head. The look in his eyes was so full of love and amazed longing that Cassandra felt tears sting her eyes. She held them back by the sheer force of the goddess. "Fuck my mouth, big boy."

The thick head of Aiden's cock passed her lips. Although her view was blocked, she felt Travis' movements. His firm hands spread her legs and held them open. Powerfully muscular thighs moved between her legs. At the first touch of the broad head of Travis' cock to her slit, chills ran down Cassandra's spine. A shallow thrust sunk the wide, bulbous head a few inches into the clutching depths of her pussy.

"Fuck, she's so tight," rasped Travis.

"Mmm, her pussy is gonna milk your cock when she comes again," Aiden commented distractedly.

In one smooth thrust Travis drove forward, pressing up against her womb. At the same time, Aiden pressed his cock deeper into her hungry mouth. Oh, this was so much better than anything she had read or fantasized.

Wrapping her legs around Travis' hips, Cass matched him thrust for thrust. With the same rhythm she sucked the satiny flesh of Aiden's cock. One hand cupped his scrotum, caressing the weight held in her palm. Her other hand held onto Travis, her short fingernails biting into his back.

As the force of each thrust increased, so did the force of her sucking. Soon, Aiden was fucking into her mouth, matching Travis' motions. The world spiraled away as her entire focus narrowed to the two cocks.

"Oh, yes…suck me, baby," Aiden gasped. "I'm not gonna last much longer, Travis," he warned.

"Unh…me either," Travis grunted.

Cassandra cried out around Aiden's cock as her body soared into oblivion. Feeling her release triggered both men. Hot jets of sperm filled her mouth as warmth blasted her spasming pussy. She could feel Travis' incredible heat right through the condom. Both cocks pulsed as the men cried out their climaxes, their faces distorted with ecstasy.

Bright, colorful lights exploded behind Cassandra's eyelids before darkness descended over the world.

The men collapsed next to her on the bed. "Shit, Aiden. We fucked her unconscious," Travis said with awe.

Aiden barely managed to rise up on his elbows to look at her peaceful, sated expression. "Shit," he agreed as his body collapsed back into the mattress.

Chapter Twenty-One

Cassandra woke trapped in a tangle of arms and legs. Too many arms and legs. What the heck? Her eyes slowly fluttered opened. Not her bed, not her room. She stretched her body lazily.

Hands tightened around her. One hand on a breast, an arm over her abdomen, fingers gripping her hip, another hand on her thigh, and one hand cupping an ass cheek. She performed a quick mental count. Hairy male legs abraded her tender skin. Memories, images, sounds, and smells played through her memory. A low moan escaped her lips. Oh, what a night.

Hmm, and now it was her turn. How delicious was that? Oh the possibilities. It took several minutes to extricate herself from the men. She felt light, bubbly, and adventurous.

In the bathroom she washed her face, used some mouthwash, and looked at the stranger in the mirror. They had turned her into a wild, sexy, thoroughly fucked woman. She sure looked the part. Her tousled caramel tresses flowed over naked shoulders. A hot shower was the first order of business.

Feeling wild and free, she searched through Aiden's walk-in closet. Nothing was sexier than wearing a man's clothes. Aiden was an impeccable dresser. His closet contained everything from casual T-shirts and jeans to tailored suits.

Selecting a teal shirt, Cassandra luxuriated in the soft, cool feel of the silk against her heated flesh. She left several buttons open at the top to allow a generous view of the swell of her breasts. She rolled up the sleeves which hung over her hands. The tails of material hung to mid-thigh. She belted his long black leather trench coat over the shirt.

Several large boxes on the top shelf caught her attention. Pulling them down, she discovered his hat collection. She chose a black fedora with a leather sweatband. It looked sexy to her resting on her head at a jaunty angle. Her black heels completed the provocative ensemble.

Hmm, what now? The boys were still tangled in the bed linens, sleeping. They were so tempting, but she steeled her spine, resisting the tantalizing sight. In the living room she looked through Aiden's extensive CD collection. She loved to dance. Delicious possibilities came to mind. Could she pull off something so daring?

The sex goddess in her mind answered, *Why the hell not?*

Indeed, why the hell not. The music needed to be sexy, something with a driving rhythm. "Ah, perfect," she whispered.

Removing the CD from its jewel case, Cassandra inserted it into the player. The soulful, gravely voice of Joe Cocker singing "Unchain My Heart" brought a seductive smile to her lips.

Looking over the songs she decided that the second track was just what she needed. Turning up the volume, Cassandra let her body move to the music.

* * * * *

Loud music caused Travis to stir. His body protested his movements, but he fought the urge to slip back into sleep. He stretched his tired muscles. Damn, what a night. His eyes opened slowly. Aiden lay sleeping soundly next to him in the big bed. Cass was nowhere in sight. Now where did that woman get to?

He sat up and cushioned his back against several pillows, leaning against the headboard. Movement at the doorway caught his eye, as Cass peeked around the frame to see if they were awake. The sight of the hat got his heart pumping.

Jabbing Aiden in the side with an elbow he muttered, "Better wake up."

Aiden mumbled a protest, but Travis was insistent. "You'll kick yourself if you miss this, Aiden. Wake up."

Aiden sat up and rubbed his eyes sleepily. "What the heck's going on?" he questioned. "What's with the music?"

Travis' laugh was deep and husky. "I think that wild little girl of yours is about to put on a show. I have a feeling it's gonna be real hot."

Pushing some pillows against the headboard, Aiden joined Travis. They both reclined against the bed, arms crossed over broad chests, ankles crossed casually.

"I think she's been rummaging in your closet," Travis confided, glancing toward the foot of the bed. "She dragged a kitchen chair in here, too." He stared in the direction of the open door, anticipation driving his pulse rate higher.

"Oh, shit. She must be waiting for the next track." Aiden looked over at Travis. "You have this CD, don't you?"

"Damn straight. I know what's coming, and I can't wait."

The sultry strains of "You Can Leave Your Hat On" poured through the room. Both men got an instant hard-on listening to the most perfect song ever made for stripping.

"What a way to wake up," Travis mumbled.

One long, bare leg snaked around the doorway. It undulated up and down seductively for several beats before disappearing. Next an arm covered in leather slid over the wall, followed by the leg. An admirably curved hip swayed in and out of view. Finally she sashayed into the room. The hat was tilted down over her face.

Catcalls and whistles from the men gave her courage. She felt sexy. The longer she moved to the music, the more freedom she felt. She was a young, pretty woman, totally capable of seducing two red-blooded men.

Cass had always been an extraordinary dancer, but this went beyond anything either man could have ever imagined. She was sex personified.

Without raising her head, Cassandra untied the belt and let the coat flap open. In a sensual move she stood with her legs spread wide, and rolled her shoulders. The heavy leather material slid salaciously down her body.

They groaned in unison as she swayed seductively before them in a silk shirt, hat, and heels. Peeking out from below the brim of the hat her smile was filled with carnal desire. Both men had taken their rock-hard cocks in their big hands, slowly stroking the thick shafts. Damn, watching them was making her so wet.

Dancing over to the chair her long legs straddled it with hedonistic delight. One slender hand held onto the back as she provocatively pumped her body up and down, riding the chair to the beat of the music. The muscles in her legs flexed and contracted with each motion. Long, luxurious waves of caramel hair streamed down to the floor.

Moving in counterpoint to the syncopated beat she turned her back to them. Wrapping her arms across her chest, Cassandra splayed her hands over her back. Moving them up and down caused the hem of the shirt to rise and fall. Her muscular ass cheeks flexed sensuously.

Looking over her shoulder at the men, she began to unbutton the shirt slowly. Aiden wished he'd had enough sense to have grabbed his camcorder. Although he knew that the images would stay with him forever. He'd never seen anything as beautiful.

Once the shirt was unbuttoned she allowed it to slip over her shoulder, revealing a glimpse of skin. When she spun around to face them the material slid deliciously over her pebbled nipples. She was blissfully naked under the silky garment.

Travis sharply sucked in a breath as she rolled her shoulders back and let the material slide seductively down her body. Her naughty smile sent heat rushing through his cock.

Taking the hat in her hand she flicked her wrist and sent it flying over to the men. Aiden caught it and held the fedora over his heart.

"Fuck, baby. You are so damn hot."

Her grin spread considerably, revealing a brilliant flash of white teeth. She seductively moved over and around the chair. Sitting on it sideways she leaned back, holding onto the top with one hand, the other braced against the floor. Her knees were bent, back arched. Cassandra began thrusting her hips up and down.

Watching both men carefully she saw them melt. Pure feminine power surged through her veins. Their responses made her feel wanton, sexy, and wild. Their tawny eyes were dark, glazed with lust. Little groans and growls escaped from the back of their throats, driving her further.

Sitting on the chair she spread her legs wide. One hand trailed over her left breast, fingers swirling around the distended, rosy nipple. She teased the other nipple before slowly running her hand down her abdomen. When she reached the junction of her thighs, Cassandra spread her pussy lips wide.

Her other hand joined in the fun, fingers sliding through the slick juices coating her sex. She held both men's rapt attention. Feeling wild, she coated her fingers in her juices and then rubbed them over her lips. The men's groans urged her on. Cassandra flicked out her tongue, letting it slide over her glistening lips.

"Holy shit," Travis gasped.

When she sucked a wet finger into her mouth, Aiden growled.

"Come here, baby."

Rising, she swayed seductively while moving to the foot of the bed. With the final strains of the song she stepped out of her shoes, and crawled up onto the mattress. "Fuck me hard, boys," she huskily intoned.

"With pleasure, sugar," drawled Travis.

"Come here, baby," Aiden said again, holding out his hand. Pulling her over his legs he asked, "Are you ready for us, Cass?"

Unable to find her voice she nodded her head.

"Damn, baby. That was so hot. You are so beautiful and sexy."

Aiden slid a finger over her weeping slit. A feral growl was his response. Setting her astride his legs he caressed her slit with the length of his cock. "Damn, baby. You are so fucking hot and wet!"

Every fiber of her being was so focused on the man she loved. Yet she felt confused, torn. Aiden was her everything, but Travis also held her heart. Her feelings for him were still emerging, taking shape. What would happen when this encounter ended?

Aiden's strong fingers kneaded her ass cheeks. With his thumb he stroked down the deep crevice then circled around her anus. Heavenly shivers coursed through her body.

Another set of hands stroked over her back. Aiden's knees pressed out against her thighs, spreading her wider. Travis knelt behind her, between Aiden's legs. Cassandra leaned back against his broad chest. Her emerald eyes sparkled. Gloriously soft caramel locks of hair teasing his torso.

"Do you want us, Cass?" Aiden whispered. His dark eyes pierced into the depths of her soul, searching for her true feelings.

"More than you can know," she replied. Cassandra almost did not recognize her own voice. It was husky with desire and need. "I want both of you to fuck me."

Aiden looked over her shoulder, and made eye contact with Travis. Silent communication flowed between the two men. Firm hands spread her ass cheeks wide. Travis' breath hissed warmly over her ear. "So beautiful," he whispered.

With his thumb, Travis began to spread lubricating gel over the puckered pink hole in a slow, circular motion. As he penetrated her anus she pushed back against his thumb. His breathing became harsh. Using generous amounts of lubrication he repeatedly pushed more of the gel into her hot channel. At the same time, Aiden rubbed her pussy with his hard shaft.

She moaned in pleasure. With each rocking motion of her hips, Travis' finger sunk deeper into her ass, and Aiden's cock rubbed over her swollen clit. "I'm gonna come," she said on a moan.

"Come for us, baby. Let us feel you surrender completely."

"Aiden," she called out as waves of bliss surged through her body. "Travis," she gasped.

Travis moaned against her ear as her muscles contracted over his thumb, pulling the digit in deeper. He pulled out then thrust with two fingers, stretching the pulsing channel, sending her orgasm spiraling higher.

"Oh, yes," she cried.

When the spasms had barely subsided, Travis tore open a foil packet and rolled a condom over his cock. He pressed his sheathed head against her anus, and Cass pushed back against him, quickly enveloping the broad tip in her tight channel.

"Ahh," he moaned deeply. His hands grasped her hips tightly as he took control of the rhythm. Using rocking motions, he slowly sheathed himself in the volcanic heat of her ass.

"Shit, so fucking tight," he gasped.

Juices poured from her slit, soaking Aiden's cock. Using his hands, he spread her ass cheeks wide. He waited until Travis was buried to the hilt. He could hear Travis' balls slapping lightly against her flesh. Lifting her slightly, Aiden sunk two fingers into her dripping wet pussy.

He stroked his fingers in and out of her narrowed opening, waiting to feel her muscles relax around Travis. With each stroke he was caressing Travis' cock through the thin membrane separating the channels. Strangely, the realization made his cock grow harder.

Looking over his shoulder into Travis' eyes they shared the knowledge of what the caress was doing to both of them. When he was sure Cass was ready, Aiden guided his cock to the mouth of her vagina. With Travis' cock in her ass, her pussy was even tighter than normal.

Working slowly he sheathed his cock to the hilt. Because of his reclining position, his balls slapped against Travis', sending an electric current through both men. They moaned in unison.

"Oh, boys. I'm so full." Cassandra's voice was raspy. She was amazed that she could take both of them at once. The feeling was so intense. She was stuffed beyond belief.

Both men remained perfectly still. "Open your eyes, Cass. Look at me." When she complied, Aiden asked, "Are you okay?"

Her eyes were glazed and she could barely speak, but both men heard every whispered word. "I can't... Oh, God...so good." Her tone became pleading. "Fuck me, hard."

The connection between the two men became stronger than they would have ever believed possible. They had shared women before, but never filling her at the same time. Moving in concert, each stroke was a caress shared by all three. They felt each inch of the other's cock with every movement along the thin membrane separating them.

Travis gasped with each movement as Aiden's shaft penetrated Cass, and brushed against the length of his own cock, buried deep inside her ass. The multiple sensations made him wonder what it would be like to fuck his friend's ass while Aiden fucked Cass' pussy.

Cassandra leaned back against Travis while he reached around and massaged her breasts. Aiden's hands took control of her hips, setting the pace. Looking into his friend's eyes, Aiden saw his intent, as Travis' hands held a breast out toward him.

Leaning forward, Aiden suckled the nipple held up in silent offering. The shudders that took Cass' body were felt by both men. With silent agreement they increased their pace, driving her higher with each stroke. Within moments she shattered around them, clamping down on both cocks held deep inside her heat.

Cassandra was lost to the sensations claiming control of her entire being. She knew that all three of them were joining completely, body to body, soul to soul. The communication the men shared was no longer a mystery to her. She felt and understood everything that crossed between the two of them, and through her.

Next to the birth of her daughter, it was the most life-altering, beautiful experience she'd ever known. A deep, binding connection opened between them that could never be broken. Time, nor distance, nor even death would separate the three lovers.

A loud noise was created by the three bodies moving together. All three of them broke into hysterical fits of laughter. It sounded similar to someone farting. Kind of like the sound a whoopee cushion makes. Cass stopped laughing suddenly, holding perfectly still, her breath coming out on a hiss. The men's laughter had their cocks jiggling wildly inside her body. Wild need suffused her as she again began the climb toward climax.

"Don't hold back. Aiden, Travis, I want everything you have to give." With one arm she pulled Aiden up into a sitting position, his chest and torso pressing into her own. With the other arm she pulled Travis tightly against her back. From hips to shoulders they were as close as three people could become. "Now, boys," she demanded. "I need you now."

The new position pressed Aiden's pelvic bone against her straining clit. Electric sensations coursed through her body, tightening her muscles. The multiple sensations were too much.

The two men totally lost control, driving into her with stroke after powerful stroke. She clung to them as the orgasms overtook her, faster and harder, one on top of the other. She cried out in ecstasy.

They shared each other's emotions, sensations, and bodies. Cassandra's body convulsed around the two cocks again and again, sending all three spiraling into a mind-blowing, shared orgasm that rocked their worlds. Their cries of pleasure and joy mingled as each shouted in violent release.

Together they fell into a combination of release and joining. Hot jets of semen filled her pussy as Travis' incredible warmth filled her ass, turning Cassandra into a boneless mass of quivering sensation.

Collapsing over onto their sides the three stayed joined together. As they caught their breath, their hands wandered over each other's bodies with awestruck wonder. They were truly one now.

None of them could have anticipated the effects of their sharing. A bond had been created between the three of them. Pleasantly overwhelmed and sated, they gave no thought as to how they'd handle the aftermath.

Chapter Twenty-Two

The weekend flew by. The three of them shared in pleasuring each other with reckless abandon. By Sunday evening, they were all beginning to get a little bit of cabin fever. After a long, sensual, shared shower they got dressed and went out to dinner.

Cassandra felt wild and crazy. She had never let herself go so completely before. And she would have never imagined Travis and Aiden becoming so consumed by passion. At first they had been very tentative as she continued to put them into positions where they came into very intimate contact with each other. As she continued to encourage their closeness the men relaxed, becoming more comfortable with adding to each other's pleasure. She hoped they would continue to move further in their explorations.

Regardless of her buoyant mood, she could tell something was bothering Travis. His mood rapidly darkened, his tension becoming palpable.

The waiter seated them in a quiet corner. A long, red linen cloth covered the intimate table. Cassandra sat with her back to the wall, a man at each side. She was careful to ensure she remained covered. She had not worn panties beneath the jade dress, and the hem only reached mid-thigh. Thankfully the tablecloth would conceal her.

After they ordered dinner, Travis excused himself and went to the restroom. She took the opportunity to talk with Aiden privately.

"You need to talk with Travis. Something is bothering him, and it's only getting worse."

Aiden sighed deeply. "I know. I've felt his tension growing all day. I'll get him alone later, and find out what's wrong. Don't worry, baby."

Taking her hand he brushed light kisses across her knuckles. "Are you okay with everything that's happened?" He held his breath while he waited for her answer. She seemed to be walking on clouds, but he had to be certain.

"I…there are no words to explain how I feel. Something has awakened within me. I have never been so wanton or horny in my life." She giggled with joy. "You boys have turned me into a wild, adventurous sex maniac."

"I think you just described yourself very well," Travis stated as he seated himself at the table once again.

Reaching out, Cassandra tenderly trailed a hand over his cheek. "I'll take that as a compliment." She held one of each of their hands in her own. Life just didn't get any better than having two hot men by your side.

It amazed her that she was feeling wet and ready for more action after how much they'd already shared. She fidgeted restlessly, her movements catching Aiden's attention. He leaned in close.

"What's wrong, baby?" he whispered against her ear.

She giggled shyly. "Believe it or not, I'm getting wet again. I just can't get enough of you boys." She wiggled helplessly. "The problem is I didn't wear any panties. I'm going to have a wet spot on my dress by the time we leave."

Aiden chuckled at her predicament. Taking the cloth napkin from his lap he whispered, "Lift up for me, baby."

Trusting him completely, Cassandra lifted her hips from the chair. Aiden put the square of linen between her and the chair, moving her dress up over her hips. She sharply sucked in a breath as his fingers brushed across her hot flesh.

Whispered words against her ear felt like another caress. "Okay, baby. You can sit back now." She moved slowly, waiting for Aiden to move his hand back. As she lowered herself to the seat his fingers brushed over her damp pussy.

Leaning across the table he motioned Travis closer. "She didn't wear any panties." The two of them shared a conspiratorial grin.

"Damn, that's hot as hell," Travis stated.

His hand joined Aiden's, sliding under her dress. Cassandra felt herself growing wetter by the second. Travis brought his hand out from under the table, his fingers glistening with her juices. With obvious pleasure he licked his fingers clean.

"Umm. They have wonderful appetizers here."

While Aiden tasted his own fingers, Travis' hand returned to her pussy. Soon both men had two of their thick fingers sunk deep inside her. Cassandra's fidgeting became more pronounced as they thrust into her heated depths, over and over again.

The fear of discovery was overridden by her increasing need for the two men. Her face and neck became flushed, and a thin line of perspiration broke out over her forehead. To keep from moaning, her teeth sank into her full lower lip as her clit was rubbed mercilessly.

When the waiter arrived with their meals neither man paused in finger-fucking her for even a moment. He gave her a curious glance, and quickly left the table after ensuring they had everything they needed.

Cassandra's breasts rose and fell rapidly with her quickened breathing. Her nipples stood out clearly against the bodice of her dress. She watched the men share a silent communication which had her juices gushing. They each moved in closer. Moments later each pulled one of her thighs over a knee, spreading her wide.

Slumping down in her chair, Cassandra gave herself over to her lover's touches. Her thighs were tenderly caressed as they fingered her all through their meal.

Briefly, she wondered what would happen when the weekend was over. Would they continue on as a trio, or would Travis step away. Pain coursed through her body with the thought. She was jolted with the realization that she loved both men. How could she choose one over the other now?

With a white-knuckled grip she held onto the table. Aiden ran his tongue over the outer shell of her ear. She shivered thinking of his talented tongue on her pussy. Travis whispered at the other ear, "Come for us, Cass."

Aiden covered her whimper with his lips. Taking her mouth in a deep kiss he swallowed her cries as she shattered around their fingers, covering their hands with her wet response. They continued to stroke her until her feet were back on solid ground once again.

Removing their hands from her pussy both men feasted on her juices. They made small sounds of pleasure, before casually picking up their forks and eating their meal as if nothing had happened.

Feeling slightly wicked she decided that since the men got appetizers, she'd get dessert. Trying to move inconspicuously she released Travis' cock from his pants, and then Aiden's. With a wicked smile she stroked the two magnificent shafts under the table.

"You know, I think dessert is definitely going to be better than the appetizers," she teased. "There's nothing better than two hot, firm cocks."

Feminine power surged through her. Both men held strained expressions when the waiter brought the check. Three peppermint candies sat on top of the bill. She did not catch the look of wicked intent that passed between her men.

Travis opened a candy, and popped it into his mouth. He leaned close to Cassandra and passed the candy to her during a scorching kiss. Soon all three of them were sucking on the strong mints.

"Hmm. I think my dessert needs a little more sugar," Aiden said. He removed the wet candy from his mouth and reached under the table. Cassandra nearly jumped from her chair as the hard, round mint rolled over her clit, leaving a sticky feeling in its wake. Before she knew what was happening he parted her lips and pushed the candy deep into her vagina.

Travis winked as Aiden licked his fingers. He removed the wet candy from his mouth, and his hand went under the table. A small whimper escaped Cass as he pushed the wet candy deep inside her. His fingers thrust against her g-spot a few times before he retreated to lick his fingers again.

After paying the bill the men struggled to encase their erect cocks back inside their pants and then helped her up. Leaning into Aiden's side she whispered naïvely, "What if they fall out?"

Aiden's robust laughter filled the restaurant, drawing attention to the handsome trio. He kissed her deeply before responding. "Just tighten your muscles like you do around my cock."

The drive back to the condo seemed to take forever. The men played with her labia while she stroked their beautiful cocks. Aiden stole Cassandra's mint during a probing kiss. Taking the wet candy, he rolled it all over her wet pussy. She was quickly becoming a sticky mess.

"I hope you plan on cleaning up that mess," she said in a stern tone.

Both men laughed with delight. "Well, of course we'll clean up after ourselves, Cass. Don't you worry about that. It'll be our pleasure."

She realized some time during the drive that she'd been cheated out of the dessert she'd planned. Umm, but the men more than made up for her loss. Their sensual play with the mints was driving her insane. She needed to come, needed to be fucked so badly. Her swollen breasts ached to be licked, suckled.

By the time they got inside, Cassandra felt like she was on fire. The melting mints sensitizing everywhere they touched. She stripped off her dress and bra while making a beeline straight for the bedroom. Lying in the middle of the bed she spread her legs and waited on her men.

Aiden and Travis looked like two little boys when they walked into the room. They were laughing, joking, and grinning from ear to ear. Stopping just inside the doorway, Aiden teased, "Damn, Travis. Look what the tooth fairy left for us."

Bounding onto the bed they took turns licking her sticky pussy lips. When one of them blew over her slick folds the mint heated her tender tissues. Writhing with need, Cassandra moaned deeply. Orgasm after orgasm racked her body as they ate her pussy for dessert.

She wanted them to feel as much pleasure as possible, but was too shaky to see to their needs. Reaching along their bodies she took Aiden's hand, guiding it to Travis' hard cock. She kept her fingers cupped over his for the first few strokes, then reached for Travis. Once she had each man stroking the other, Cassandra laid back, surrendering to how right it felt for the three of them to come together so perfectly.

* * * * *

When Cassandra woke during the night, she immediately knew one of the men was missing. Propping herself up on her elbows she looked lovingly at Aiden, who slept contentedly. His face held the relaxation of a man well-loved, and satisfied.

Rising from the bed she put on a short silk robe. Travis was nowhere to be found in the condo, but his car keys and wallet still lay on the dresser. She finally found him out on the patio in the dark, deep in thought.

Going to him, she curled up in his lap. She knew that Aiden had not found time to speak with Travis alone. "I'm worried about you, Travis. What's wrong?" Her voice carried a great depth of emotion. "Are you bothered by what happened with Aiden?"

He shrugged off her concern. "No. Surprisingly, I'm fine with it, Cass. What are you doing up?" His fingers lightly trailed over her face. The tenderness of his caress touched her heart. The tormented look in his dark eyes caused her stomach to flip-flop.

"Hmm. I woke up and one of my men was missing." Unconsciously she toyed with his chest hair. Her ear lay over his heart, and she listened to the reassuring rhythm. "Please talk to me, Travis. I know something is bothering you."

His chest rumbled with some unintelligible, muttered response. Leaning back she took his face in her hands, forcing him to look into her eyes. "I can see and feel your tension, Travis. It's eating you up inside, and tearing my heart out. Please talk to me."

He sighed deeply, sensing the truth of her words in the emerald depths of her expressive eyes.

"I'm just thinking about life after this weekend. It's going to be really hard for me to walk away from you now." One big hand stroked over her long hair. Frustration and uncertainty overwhelmed him.

What the hell was he supposed to say? He didn't want to upset Cass. He'd go to great pains to prevent that from happening. Damn it, she felt so good in his arms. He had fallen under her spell during the past week, fallen hard. No matter what, he couldn't escape the facts. She belonged to another man, his best friend.

Agreeing to help Cass with her plan had been a big mistake. He'd known how difficult it would be for him to walk away, and that was before he'd made love to her, held her in his arms, and sunk his cock in her tight, pretty little pussy. Now it would kill him, rip his still beating heart from his chest.

"Things are going to be different between the three of us now. To tell you the truth, I'm not sure I'll be able to be around you two after this weekend." He stared out into space for a long time. Cass remained silent, waiting for him to go on.

While he enjoyed working with Aiden, it would tear him apart to be so close to them, but on the outside looking in. It would be difficult to walk away from the indelible bond he shared with Aiden. Their closeness was something that Travis had always valued. His most priceless treasure.

He was pretty sure Aiden would ask Cass to marry him now. That was just not something he could stand by and watch. No matter how devastating the pain of separating from Aiden, watching the two of them live happily ever after as an outsider would be worse.

Thinking back he remembered helping Aiden land his job with the company. Working in marketing kept him and Aiden in separate departments, but still working closely. On Thursday the company CEO had come and offered Travis a promotion to Director of Marketing. It was a hard-earned honor, but required relocation to the Knoxville office.

The answer he gave on Monday morning would be entirely dependent on what happened with the three of them. Sometime over the past week everything had changed. He'd fallen in love with Cass. Sharing her with Aiden was better than anything he'd ever experienced.

It would be torture to stay in Florida. He couldn't imagine going to the club and seeing Cass, or dancing with the couple. There was no way he could be so close to her, but not hold her. He could not go back to just being a friend.

His entire life had taken a drastic shift over the amazing, unexpected weekend. Everything had changed the moment he had touched her. "I've been offered a promotion at work," he finally said. He held his breath while waiting for her response.

Smiling up at him with pride she said, "That's wonderful, Travis. Congratulations."

"It would be wonderful, but it means relocating to Tennessee...permanently." He sighed with frustration. "It's a difficult decision, and it's weighing on my mind. I have to let Danbury know my decision tomorrow."

Panic seized her heart. Relocate. How could he relocate? She needed Travis with her. He'd become a very important part of her life. Hell, she had woken up because his body was no longer next to hers in bed. She had fallen in love with Travis, just as deeply as she loved Aiden.

Uncertainty now clouded her thoughts. What would happen with the three of them after the weekend? When Travis had been invited into bed they had not discussed the future. The focus had remained on immediate gratification. Cassandra began to understand his turmoil. They could not go back to just being friends. She didn't want that. Oh God, what a mess. She'd gone from being alone to falling in love with two men.

Both men were so incredibly sexy, charming, and strong. Travis had become someone she could trust implicitly with anything. So honorable, loyal, and caring. Aiden was someone she could count on. Dependable, responsible, and smart. She needed both of them, loved both of them, completely.

The thought of turning away from either man brought searing pain. Each man held her heart. She would never be whole again without having them both in her life. A restless urgency claimed her. She needed to hold Travis tight within her body for however long they had remaining…for what might be the last time.

Tentatively she questioned, "What did you decide?" She wasn't sure she was ready to hear his answer.

It took him a moment before he quietly answered, "I haven't."

Standing, she opened her robe and let it fall to the ground.

"Cass, what are you doing?" Confusion clouded his eyes.

"I need you, Travis. Now!"

Taking hold of his boxers she waited for him to lift his hips off the lounge chair.

"What about Aiden?" he questioned.

"I need you inside me, Travis, with or without Aiden."

Travis stared into her eyes, seeing her raw need, but also the underlying emotions driving Cass. He lifted his hips and helped her remove the boxers, then pulled her into a crushing embrace. It might be the last time he held her in his arms. He sure as hell was going to enjoy the experience.

Both of them remained still, just holding tight to the other. Their hearts raced frantically. "Travis, please," she whispered.

"Shit, I have to get a condom, sugar."

"No. I'm going to tell you the same thing I told Aiden. I only want to feel you. I'm on the pill. I need you, now!" She paused for a moment, staring into his dark eyes. "I don't have to worry about anything, do I? Have you had unprotected sex?"

"No, never."

"Good, because I need you. Just you inside me. No barriers." Kneeling over him on the chair she kissed Travis. What started as a sweet, tender kiss quickly became a mating of their mouths. Tongues twined around each other, fighting for a total joining. They tried to absorb each other's essences, draw the other into their souls.

With each breath her taut nipples rasped over his chest hair, sending electric sensations to her pussy. Her juices spread down onto his thighs. A frenzied need overcame Cassandra.

"Now, Travis, please." She raised her hips, sliding over his bulging cock.

Travis guided the tip of his cock to the mouth of her pussy. Hot, slick juices dripped down his shaft. With one swift thrust he buried himself in her warm folds then froze. He had never been inside a woman without a condom before. The intense intimacy of the sensations tested his control. He wanted to make this last forever, but needed to take her hard with the animalistic hunger surging through his veins.

"Oh, God. You are so hot and tight. I want to bury myself deep inside your womb and never find my way out." His breath came out as a hiss.

She started slowly rocking her hips. With each motion her engorged clit stroked over his pelvis. Her breathing became ragged as Cassandra fought to take things slowly. She wanted to burn every stroke, sensation, and feeling into her being. Brand herself with his steely cock.

Travis raised his knees slightly, propping his feet against the end of the long chair. "Lean back, Cass," he whispered.

The new position took the pressure off her clit, and put it against her g-spot. With each motion the sensitive spot was stroked. Moving in a circular motion, his cock caressed her in a whole new, tantalizing way.

Cass moaned and ground her pussy against his cock. He thrust forward, butting the tip against her womb. She felt him in every fiber of her being. He was everywhere, filling her completely.

"Oh, Travis. I can feel you all the way up in my throat. You fill me up." She moved slowly, almost carefully. Reaching behind herself, and between his legs she cupped his scrotum. The weight felt good in her hand as she massaged the tightening globes.

"Cass…oh, shit. I won't last…if you keep that up." His breathing was broken. The words came out between gasping breaths. His jaw was tense, his pulse beating wildly in his strong neck.

Moving slowly over his cock she fought for control. Her orgasm peaked suddenly, surprising them both.

Travis was sure he had died and gone to heaven. That was the only explanation. Nothing had ever felt half as good as having Cass' body clamp down on his cock with nothing between them, drawing him in deeper. He didn't think it was possible to sink any further into her, but it happened.

The sweet little writer in his arms had just signed her name across his heart, claiming it as her own. Signed, sealed, and delivered, she took possession, locking his emotions up tightly with her own.

Cassandra's head was swimming. A confusing surge of emotion sent her on an out of control roller coaster ride. This was not just sex. It went way beyond mere sex, beyond the way he made her burn, the way he felt like he belonged inside her body.

Somehow Cassandra felt there was no way this would end well. Someone was going to be hurt, most likely all three of them. A slow stream of silent tears trickled down her cheeks.

Then and there she decided to not worry about the future, just revel in the present. Tonight she would love her men. In the morning she would sit them down and discuss the future. She would plead and beg Travis not to go, and Aiden to accept that she loved them both equally. Between the three of them they would figure out how to make this unconventional relationship work.

Her body fought to draw Travis in deeper, hold him captured within her depths. She felt his cock pulse, and Travis tremble as his climax seized him. Hot jets of his seed filled her body, triggering a second orgasm within her.

Once sated she lay against his chest, fighting for each breath. She was not ready to let him go from her body. She was unaware of anything but the man cradled within her warmth. She didn't even hear the words he whispered against her hair.

"I love you, Cass."

* * * * *

Aiden stood cloaked in shadow, watching Cass and Travis, wondering what he'd done by inviting him to join them. Travis had not told him about the promotion. God, everything had become such a disjointed mess, and he didn't see a way around someone getting hurt.

It tore his heart out to watch the love pouring from them, filling each other. He pictured himself alone and cold outside a house, peering through a window on the warm domestic scene taking place inside. Wishing desperately to be part of what he saw.

Chapter Twenty-Three

Aiden and Travis spent some time talking while Cass slept. After Aiden had helped dress their groggy lover, Travis carried her out to his truck. She barely twitched as he strapped her sleepy form into the seat belt. They had thoroughly worn her out.

Street lights sporadically illuminated his sleeping lover's face. Each time he got a glimpse of her features relaxed in sleep, a knife turned in his chest. He ached to hold her again, feel the warmth of her body molded along his own. For the millionth time, Travis told himself that everything would work out for the three of them. Then he prayed he was right.

As he carried her into the house, Cassandra trustingly snuggled into his warmth. Travis mumbled sweet nothings while once again removing her clothes.

He gently lay her down in the big bed, pulling the covers high over her slender form. He brushed a light kiss over her forehead. She muttered something he couldn't quite make out, then curled deeper under the comforter. An indeterminable amount of time passed before he finally moved away. The temptation to curl up next to her nearly breaking his will.

The future held so many unknown variables. Travis prayed for things to go his way. The day would be excruciatingly long as he waited for his path to be determined. No one could have ever predicted the circumstances in which he now found himself.

The walk from the driveway into his house seemed like miles. Exhaustion slowed each step he took. Finally lying naked in his bed, sleep evaded his grasp. No matter how tired his body, Travis' mind refused to shut down.

Across town, Aiden lay in the same state. So many things would have to fall precisely into place for the outcome to be good. He felt like a juggler with too many balls in the air, just waiting for the inevitable crash as gravity asserted itself.

Somehow, someway, the three of them would work this out. He couldn't bear the thought of losing either of the two most important people in his life. Once everything was settled in Knoxville things would hopefully fall into place.

* * * * *

Awaking with a start she immediately realized something was wrong. Sitting up in the bed, Cassandra took in her surroundings. She was at home, but had no idea how she had gotten there. Distantly she remembered Travis tucking her into bed.

Lying back against the pillows, Cassandra was very close to drifting back into a deep sleep. Suddenly she jumped from the bed. *Oh no.* It was Monday morning, and she was alone. A quick glance at the alarm clock had her heart thudding painfully against her ribs.

She never slept in, but the numbers didn't lie. It was ten o'clock. Bright light streamed in around the edges of the curtains. Travis had brought her home, and left her there alone.

Travis. Panic surged through her. She had planned to sit down and talk with the men this morning. Travis had to give his decision today about the promotion and relocation.

Grabbing the cordless phone from the cradle, she first tried Travis' cellular phone. At the end of the voicemail greeting she left a message for him to call her immediately. The process was repeated when she called Aiden. Neither man answered their office phones, so again she left messages.

She had to get to them quickly, before Travis spoke with the CEO. Snatching up the first clothes she found in the closet, Cassandra jumped into a pair of jeans and T-shirt. She did not waste time on finding a bra or panties. White canvas slip-on sneakers completed the hastily chosen outfit.

In the bathroom she brushed her teeth, washed her face, and quickly brushed her hair into a ponytail. Her wallet and car keys were the only things she took as she left the house. She never saw the note Aiden and Travis had left on the kitchen counter near the coffeemaker.

Pulling out of the driveway she slammed the gas peddle to the floor, smoking the expensive tires. Haste and panic made her normally smooth movements erratic. She ground Don's gears several times, but barely noticed the abuse heaped on her prized possession. Nothing mattered except reaching Travis in time.

Reaching the building she left Don parked at the curb, forgoing her normal routine. She raced through the doors and through the tropical atrium. Having no patience for the elevators, Cassandra ran up the three flights of stairs.

Fighting for each breath, she never paused at the reception desk. Reaching his office she threw opened the door and stared into the empty space. Damn. Where could he be?

Cindy let out a startled gasp as Cassandra raced by, and threw open Aiden's office door. It was also empty. She bent at the waist, sucking in great shuddering breaths of air. A cramp tightened the muscles of her right side painfully.

She jumped at the feel of a hand on her shoulder. Spinning quickly she faced Cindy.

"Cass, what the hell's wrong?"

Her words were spoken in a raspy voice between gasping breaths. "I have to…stop him… Have to tell them…can't let them go."

Taking her arm, Cindy led Cassandra to a chair in Aiden's office. "Don't move," she stated sternly.

Moments later Cindy returned with a cold bottle of water. She sank into the chair next to Cassandra, watching as half the bottle's contents disappeared within moments.

She waited until Cassandra had some of her breath back, and had calmed down. "Now, start again. This time try to make some sense."

"Oh, God. I have to stop Travis. I have to talk to him before he gives Danbury his decision about the promotion." She raked her fingers through the long ponytail lying over her shoulder. "I have to find Aiden too. Where are they?"

"They are probably in Knoxville by now. They left for the airport hours ago. They were on the first flight out, and only stopped here to pick up some paperwork. Travis has a meeting with Danbury, and Aiden had some errand to take care of out there." She looked at Cass with concern and confusion etched across her delicate features. "What promotion are you talking about?"

"It's so crazy, Cin. Travis was offered a promotion that would require he relocate to Tennessee. I have to stop him." She paused, wondering how much to tell the other woman, not wanting to hurt her. No matter how hurt and confused Cassandra was, she had to handle this situation with some finesse. How would Cindy react to the newly formed relationship? She decided to keep her words somewhat vague. "My feelings are so confused. I can't just let Travis go. We have a lot to discuss."

Cindy shook her head briefly. "I've suspected that there were strong feelings between the two of you for a while now. Must have been some weekend to have you this tied up in knots." Rising to her feet she pulled Cassandra into a friendly hug. When Cindy pulled back she walked to her desk, taking Cass with her.

Quickly, Cindy scribbled down facts on a sheet of paper, and then handed it to Cass. "Here is the flight information, address for the office, and name of the hotel where they are staying." Looking deeply into Cass' eyes she said, "Good luck, girl. They are two very strong-willed men. You seem to know what you want, so now you just have to go get it."

Yes, she knew exactly what she wanted. She'd have her cake and not only eat it, but absorb every single molecule into her being. She had a life, but now she wanted to live. Wring every drop free until it overflowed.

Many times she'd been called stubborn and determined. Well, that was nothing. She was going to grab for the brass ring, hold on with both hands and never let go. Nothing would stop her now.

The easy acceptance of the situation she saw in Cindy's eyes shocked her. She had expected jealousy, even anger. The other woman actually seemed happy for the trio. She moved down the hallway in a haze of confusion. Looking back over her shoulder she saw Cindy smiling encouragingly.

"Go get 'em, girl."

Back in the Mustang, Cassandra raced toward the airport with no clear plan of action. She had to get to the men. Her mind focused on that goal to the exclusion of almost everything else. Don once again was neglected. She parked the pony car in the garage and set the alarm.

The airport was teeming with activity. The organized chaos did little to ease her panic. Scanning the reservations desks, the long lines looked ominous. A self-service kiosk caught her attention.

With the computer generated voice grating on her nerves, Cassandra navigated the touch screen menus as quickly as possible. Searching for direct flights to Knoxville she determined the next available plane did not leave for several hours. That wouldn't work.

Okay, think. What the hell are you going to do?

Thankfully an airport employee came over to see if she needed assistance. Explaining what she needed the woman did a search of flights going anywhere near Knoxville. The computer listed planes heading for Chattanooga, Memphis, and Nashville.

None of the flights were nonstop, and all would take more than four hours. Cassandra's voice was strained as she explained that she needed to be there now.

"If it's an emergency you could book a private plane, but that will be expensive." The woman efficiently helped her secure a private flight which would be ready to leave in thirty minutes.

She also arranged for a rental car to be waiting at the charter company when she arrived.

Cassandra moved through the airport and security checkpoints in a daze. Her body was aching from the weekend's activities. The minor soreness was an annoyance that barely penetrated her scattered thoughts.

She was driven out to the airplane on an open air cart. Everything with the charter company was first-class. Hell, for what she was paying she should own the plane after the brief flight. She was escorted onto the plane and offered refreshments while the crew completed the preflight checks.

Sitting back in the plush leather chair she began making phone calls. Travis and Aiden's cell phones still were being answered by voicemail. Damn it, what was the point of having the infernal things if they were not going to answer calls?

Hearing Darlene's voice helped bring Cassandra out of her confused daze. The other woman was shocked to hear what was happening.

"Are you crazy? You're taking off on a ridiculously expensive chartered flight without even a change of clothes. How do you expect to find them when you get to Knoxville?"

She sighed deeply before replying. "With a hell of a lot of luck," she stated. The reality of her actions was just beginning to hit home. She had never flown before, never been outside Florida. What did she think she was doing taking off on a jet chasing after two men?

All she knew for sure was that no matter what it took she had to get to her men. She had to convince Travis not to take the promotion. How she would do that was beyond Cassandra. What did she have to offer? A love triangle? What made her think he would give up a major promotion for a woman he would have to share? God, she was so mad at them for leaving her like that. She was going to kick both their asses.

"I don't know what to say, Cass. Please be careful, and keep me updated."

"I will, Darlene. Tell Sam that I'll call her tonight before bedtime." She hated being away from her daughter and felt like she was always dumping her on Darlene. "Thanks for everything."

After disconnecting the call she sipped the soda the stewardess had provided. The effects of exhaustion and stress finally took hold. Within moments of takeoff she was sound asleep.

* * * * *

Lunch with George Danbury, CEO of Danbury Industries, did not go well. Aiden's presence had not helped matters as Travis had hoped. At least with the meeting out of the way he could concentrate on the future.

Accompanying Aiden to the posh shop for his appointment was a much more pleasant experience. After concluding their business they walked aimlessly through the glitzy downtown shopping area.

"You realize that Cass is going to be pissed about waking up alone at her house, don't you?" Aiden asked.

"Uh-huh. Tomorrow is going to be rough. How do you think she will react?"

Aiden wished he could reassure Travis. The truth was he had no idea how Cass would react to what they had to say. She was so damn independent. And she would justifiably be concerned about how everything would affect Sam.

"I wish I knew, Travis. There's really no telling with Cass. I've seen her claw her way over obstacles while under severe pressure that would send most people running for cover. I've also seen her crumble into a weepy mass over a crayon stick figure drawing created by Sam."

Aiden remained lost in thought for a long time. When he finally spoke his voice was very quiet. "She is unpredictable, Travis. That's part of her incredible appeal. Cass has a quick, sharp mind. She also has a quick, wicked temper."

Travis considered Aiden's words. He prayed that her mind would be open, and her temper would remain in check when they talked. He didn't want to lose what the three of them had found over the weekend.

* * * * *

Her body floated on fluffy white clouds. The azure blue sky soothed her weary soul. She felt nothing except the warmth of the sun enveloping her body. Ripples of heat washed over her skin, sensitizing nerve endings. She dreamed of two men, so very similar, but different at the same time.

The clouds held her wrapped securely. It felt like the softest downy blankets feathered over her body. A smile curled the corners of her lips.

Her name came on a whispered breath of wind. "Ms. McCarthy." She tried to sink further down into the clouds, but her shoulder was shaken forcefully. "Ms. McCarthy, we're landing now. You'll need to fasten your seat belt."

Reality crashed into Cassandra like a ton of bricks. Somehow she had slept through her first airplane trip. Exhaustion had conquered her fears, leaving her in blissful oblivion.

The stewardess clasped the belt and patted her hand reassuringly. "Everything is ready for your arrival. The rental car is waiting at the hangar."

Before she knew it they were landing. The process was much smoother then she had imagined. Still, she'd held her breath during the long moments before the wheels finally hit the ground.

Once off the plane she signed for the car. With several maps in hand she headed out on the biggest adventure she'd had ever undertaken.

Knoxville was both large and confusing. Following instructions she'd been given it took almost twenty minutes, and two wrong turns to find the home office of Danbury Industries.

The sprawling buildings were very modern and appealing. She could easily picture Travis walking the posh hallways wearing one of his impeccably tailored suits.

A bright smile flitted across her lips. There was nothing quite like the sight of the two men dressed sharply for work, ready to conquer the world. They radiated confidence, power, and testosterone. You would think business suits would hide their muscular beauty, but not her men. Their deliciously powerful bodies could not be masked by clothing.

Cassandra approached the snooty-looking receptionist with a smile. "Hello. I'm looking for Travis Lundy, and Aiden McCarthy." She forced herself to stand still, head held high as the woman looked at her down her long nose.

"And who are you to Mr. Lundy, and Mr. McCarthy?"

What a bitch, Cassandra thought. "I am Mr. McCarthy's sister-in-law. I just flew in from Florida on a family emergency." Okay, so that was fudging things, but this bitch didn't need to know why she was there.

"I'm sorry, ma'am. Mr. Lundy and Mr. McCarthy are out of the office." She turned away from Cassandra dismissively.

Counting to ten she fought to keep her temper under control. Oh, how she would love to provide the snooty woman with a proper dressing down. Until she found out where her men were she'd have to remain calm.

"Um, excuse me. Do you happen to know where they went?" She tried to smile but was certain the look on her face was anything other than friendly. "It is very important that I locate them quickly."

The woman just stood there staring at Cassandra like she was a stain on the floor. *Not smart, lady. You really don't want to push me right now.*

"I'm certain that I have no idea where they would have gone after their meeting. Maybe you should try their hotel." She gave Cassandra a superior look, eyebrow raised in challenge. "If they wanted you to know where they were, don't you think they would have told you?"

Once again the woman turned away dismissively. It took every ounce of her will power not to reach out and slap the hoity bitch upside the back of her head. On second thought...the stakes were too high.

Cassandra cleared her throat, and the receptionist turned toward her once again. She grabbed the woman by the big silk bow around her neck. She pulled her halfway across the counter, the woman's nose barely an inch from her own.

"Now listen here, bitch. Those are my men you're talking about, and I'm on the edge. It would be really smart of you to change your crappy attitude."

Her level of anxiety prohibited Cassandra from really enjoying the other woman's shovel full of crow.

The receptionist sputtered out, "I'm s-sorry."

The now properly dressed-down receptionist ended up giving her directions to the hotel. Still, Cassandra felt little satisfaction from her new attitude. It just didn't matter when compared to tracking down Travis and Aiden.

Chapter Twenty-Four

Finding the hotel was a challenge. Even after stopping at two different gas stations for directions, she still ended up on the wrong side of town. Cassandra felt incredibly lost and intimidated by the unfamiliar surroundings. It was a foreign feeling that she did not know how to cope with.

At the hotel, a valet parking attendant took her rental car. It was frightening to give up the one thing that had become familiar. Entering the lobby she felt very small, insignificant. Everything in the hotel was of gargantuan proportions.

She stood gaping up at the soaring ceilings adorned with intricate murals. The furnishings in the lobby could easily fit in the richest of mansions. The whole place was so lifestyles-of-the-rich-and-famous. Cassandra had seen opulence before, but never anything quite so ostentatious as the fancy lobby.

The employees were all impeccably dressed in perfectly pressed uniforms that must sport designer labels. Looking down over her body, Cassandra cringed at her rumpled state. All she had were the wrinkled jeans and T-shirt she'd worn all day.

"Good afternoon, ma'am. How may I be of service?" queried the clerk.

She leaned against the tall desk. "Hi. Can you please tell me if either Travis Lundy or Aiden McCarthy have checked in yet?"

The clerk's expression hardened. "I am sorry, ma'am. I cannot give out information concerning our guests."

"Oh, well, I am Mrs. McCarthy," Cassandra stated. "I am joining my husband, and his co-worker." Okay, so she was Mike McCarthy's widow, but the grumpy clerk did not need to know that. "Have they arrived yet?"

"Ah, Mrs. McCarthy. I was unaware that you would be joining your husband." His fingers clicked over the keyboard. Frowning he said, "I am sorry, ma'am, but they have not checked in." He stood looking expectantly at Cassandra. "Is there any other way I may be of service?"

Jeez, this guy could teach pompous to royalty. She considered his last statement. Exactly how could he be of service? She looked quickly at the name tag pinned to his black jacket. "Yes, Reginald. I would like a key to our room so that I may freshen up. It has been a difficult trip to say the least." Hmm, that sounded pretty good.

"Yes, Mrs. McCarthy. I will just need to make an imprint of your credit card first." Reginald stood looking at her expectantly once again.

Oh, what the hell. This would be her best chance of finding them. She handed over her thoroughly abused credit card, wondering how much a night in this hoity-toity place would set her back.

Smug satisfaction surged through Cassandra at the look on Reginald's face. He had not expected her to pay for the room, or to produce something bearing the McCarthy name. *Ha, take that you overbearing stuffed shirt.*

Reginald got in a final parting shot, his lips set in a smirk. "Shall I ring the bell captain to help with your bags?"

Shit, thought Cass. "No, thank you, Reginald. My husband has my luggage."

Naaahhh. She wanted to stick her tongue out, but somehow resisted the urge. Digging in her wallet she pulled out a twenty-dollar bill. Folding it in half she turned back to the clerk. "Reginald?"

"Yes, ma'am?" His voice held an unmistakable edge of frustration.

"Please do not tell my husband that I have arrived. I would like it to be a surprise." She passed him the bill praying that it was enough. She did not have much experience in buying off pompous hotel clerks.

Reginald nodded slightly. "As you wish, ma'am."

The fine appointments of the expensive room were lost on Cassandra. She paced miles across the thick carpet after once again leaving messages on both Aiden's and Travis' cell phones. When she finally caught up with them, those boys were in for quite the lecture.

Frustration was becoming a permanent state for her. She hadn't made it in time to talk to Travis before the meeting. Everyone in Knoxville seemed unhappy. Now she could not find her men. She was in a strange hotel, in a strange city, and she didn't even have any change of underwear. Her whole world was upside down, but yet she felt terrific, strong, and totally in command.

* * * * *

Riding in the elevator, Aiden felt the hair on the back of his neck standing on end. The desk clerk had acted very strange after hearing his name. What the hell was that all about?

"Reginald gave me the creeps," Travis stated as if reading his mind.

"I'm glad it wasn't only me. As soon as I said my name he got all squirrelly acting. It was really weird."

Aiden couldn't wait to get into a hot shower. It had been a long day after a relatively sleepless night. Tonight would most likely be more of the same. At least he and Travis had worked out their issues and come up with a game plan. Now they would just have to face Cass.

Their rooms were right next to each other, and they stood in the hallway discussing dinner arrangements. "How about we head downstairs in an hour," Travis suggested.

"Yeah, that sounds good to me. I need a shower."

Both men stood in shock as the door to Aiden's room flew open. He was almost knocked to the ground as Cassandra launched herself into his arms, her legs wrapping around his hips. Using both hands she pulled his head forward and claimed his mouth with a fierce kiss.

Her words were spoken between sobs. "I love you."

Aiden stood frozen in shock for several long moments. "Say it again," he finally whispered reverently.

"I love you. I love you. I love you." The kiss only became more intense as she opened herself up to Aiden. Clinging to him with all her strength, Cassandra tried to absorb him into her body.

Travis felt his heart being ripped from his chest. There was no way he could stand there while Cass clung to Aiden, professing her love. He turned away and fumbled with the key card to open his room. The lock clicked open and he moved quickly away.

Cassandra released Aiden and slid down his long frame. She was reluctant to let him go, but needed to go to Travis. Hearing the door open she turned. Her voice became harsh. "Travis Lundy, don't you dare turn away from me."

He slowly turned back around, letting the door close again. Cass moved forward, fisting both hands in his jacket lapels, pulling him up against her body. She stood on tiptoes, her face barely an inch from his.

"What did you do, Travis?"

He just stared in confusion. "Wh-What do you mean?"

A rumbling feline growl issued from somewhere deep in her chest. "What did you do at the meeting? What did you decide?" Her frustration grew as he just continued to stare at her. "Damn it, Travis. Did you take the promotion?"

He just stared at her for a moment before finally answering. "No, I couldn't."

With lightning-fast speed she jumped into his arms, tears streaming down her face. "Oh, thank God. I love you too." Grabbing his head she pulled Travis into a searing kiss.

The force of the wild mating of their mouths took his breath away. His legs trembled, knees giving out. Travis collapsed back against the wall as she clung to him in desperation.

"You what?" he asked, afraid to believe the words.

Cassandra was laughing through her happy tears now. "You heard me. I love you, Travis." It was several moments before she finally released him from the fierce embrace. She stood with her hands fisted on her hips, face turning grave.

"Now, get your butts into this room," she demanded. "We need to talk, boys." Her words and tone left no room for argument.

"Yes, ma'am," the two men said in unison.

* * * * *

They sat in chairs near the window anxiously watching Cass pace the room. Agitation rolled off her in palpable waves. She held her hands fisted tightly at her sides. Every so often a feral growl would issue from deep within her throat.

Now what was she going to do? They both sat there looking like chastised little boys. No scratch that. There was nothing little about her men. And there was enough testosterone in the room to choke her.

"Cass, what are you doing here?" Aiden thought about it for a moment. She could not have driven. Excitement crept into his voice as he asked, "Did you get on a plane?"

She stopped her pacing and stood facing them, eyes narrowing. "No. Not just any plane. Do you realize there are no direct flights from Tampa to Knoxville? You have to change planes somewhere along the way, which makes the trip twice as long." Her voice held accusation.

Shaking her head she said, "I'll get to all that." For a moment she just glared at the two men.

"How dare you two leave me alone without telling me what's going on?" Another deep growl rumbled through her chest. "I have never been so mad before in all my life." She turned, facing directly toward Travis. "And you. You tell me you have an important, life-altering decision to make and then take off without telling me what you decided." Her expression was incredulous.

Dropping down onto his lap she raised his chin so Travis was looking into her eyes. "You didn't give me a chance to discuss it with you." She stared intently into his eyes for several long moments. "I was so scared. Don't ever do that to me again."

He shook his head in acknowledgement then slipped his arms around her as she tenderly spread kisses over his face. Cassandra rubbed her face over his shoulder, breathing in the incredible scent that was distinctively Travis.

She rose and stood before Aiden. "And you. You should know better," she charged, giving him the same disappointed look. She began pacing again in front of the men.

"I fell asleep in your arms, but woke up alone in another bed. There was no note explaining anything. I threw on the first clothes I found, not even taking time to put on underwear. I raced over to the office only to find out you've flown off to Tennessee."

Her hurt and torment were evident. Aiden wanted nothing more than to hold her, but remained sitting while she spoke.

"I raced to the airport and left poor Don in a public parking garage." Her forehead crinkled with concern thinking of her prized Mustang getting dings in the doors. "I maxed out my credit card for an extremely expensive chartered jet, and flew for the first time, alone."

Travis cringed, thinking of how afraid she must have been.

"I ended up in a strange city driving around in a smelly rented Chevy. Finally finding the office, I had to face a snooty bitch receptionist who refused to tell me where you were."

Aiden rose, needing to hold her, provide comfort. Planting both hands on his chest, Cass effortlessly pushed him back into the chair. "I'm not done yet." Returning her fisted hands to her hips she stared at him for a moment.

"I got lost several times looking for this place. Then I get here, and have to lie to the pompous desk clerk to even find out if you two have checked in. I had to pay him off and say I was your wife," she said narrowing her eyes at Aiden. "He looked at me like I was trailer park trash. I had to put this room on my credit card just to get a key."

Pacing again in frustration she continued. "I have practically worn a trench in the carpet waiting for you two to finally get here." She stopped short. "Where the hell are your cell phones?"

Realization dawned on Aiden. "Shit. I left it in my desk again." He raked his fingers through his dark hair. "I'm so sorry, Cass."

Travis pulled his phone from his pocket and hit the power button. Nothing happened. He turned it for her to see the screen. "Dead battery, sugar. I'm sorry."

She mumbled something unintelligible. "Why bother to have the damn things then? From now on you will both have your phones charged up and turned on whenever you're not with me." Her tone left no room for argument.

Both men nodded their heads in agreement. They shared a silent communication at her last words. Was she saying that she intended to keep both of them? Hope surged in both men.

The adrenaline rush from her anger finally faded, leaving Cassandra weak. Her body began to tremble with increasing intensity. Before she knew it both men were at her side. They scooped her up then gently lay her on the huge bed.

Her thoughts were confused and jumbled. "Everything in this place is gargantuan size." She rubbed her head. "Oh, poor Don." She growled again, but it lacked her previous ferocious energy. "I hope he's okay."

The warmth of their bodies sheltering her soon eased the trembling. "I was so scared and alone." Her voice was weak now. "I never want to feel like that again."

Warm hands soothed her frazzled nerves. "We are so sorry, baby. It won't happen again," Aiden soothed.

"You'll always have at least one, if not both of us, nearby," Travis said in his velvety voice.

Silent tears began to slide down her cheeks again. Two mouths quickly moved to kiss away her pain. She looked between the two men, cupping a face in each hand. "I love you both so much. I can't choose one over the other." Worry creased her brow.

Travis soothed the lines with his finger tips. "It's okay, Cass. You don't have to choose. We figured everything out."

She fought against the hope the softly spoken words sent through her heart. "It's impossible." Her eyes fluttered as she fought against the exhaustion that stole over her body now that the adrenaline ebbed.

"Okay, baby. Sleep now. We're here. Everything is going to be all right." Their silky voices wrapped around Cassandra like a warm blanket. "Just sleep, Cass. We'll tell you everything later."

"Wait," Travis whispered. "Are you really not wearing any underwear?"

She just chuckled and shook her head. Feeling sheltered and safe, Cassandra allowed sleep to take her. She was enveloped in the scents, sounds, and touch of her men. She let go and placed herself completely in their strong hands. Finally she could relax and depend on someone else. Now this was heaven.

Chapter Twenty-Five

The grumbling protest of her empty stomach woke Cassandra. She sat up and rubbed her eyes. Soft candlelight filled the room along with relaxing strains of piano music. It took her a few moments to remember where she was.

Wild woman had struck out on a big-time adventure. Thinking back over the day she shuddered. Had she really taken off on a private plane in search of her men? Wow, what happened to the practical, cautious woman she normally was?

Feeling her way along the wall, she went into the bathroom. After washing her face she began to feel more alert. It would have been nice to have a change of clothes.

Looking around the large room she admired the marbled countertops and fine appointments. Steam rose off the large Jacuzzi tub. Sitting on the edge Cassandra trailed a hand through the warm, inviting water. Pink, red, and white rose petals floated along the surface.

Stripping out of her rumpled clothes, she sunk slowly into the inviting tub. Her tired muscles reveled in the warm embrace of the scented water. She leaned back against the pillowed edge, letting her hair stream out over the side.

Not bothering to hide her smile, she kept her eyes shut as large hands began to wash her body. Long fingers floated tenderly across her skin, sensitizing every nerve ending. "I could get used to being pampered like this," she purred.

Travis' deep sultry voice was another caress. "Good, because that's exactly what we intend to do. Just relax and let us take care of you."

Cassandra had never felt half as carefree and light. Still she was plagued by questions. Making a conscious decision to trust in the men, she allowed herself to be swept away by their loving care.

Strong fingers massaged shampoo into her hair and scalp. One man held a towel over her face while the other rinsed the long tresses. No one had washed her hair for her since Cassandra was a small child. It felt so good.

Her tears were soaked up by the towel. Once it was removed, Aiden's concerned voice filtered through her senses.

"Cass? What's wrong, baby?" Tender kisses feathered across her cheeks.

Emotions clogged her throat, stealing her voice. When she finally was able to answer her voice became husky. "No one's ever taken care of me like this before." Love shone in her green eyes.

Travis' words were spoken against her ear. "Well, get used to it, sugar. It's time to lean on us."

When the water began to cool, Aiden drained the tub. Travis helped her out, and two towels were rubbed over her body. Aiden carried her to the bed and laid her down in the center. The two men knelt on either side and began to massage vanilla-scented lotion into her skin. Strong fingers rubbed away any remaining tension as they stroked her. Their touches were soothing, but she felt streamers of sexual tension spread through her body.

"How do you feel, baby?"

"Mmmm. I've died and gone to heaven." She thought for a moment. "No, actually I'm on Mount Olympus being tended to by two Grecian gods." She smiled brightly. "Maybe we can find you two some togas," she said with a smile in her voice.

The two men joined in with her laughter. "Actually, it's about time we get dressed for dinner."

Her stomach rumbled in agreement.

"When's the last time you had something to eat?" Aiden questioned with concern clear in his voice.

She had to think back for several moments. "Um, I guess it was Chinese food in bed yesterday afternoon." The memory brought a mischievous glint to her eyes.

Travis gave Aiden a serious look. "We are going to have to stay very close to her. Obviously she needs someone to constantly take care of her."

Aiden shook his head in agreement. "Hmm. We can't let her out of our sight."

Giggles bubbled up past her lips. "You two are impossible."

Sometime while she'd slept one of the men had gone shopping. After helping her up, Travis raised her arms and slipped a silky gown over her head. The fine emerald material draped her curves lovingly. Spaghetti straps led to a plunging neckline. The sinuous material flowed down to her ankles.

Aiden moved behind her, holding out a matching robe. After draping it over her shoulders he turned her in his arms. With deft movements the belt was cinched around her slender waist.

"It's beautiful. Thank you, boys."

Leaning in for a chaste kiss, Aiden whispered, "You're beautiful, Cass."

The men both wore silk pajama pants, choosing to remain bare-chested. Cassandra felt that this was a good choice. It allowed her to enjoy every ripple of their muscular arms and torsos.

She placed a quick call to Sam. Her daughter was amazed to hear about the private plane, and palace of a hotel. After saying good night a little more of her tension dissipated.

Travis settled her across his lap while Aiden knelt close by and gently tended to her hair. First he blow-dried the long silken strands. Then he brushed the thick mass until it shone. He delighted in the way the spun silk clung to his hands, and wrapped lovingly around his fingers.

It felt so decadent to give herself over completely to the men, to not worry about anything, letting them take care of her.

"I don't think I have ever felt so utterly at peace before, but we still need to talk."

Travis trailed his fingers over the curve of her bottom lip. "Cass, just relax for right now. Let us enjoy just being with you for a little while longer. We'll talk after dinner."

It wasn't long before the room service waiter arrived and set up a fabulous meal on the large balcony. The nighttime view of the downtown lights was breathtaking. It was a crisp, clear night, perfect for dining outside.

The room was on the sixteenth floor. Looking out over the spectacular view, Cassandra could see the Tennessee River rolling sedately through the countryside.

An incredible feast was spread on the table before them. Thick steaks, enormous sautéed shrimp, baked potatoes covered in butter, crisp tossed salad, and fluffy rolls. The trio ate with gusto, their appetites insatiable. They drank champagne from elegant crystal flutes.

Travis removed the plates and stacked them on the room service cart when they'd finished. Aiden brought over cups of dark, rich espresso, and plates of tiramisu. How could the night get any better? Her hands trembled in anticipation.

Aiden slid a forkful of the dessert into her mouth. The rich scents were heavenly. Her eyelids drooped as waves of ecstasy flooded her senses. The ambient sounds of the city melted away. Her shoulders slumped, and her body floated on the sweet blissful tastes suffusing her mouth.

Creamy, light mocha kissed the fullness of ladyfinger pastry, accompanied by the strong, rich taste of coffee and the slight, tantalizing hint of liquor. The wonderful combination exploded across her tongue. Her toes curled, and a soft, contented sigh passed her lips.

Travis sat marveling at her sensual abandon in response to the sweet treat. "Holy shit," he exclaimed.

Aiden just smiled and said, "I told you so."

Travis held a fine china cup to her lips, watching as she slowly sipped the rich espresso. He was amazed by the dreamy look on her face as they took turns feeding her the dessert and sips of coffee.

The small sounds of pleasure that she made were making the men crazy. Never before had Travis gotten a hard-on watching someone eat. He came to realize that it was more than just enjoyment of the flavors for Cass, it was a sexual experience. The looks that crossed her expressive face were nearly indistinguishable from the way she looked when she climaxed.

When the last drops of the dessert had been licked from the fork, Cass opened her eyes. They were glazed over with passion. Her expression was sated, and sexy as hell. Both men were nearly drooling.

"Wow," was all Travis could manage to say.

"Mmm. Okay, boys. I've been thoroughly cared for, bathed, pampered, fed, and relaxed. Now it's time that we talk. I want to hear what you two have 'figured out' about this impossible situation."

The trio quietly moved back inside. Cassandra sat on the loveseat, wrapped up in Travis' arms. Aiden sat on the floor draped over her long legs. She was pleasantly surrounded by the warm masculine presence of the men she loved.

The two men shared a quick glance and nod. Aiden took her hands in his, holding firmly. "I've never met anyone as incredible as you, Cass. You're the strongest woman I know, and a wonderful mother to Sam. You have an enormous heart, and I love you completely."

Travis leaned forward. "You are so beautiful, sexy, and passionate. You're the most feminine, adventurous, seductive woman I've ever known. I love you too." He sat her aside and both men knelt at her feet.

Had they not been holding her hands she would have buried her face in them. Unshed tears shimmered in her eyes.

No, she would be strong, she wouldn't cry. She would find a way to keep them all together.

Aiden held out a small black velvet jeweler's box. Travis opened the top. Inside was nestled the most dazzling ring she had ever seen. The large princess-cut diamond sparkled between two smaller channel-set stones in a platinum band.

"We picked it out together this afternoon," Travis explained. "You have captured both of our hearts, bound all three of us together."

"Will you marry me, Cass?" Aiden asked.

"And me," echoed Travis.

Cassandra's head swam wildly. Emotions clogged her throat only allowing a small squeak to escape. She sat turning her head from one to the other. Pulling her hands away she wrapped her arms tightly around herself.

"That's…oh, God…that's crazy. Are you suggesting… P-polygamy is against the law." Was that their solution?

The men shared a glance. Travis nodded his head toward Aiden.

"Cass, I've loved you for so long. Officially you and I will be married. We will buy a big house, and our friend will come to live with us. That's how it will appear to everyone." He nodded to Travis.

"I fell for you so quickly and totally," Travis continued. "Unofficially you will be married to both of us. We will each have our own bedrooms and private spaces, but will sleep together in one bed. Neither one of us is willing to turn away."

Cassandra could picture what they described in her head. She could have both of them. Two Greek gods fallen to earth to pleasure her. Two intelligent, strong, hot men to love. She'd never be alone again.

She watched as Travis took the ring from the box. Aiden gently pulled her left hand forward. Together the two men slid the ring onto her finger. The tears flowed freely down her cheeks. She could no longer hold back the emotions. "Damn it, you boys keep making me cry."

"We love you and Sam. We will both protect and cherish the two of you until the day we die," Aiden stated.

"We want to make babies with you. They will have two fathers watching over them as they grow, as our family grows," Travis said. "Neither you or the children will ever want for anything."

Aiden nodded his agreement. Two sets of dark chocolate eyes gazed at her lovingly. Four strong hands held hers. What could she do? There were only two options that Cassandra could see. She could walk away from both of the men she loved, and be alone. Or she could marry them both, and bask in a glorious abundance of love.

Sliding to her knees between them she wrapped an arm around each man's back, pulling them close. Tremors racked her body, but were eased by the reassuring male presence surrounding her. It would always be this way. There was really only one choice to be made.

She leaned back slightly looking into their eyes. "I'm afraid that you will become jealous of each other. And how would it feel to not know who is the father of the children we have. Will you grow bitter, dissatisfied? Then we would all end up alone again."

Aiden sighed deeply. "Cass, Travis and I grew up closer than brothers. We share a bond that connects us almost like twins. You've felt it. You make that bond stronger."

Travis joined in. "We have always shared almost everything. Clothes, cars, successes, and failures. There will be no jealousy. Loving you makes our bond even stronger. I know you feel it too."

Yes, she did feel it. She did not need a ring or a wedding ceremony to bind her to the two men she loved. They were already bound by their hearts. At that moment, Cassandra felt the last of her fears melt away. Her uncertainty disappeared.

What they shared was so perfect, so right. Suddenly she realized that everything was complete now. There was no longer anything missing.

In unison the two men asked, "Will you marry us?"

"Yes...yes...yes," she repeated between the kisses she spread over both men's faces. "I love you both so much."

Chapter Twenty-Six

Travis got to his feet, and then pulled Cass up. Aiden rose behind her, reaching around to unfasten the robe, letting it fall to the floor. Travis pushed the thin straps of her gown over her shoulders, watching it pool at her feet.

They each removed their pants and laid their lover down on the big bed. They stared down at her for several moments, elbowing each other in the ribs.

"Oh, boys," Cassandra whispered. "C'mere."

Travis crawled up onto the bed, rolling her onto her side as he moved. When he reached her bare pussy lips, Cass was already wet and ready. He licked her in a long stroke from anus to clitoris.

Aiden moved in behind, pressing his hard cock against her crevice. "Just imagine spending the next fifty years sandwiched between the two of us," he whispered against her ear. He chuckled when she gasped.

Grabbing a tube of lubricating gel from a valise on the nightstand, he spread a generous amount over her anus while Travis licked her throbbing pussy. With his thumb, Aiden made slow circles around the tight bud. "Relax for me, baby."

As he worked his thumb into her tight channel, Aiden licked the delicate outer edge of her ear. Travis sank two fingers into her pussy, moving in counterpoint to Aiden. Shudders racked her body.

"Travis," she gasped. "Turn around so I can suck on that gorgeous cock."

He didn't need to be asked twice. He repositioned himself quickly, then resumed lapping at her lips. In the meantime

Aiden now had two fingers buried in her ass, preparing her for his cock. He thoroughly lubricated his cock before placing the tip against her tight hole.

Travis had a clear view of everything that was happening. He angled his fingers and began stroking her g-spot while sucking her clit between his lips. She gasped around his cock as Aiden began slow, shallow thrusts.

In their current position every time Aiden drove forward his scrotum slapped Travis in the face. But Cass sucking his cock deep into her throat somewhat made up for the inconvenience.

So this is what the future will be like, Travis thought. *I do believe that Aiden and I are going to be getting a whole lot closer than either of us would have ever imagined.*

Inspired by Aiden, Cassandra pressed her finger against Travis' anus. Using her saliva for lubrication she slowly worked the digit deeply inside the tight, puckered hole. Travis moaned against her clit, setting off a chain reaction. She clamped her muscles down on Aiden's cock, and moaned against Travis' shaft. Aiden jerked his hips forward, moaning with his own pleasure.

Travis plunged his fingers in and out of her pussy, while stroking her clit with his thumb. His tongue teased her swollen, sensitive folds. Tilting his head back he watched his rhythm. The next time Aiden pulled back, Travis licked his tight sac. Aiden thrust forward with more force, moaning deeply.

What the hell, Travis thought. He began enthusiastically licking Aiden's balls while working Cass' pussy. He worked his other arm between his legs, pressing his index finger against his anus.

At first Aiden froze. Travis circled the tight hole, waiting for Aiden to push back, if that's what he wanted. Eventually Aiden's thrusts began again, each one driving Travis' finger deep into his ass.

Cassandra could not see what was happening, but knew that Travis was doing something to Aiden. His breathing became raspy against her neck, and his entire body tensed. She could tell he was close to coming.

She could imagine nothing more erotic than the picture they must make. One lover faced her pussy while she sucked his cock and stimulated his anus, while her second lover thrust his dick deep into her ass.

She increased her suction on Travis' cock. Her finger gently stroked his prostate, while her tongue twirled over his shaft. He gasped in response to the teasing nips from her teeth.

Aiden couldn't believe what he was feeling. He never would have imagined Travis stimulating him anally. Aiden thrust frantically into Cass' ass, and massaged her breasts, tweaking her taut nipples. Travis licked his balls, and plunged two fingers in and out of his ass. All the while, Cass sucked Travis' cock.

The fingers Travis used in Cass' pussy stroked Aiden's cock through the thin tissues. As Travis stroked over his prostate, Aiden exploded into her tight ass with a shout.

Travis continued stimulating both of them while Cass drew his cock down her throat. He exploded within seconds of feeling Aiden's release. Moving his mouth to her clit he sucked deeply, stroking his tongue over the sensitive nub. She continued to lick his cock as her own orgasm shook her body. He greedily drank in her hot release.

The two men shared a silent communication over her body. They reached an understanding, before finally relaxing back into the bed. The three of them lay in a sated, contented tangle. No one could have determined where one ended and the others began.

* * * * *

Waking some time later, Cassandra felt sheltered and protected between the muscular bodies of her soon-to-be husbands. It would take quite a while to get used to the thought of having two husbands. Two strong, sexy, fuck-tastic men. Delicious.

At some point Travis had turned around on the bed. He and Aiden each had an arm draped over her abdomen, lying on their sides. She could feel Travis' cock against her hip, thick and long.

Umm. Two luscious cocks, two hot mouths, four big hands, and they were all hers. Now that held some definite possibilities. Her juices flowed over her bare pussy lips from the images floating through her mind.

Travis stirred next to her, opening his tawny eyes. "Hi, beautiful."

"Hi yourself, stud." She smiled when his cock thumped its hello against her hip. "You certainly wake up quickly."

Tracing his fingers down her cheek in a tender caress, Travis asked, "Are you okay with all this, Cass?" He stared intently into her eyes.

She smiled brightly. "Travis, there really is no other possibility. I love you both. I think that I have since I met the two of you. There is no way I could choose one over the other."

Gently she moved Aiden's arm from her abdomen. She took Travis' face in her hands. "C'mere, lover," she whispered. "I need to show you what words can never express."

He covered her with his warmth, and claimed her mouth in a heated kiss. Sliding between her legs his cock was cradled in the vee between her thighs. Heat rose up from her core, quickly engulfing Travis.

"I don't think I'll ever get enough of you." His voice was raspy with need.

"I sure hope not," she teased. "I need you, Travis."

He stroked the head of his cock over her weeping pussy lips, covering himself in her hot juices. Positioning himself at her opening he stared down into her eyes for several long moments.

"Travis, please."

Her words snapped his control. He sheathed himself in her warmth with one powerful thrust. He moved slowly, wanting to make their loving last. His jaw clenched against the need to fuck her hard and fast.

Aiden woke to the sound of their gentle moans. "Hey, you started without me," he complained.

Cassandra turned her head toward him. "Mmm. Hi, lover."

Leaning forward he mated his mouth to hers. With his eyes, Aiden connected with Travis' eyes and found him watching them. With a mischievous gleam in his tawny eyes, Aiden ended the kiss. He grabbed up the tube of gel then silently moved behind Travis, kneeling between his spread thighs.

Resting his hands on Travis' muscular ass, Aiden began stroking the rippling tissues. Squirting out a large glob of gel, Aiden warmed the lubricant between his fingers before spreading it over Travis' anus. He had an incredible view of where his cock joined with their lover's pussy.

Travis moaned as a big finger began rimming his anus. He wasn't sure what Aiden had in mind, but was game for just about anything.

The broad finger moved in the same languid rhythm, stretching his sensitive tissues. Travis knew that he would not last long. Reaching between their bodies he began to stroke Cass' clit.

He cried out when Aiden sunk a second finger into his ass. Incredibly, his cock grew harder, after the initial searing bite of pain spread through his ass. He'd never been so hard before, so ready to explode at any moment.

"Stop," he cried holding perfectly still. "I don't want to come yet."

With his other hand Aiden pinched the tissue connecting Travis' scrotum to his body, and pulled gently back. Travis growled deeply, then slowly began moving again.

Aiden smeared lubricant thickly over his cock. Relief washed through Travis as he removed his fingers from his ass. When they were replaced with the pressure of Aiden's cock against the tight hole, he gasped. His hips thrust harder into Cass then back into Aiden with each stroke.

He wasn't sure how he felt about this turn of events. When the broad head of Aiden's cock breached his tight sphincter, he growled. Burning waves of pleasure and pain surged through his body.

"Are you okay, Travis?" Aiden asked in a strangled voice. He did not want to hurt him, but the hot, tight channel felt so damn good. He knew it would not take long for him to climax.

Travis' breathing came in harsh pants. "Fine," he grumbled from between clenched teeth. On his next stroke his hips pushed back against Aiden, driving his cock deeper. Now he understood how overwhelmed Cass was when they took her from both directions at once. With each movement he thrust into her pussy, then was impaled on Aiden's cock.

Cass pulled his face forward, claiming his mouth. He kissed her deeply as each thrust drove Aiden deeper until their balls and thighs slapped together. The sensations coursing through his body were so overpowering that his fragile control snapped.

"Damn, this is so hot," Cass said in a raspy tone. "I bet his ass feels good." Her words encouraged the men to give themselves over to the moment. Her approval making their coming together that much better.

She made eye contact with each of the men, making sure they saw the love and approval in her gaze. Both sets of heavy-lidded chocolate eyes were smoldering with desire. It was such a turn-on to see one man pleasuring the other.

A frantic, primal rhythm overtook Travis. He pulled Cass' knees over his elbows, sinking deeper into her with each forward motion. Each backwards motion drove Aiden's cock deeper into his ass. Every muscle in his body tightened. Cass' pussy muscles clamped down on his cock, and Travis bellowed out his release as Aiden's hot cum filled his ass.

Aiden knew they had to be crushing Cass, and that Travis would be unable to move. Holding on to his hips he rolled the three of them over onto their sides. His cock remained locked in Aiden's ass, still semi-erect. Travis' cock remained in Cass' pussy.

A deep feeling of joy surged through Aiden at the realization that nothing would ever be able to break the bond that tied the three of them together. He smiled, considering what an incredible, uninhibited sex life they were going to have.

Eventually they would have to think about heading to the showers, but it would have to wait. The feelings of satiated contentment surging through the trio would not let them move from the bed.

The slow movement of Aiden's cock as it slid from his ass had Travis' cock springing back to life. Unfortunately he did not have the strength to do anything about it, so he slid from Cass' warmth. The three of them spent the night wrapped tightly in each other's arms.

"I love you both," Cassandra whispered.

"We love you, too," they said in unison.

Epilogue

Cassandra swung lazily in a hammock, looking out over the backyard, lost in thought. The small wedding ceremony had been conducted under an arbor covered in roses erected on the beach behind their new home. Darlene, Jared, and Jessica were all there. Their small, close-knit group of friends completed the guests.

Aiden and Travis had stood side by side in matching black tuxedos looking sexier than ever. Sam had smiled proudly as she walked toward the two handsome men whom she had quickly come to love as fathers. She had told Cassandra that she was the luckiest girl in the world to be getting two awesome dads. The idea of living with them both had filled her with joy. Her relationship with both of them had always been strong. Having both in her life was a dream come true.

It hadn't taken much convincing to get Bryce to sign over parental rights. The small adoption ceremony had taken place a week ago with the same group of witnesses, officially making Aiden her father. She had no qualms in accepting Travis as an unofficial father, or moving to the new house to start their new family. Sam had said it was the best day of her life.

When Cassandra had appeared, a collective sigh had spread over the assembled group. She'd been breathtaking with the glow of love and happiness that surrounded her. Her gown was made from antique ivory lace over silk. It swooped low over her full breasts, the material hugging her luscious body. The hem came to just above her knees in front, and angled down to her ankles in the back.

She'd held a bouquet of calla lilies wrapped with a thick ivory satin bow. Baby's breath had been woven into her thick caramel tresses and swept up into an elegant, yet sexy do. Long wispy tendrils curled around her face and shoulders, softening the look.

The two men had stood elbowing each other. Their broad grins expressed the happiness that threatened to overwhelm them. As she had moved toward them, their hearts soared.

Cassandra had stood between the two men, holding tightly to their hands. As Aiden had stated his vows, Travis had quietly whispered the words next to her ear. A band of three entwined platinum strands was placed on her finger next to the sparkling engagement ring. Its mate had gone onto Aiden's finger. Later, in private, Cassandra had placed a matching ring on Travis' finger.

The first week of their honeymoon was spent at a very private resort in Bora Bora. Their luxurious, thatched bungalow sat over a sparkling blue lagoon. It had a large bathtub with a clear glass bottom that looked down into the water, and quickly became a favorite spot. They made love endlessly in the warm water, while tropical fish swam below.

The bungalow also featured a private terrace from which they could dive into the crystalline waters of the lagoon whenever the mood struck. Room service was delivered on outrigger canoes. In the living room, the coffee table not only provided a view of the fish, but the top could be slid to the side to allow them to feed the exotic, colorful creatures.

The second week of their honeymoon was spent in their new home with Sam. Her joy over having the love and attention of the two men was unequivocal. Aiden and Travis both basked in the glory of her love and admiration.

The house never ceased to amaze Cassandra. Huge was an understatement. It actually had separate wings for staff, family, and guests. Never in her life would she have imagined owning a house so large that it required a full-time staff to keep everything in order.

She was continually taken aback by how her life had changed so dramatically. Where once there was loneliness and pain, now she had overwhelming love and devotion. Her two husbands doted on her. She was spoiled by unexpected gifts, and constant pampering without end. Their love grew stronger with each passing day. And with each night their lovemaking became more passionate.

Eventually the small marks that had constantly marred her forearms disappeared as Cassandra no longer had to pinch herself to be sure she wasn't dreaming. The strength of her two husbands love soon relieved any lingering doubts.

Rubbing her hand over her still flat tummy, Cassandra wondered how she would tell her men. Somehow they had not only gotten her pregnant, but had given her twins. Just the word sent fear coursing through her. Intuition told her they would be boys, full of mischief, just like their fathers.

She still wrote the Lacy Harte erotica e-books for fun. Of course, the research was a big draw. Oh, how her boys loved to help with the research. But now she also wrote suspense novels, published under her own name. Her first story was due on bookshelves next month. Already, those who had reviewed the book were praising her work.

She was living a fairy tale much better than any she could have ever dreamed up. The passionate realities of life far surpassed the make-believe stories she wrote. She finally understood the happily-ever-after undying love and devotion possible when you found the right people to love.

Looking up, she saw her two handsome husbands headed across the lawn. They wore identical, totally sexy, devilish grins. Umm, she had to be about the luckiest woman in the world.

"What's going on, boys?"

Their smoldering chocolate eyes, deep dimples, and bad boy charm never failed to turn her on. She watched their powerful bodies move with that lazy, loose-hipped walk that drove her crazy. By the twinkle in their eyes, she could tell her boys were up to something.

"Got a package today, sugar," Travis drawled.

"From your favorite online store," Aiden finished.

Unconsciously her tongue slowly licked her suddenly dry lips. Both men followed the movement as she moistened her lips. Well, maybe she could wait to tell them about the twins for a few hours.

"Time for some research," they said in unison.

Umm, her boys were tireless when it came to helping with her research. She couldn't ask for anything more.

About the author:

Nicole Austin lives on the sheltered Gulf Coast of Florida, where inspiration can be readily found sitting under a big shade umbrella on the beach while sipping cold margaritas. A voracious reader, she never goes anywhere without a book. All those delicious romances combined with a vivid imagination naturally created steamy fantasies and characters in her mind.

Discovering Ellora's Cave paved the path to freeing them as well as manifesting an intoxicating passion for romantica. The positive response of family and friends to her stories propelled Nicole into an incredible world where fantasy comes boldly to life. Now she stays busy working as a certified CT scan technologist, finishing her third college degree, reading, writing, and keeping up with family. Oh yeah, and did we mention all the hard work involved with research? Well, that's the fun job— certainly a labor of love.

Nicole welcomes mail from readers. You can write to her c/o Ellora's Cave Publishing at 1056 Home Avenue, Akron OH 44310-3502.

Enjoy this excerpt from
Triple Play
Sexy Sweet
© Copyright Rhyannon Byrd 2005

"I asked if you'd like to be a birthday present. How 'bout it, beautiful?"

A birthday present?

Twisting in her chair, hands smoothing over her skirt-covered, dimpled knees, Denny cocked her head to the side, wondering what the sexy hunk was up to. Aware of the dangers that came with flirting in the workplace, Jonah and his senior partners at Atlas Associates were ever mindful of the lines they couldn't cross in the office. But something about his tone and that wicked, predatory gleam in his intense gaze warned Denny that tonight was somehow different. *A birthday present?* What on earth was he talking about? There'd been no office birthday parties that day, and she remembered that Jonah had celebrated his birthday nearly three months ago.

Plus, how could someone actually *be* a present? Maybe if they were a stripper jumping out of some gaudy, oversized birthday cake. *No*, she thought with a soft, inner sigh of relief, Jonah surely wasn't asking her to do something like *that*.

But what is he asking me?

She watched with wide eyes as he reached out, and then *felt* as he smoothed one arched brown brow with the tip of his index finger. Her breath sucked in on a sharp gasp as he moved on to flick the tiny silver hoop pierced through the upper curve of her left ear, his blue eyes burning with a fierce, seductive heat that had a warm flash of pink climbing up her cheeks. Her female intuition was going on red alert as understanding dawned and she suddenly realized this wasn't just some sort of playful banter.

Crossing her suddenly nervous arms over her silk-covered chest, Denny tried to quell the flutter of butterflies in her belly. "Just what are you getting at, Mr. Cartwright?"

He gave her another one of those slow, sin-laced grins at the formal use of his last name—and that unhurried twisting of his wide mouth nearly—*oh so nearly*—made her moan with regret. If only she dreamed of this gorgeous stud the same way she did of his best friend.

His best friend…not to mention her damn boss.

Jonah was fine, no doubt about it, but it was Mr. Harrison, *Gabriel*, who made her ache with churning, desperate, lust-filled hope that a miracle would be granted and the one man she wanted for her own would someday wake-up and finally take an interest in her.

Well, an interest that went further than what she ordered for lunch, she silently grumbled.

She was captivated by the wicked grin that curled the edges of Jonah's beautiful mouth, suggestive and teasing, and her pulse quickened, despite the knowledge that he was just toying with her. *He has to be. Right?* The guy could have any woman he wanted — *any woman* — and she was willing to bet her life savings that he had.

Moving that long-fingered hand across her cheek, he brushed a wayward strand of mahogany hair behind the shell of her ear, winking as he announced, "Today is Gabriel's birthday, Denny."

She cocked her head to the other side and blinked in surprise, wondering with heart-stopping expectation about his earlier opening statement. "He didn't mention it. *No one* mentioned it," she whispered lamely, nervously licking her bottom lip, her palms going damp when she saw Jonah follow the movement like an alley cat eyeing a slow, tasty meal of midnight mouse. "Er…how old is he?"

"Old enough, sweet stuff." The tall redhead's full smile flashed, as wickedly sinful as his reputation. For all of Gabriel's brooding darkness, Jonah was the epitome of the consummate devil, and a definite playboy. Hell, he'd even playfully flirted with her from time to time, but she'd never paid it much attention, and she'd never acted on it. Not that he wasn't a great guy, but she'd been pining away, like the lovesick idiot she'd become, for the one who made her heart shiver every time she set eyes on him.

Yeah, old enough, she silently snorted. *Lot of good it does me. Gabriel Harrison could be ninety and he still wouldn't want me.*

"And old enough to know what he wants," Jonah murmured, as if reading her mind. "Only a little too stubborn to go after it." He spread his arms wide, his dark sweater pulling taut across the solid muscles of his chest. At six-three, he was as tall and wide as Gabriel, and just as deadly when it came to masculine beauty and hard-edged sexual magnetism. "So, like any good pal, I'm here to get it for him."

Denny chewed her bottom lip, worrying away the cranberry gloss she'd applied during her last visit to the ladies' room. "And that would be what…exactly?" she asked with careful precision, almost afraid of what he'd say.

"A certain Miss Denny Abbott."

She couldn't help it—she snorted loudly this time. "Yeah, right."

Jonah clucked his tongue, giving her another playful wink. "I'm not teasing, Denny."

Without conscious thought, her eyes narrowed with beginning anger, even hurt, despite the unmistakable heat of anticipation racing through her veins. No matter how fiercely she might have wished it otherwise, men like Gabriel Harrison did *not* fall head over heels in love with women like her. Hell, they didn't even date them. They just stole their diet bars and drove them crazy with aching, unbearable longing.

"I'm sorry," she said tightly, her lips feeling strangely numb, "but I'm not as stupid as you obviously think I look."

"Cut the crap, Denny," he suddenly warned, brilliant blue eyes flashing with mild irritation at her words. "You know I think you're incredibly beautiful—inside and out—just like every other man who sets eyes on you."

As if, she silently laughed, wondering where he was going with this, but he only ignored her pointed look of disbelief. "If you trust me, you can have him. He's yours for the taking, sweet stuff."

Her heart dropped into her stomach with jolting, head-spinning speed. "Have…him?"

"Yeah," he said in that low, rough-velvet voice. "If you want it, you can have it all, Denny. Both of us can."

Both of us? Both!!!

"Just what do *you* get out of it?" she couldn't help but ask, still not really believing a word he'd said, though she was positive it'd be fueling her late night fantasies from here 'til kingdom come.

Before she realized what he intended, Jonah leaned down, braced his large hands on the padded arms of her chair, and pressed his warm, honey-flavored mouth against hers. With a rough sound of hunger, he slipped his talented tongue deep inside the warm recess of her mouth as she gasped in sudden, reeling shock against his silk-roughened lips. He tasted sexy and sinful, a heady combination that made her feel a little dizzy, as if her balance had been ripped from beneath her.

Ohmygod! It's a good thing my backside is still planted firmly in this chair, she mused in stunned disbelief, or she knew she'd have landed flat on her ass.

He took his time exploring the heat of her mouth, as if savoring what he found there, breathing into her until she felt drunk—even a little guilty with the flood of desire drenching her satin panties. Not that she owed Gabriel Harrison her self-imposed celibacy, but it felt somehow *wrong* to be kissing his best friend. Not to mention the fact that she was getting embarrassingly turned-on in the process.

Nipping her bottom lip, Jonah pulled back, some of that teasing light replaced by a physical fire in his deep blue gaze that she could all but feel stroking her tender flesh, making her pussy swell with surprising need. "If this all goes to plan, then I get to enjoy the pleasure of this—of you," he rasped, rubbing her bottom lip with his thumb, "at least until Gabe kicks me to the street."

Why an electronic book?

We live in the Information Age—an exciting time in the history of human civilization in which technology rules supreme and continues to progress in leaps and bounds every minute of every hour of every day. For a multitude of reasons, more and more avid literary fans are opting to purchase e-books instead of paperbacks. The question to those not yet initiated to the world of electronic reading is simply: *why?*

1. *Price.* An electronic title at Ellora's Cave Publishing and Cerridwen Press runs anywhere from 40-75% less than the cover price of the <u>exact same title</u> in paperback format. Why? Cold mathematics. It is less expensive to publish an e-book than it is to publish a paperback, so the savings are passed along to the consumer.

2. *Space.* Running out of room to house your paperback books? That is one worry you will never have with electronic novels. For a low one-time cost, you can purchase a handheld computer designed specifically for e-reading purposes. Many e-readers are larger than the average handheld, giving you plenty of screen room. Better yet, hundreds of titles can be stored within your new library—a single microchip. (Please note that Ellora's Cave and Cerridwen Press does not endorse any specific brands. You can check our website at www.ellorascave.com or

www.cerridwenpress.com for customer recommendations we make available to new consumers.)

3. *Mobility*. Because your new library now consists of only a microchip, your entire cache of books can be taken with you wherever you go.

4. *Personal preferences are accounted for*. Are the words you are currently reading too small? Too large? Too...**ANNOYING**? Paperback books cannot be modified according to personal preferences, but e-books can.

5. *Instant gratification*. Is it the middle of the night and all the bookstores are closed? Are you tired of waiting days—sometimes weeks—for online and offline bookstores to ship the novels you bought? Ellora's Cave Publishing sells instantaneous downloads 24 hours a day, 7 days a week, 365 days a year. Our e-book delivery system is 100% automated, meaning your order is filled as soon as you pay for it.

Those are a few of the top reasons why electronic novels are displacing paperbacks for many an avid reader. As always, Ellora's Cave and Cerridwen Press welcomes your questions and comments. We invite you to email us at service@ellorascave.com, service@cerridwenpress.com or write to us directly at: 1056 Home Ave. Akron OH 44310-3502.

Discover for yourself why readers can't get enough of the multiple award-winning publisher Ellora's Cave. Whether you prefer e-books or paperbacks, be sure to visit EC on the web at www.ellorascave.com for an erotic reading experience that will leave you breathless.

www.ellorascave.com